COACH

WALL STREET JOURNAL & *USA TODAY* BESTSELLING AUTHOR

DEVNEY PERRY

COACH

Editing:

Elizabeth Nover, Razor Sharp Editing

Proofreading:

Julie Deaton, Deaton Author Services

Judy Zweifel, Judy's Proofreading

Kaitlyn Moodie, Moodie Editing Services

Cover:

Sarah Hansen © Okay Creations

OTHER TITLES

The Edens Series

Christmas in Quincy - Prequel

Indigo Ridge

Juniper Hill

Garnet Flats

Jasper Vale

Crimson River

Clifton Forge Series

Steel King

Riven Knight

Stone Princess

Noble Prince

Fallen Jester

Tin Queen

Jamison Valley Series

The Coppersmith Farmhouse

The Clover Chapel

The Lucky Heart

The Outpost

The Bitterroot Inn

The Candle Palace

Maysen Jar Series

The Birthday List

Letters to Molly

Lark Cove Series

Tattered

Timid

Tragic

Tinsel

Timeless

Runaway Series

Runaway Road

Wild Highway

Quarter Miles

Forsaken Trail

Dotted Lines

Calamity Montana Series

The Bribe

The Bluff

The Brazen

The Bully

The Brawl

The Brood

Standalones

Ivy

Rifts and Refrains

A Little Too Wild

Coach

Holiday Brothers

The Naughty, The Nice and The Nanny

Three Bells, Two Bows and One Brother's Best Friend

A Partridge and a Pregnancy

CONTENTS

Prologue	1
Chapter 1	5
Chapter 2	17
Chapter 3	27
Chapter 4	36
Chapter 5	46
Chapter 6	57
Chapter 7	66
Chapter 8	76
Chapter 9	85
Chapter 10	95
Chapter 11	103
Chapter 12	111
Chapter 13	121
Chapter 14	129
Chapter 15	137
Chapter 16	147
Chapter 17	155
Chapter 18	165
Chapter 19	175
Chapter 20	183
Chapter 21	194
Chapter 22	203
Chapter 23	212
Chapter 24	221
Chapter 25	230
Chapter 26	241
Chapter 27	253
Chapter 28	264
Chapter 29	270

Chapter 30   276
Chapter 31   283
Chapter 32   289
Chapter 33   297
Chapter 34   303
Chapter 35   311
Chapter 36   318
Epilogue   330

Acknowledgments   339
About the Author   341
Preview to Indigo Ridge   343

PROLOGUE
FORD

M illie slammed her textbook closed so hard it shook my dining room table. "I hate philosophy."

"It's the worst." The class, definitely. Having it with Millie? Not so bad.

She groaned and, with a huff, blew a lock of smooth, brown hair out of her face. It fell right back across her cheek.

I lifted my hand, about to tuck it behind her ear, but caught myself. Millie was . . . the best. The best of the best. She deserved it from the people in her life because that was what she gave them.

She was my best friend. But damn, I wanted to kiss her. To say to hell with our friendship and see what we could make of this spark between us.

Except I'd just come out of a long-term relationship, and I wanted her to know that if—*when*—we got together, it wasn't a rebound thing.

I'd kiss her. One day soon.

Just not yet.

So I kept my hands to myself and scanned the sheet of

notes I'd taken in our philosophy lecture yesterday. Over half were to Millie and had nothing to do with the course.

Want to get pizza after this?

She'd circled the *yes* I'd written beneath.

Think Professor Smythe owns multiple versions of that sweater vest?

Another yes.

If he says absolutism one more time I might scream.

That one had earned me a muted laugh.

Beyond that, my notes were a wreck. "None of these make any sense."

"I think if I can just manage a B, this class won't entirely tank my GPA and ruin my collegiate career."

"I just want to pass." I dragged a hand through my hair, leaning back in my chair. Then I reached toward Millie, touching the button at the base of her throat. "You have a stain on your shirt."

"What?" She gasped and looked down, just in time for me to flick the tip of her nose.

I chuckled as she swatted my hand away, fighting a smile as she glared. "I can't believe you fell for that."

"Shut up." She shoved at my arm, her cheeks flushing.

Millie was never more beautiful than when she blushed. And God, she was fun to flirt with. Whenever I'd tried playing with Sienna like that, she'd thrown a temper tantrum because she couldn't take a fucking joke.

"Okay, let's finish this." I sat up straighter, inching my chair closer to Millie's to peer at her notes, hoping they were better than mine. The scent of her perfume filled my nose, citrus with a sweetness that was all Millie. I held it in, letting it sink deep, then glanced at her profile.

Our gazes locked. Those pretty hazel eyes searched mine. "I, um . . ."

Too close. We were too close. Best friends didn't sit like they were seconds from crawling into each other's laps. They didn't find ways to touch. They didn't stare at each other like they'd die without a kiss.

What were we supposed to be studying again?

But before I could back away, retreat to my side of the dining room table, she surged.

Millie's lips crashed onto mine so fast it took me a second to realize she'd kissed me. *Was* kissing me. It took my brain a moment to process that her lips were even softer than I'd imagined.

I wasn't supposed to kiss her. Not yet.

Why was that again?

Fuck it.

I licked the seam of her mouth, earning a mewl. Then she opened for me, and with one sweet taste, I was done for. The fire I'd spent too long trying to tame coursed through my veins. So I leaned into it, kissing her until she was breathless. Until I knew if I didn't stop, I'd take her to my bedroom.

Not yet.

I'd do it right this time. I'd do right by Millie. So I broke away, my heart racing, and took in the pretty color of her cheeks.

"Uh . . . sorry. Not exactly what we were supposed to be doing tonight." She nibbled on her lower lip. "Sorry."

"Don't be." I loved that she'd instigated our first kiss.

Millie wasn't bold like some girls. That was part of why I liked her. She had a shy streak that was so goddamn adorable. But fuck, it was hot that she'd taken charge.

"I think I'm going to give up on studying," she said.

3

"Are you sure?" This time, I did tuck that lock of hair behind her ear, and it made the pink in her face flame brighter.

"Yeah. I'd better go." She stood and began collecting her things, shoving them in her backpack. Her fingers fumbled with a pen. Her eyes stayed glued to the books, notepads and worksheets on the table.

There was nothing for her to be shy about, not with me. But I wouldn't push. Not yet.

So I helped her pack her things, then took her backpack before she could sling it over a shoulder, carrying it through the house. I opened the front door for her, then handed over her bag. "See ya, Mills."

"Bye, Ford." She smiled, then stepped outside, giving me a little finger wave before walking to her car.

I stayed on the threshold, lifting a hand as she reversed out of the driveway, then closed the door once her taillights disappeared. A laugh escaped, filling the entryway. "Damn."

That kiss . . . it was good. Really good. But I'd give her better.

I dug my phone from my pocket, my brain racing about what to text Millie. I wasn't ready to say good night to her yet. Except before I could decide what to type, a knock came at the door.

I ripped it open. Maybe Millie had come back and—

It wasn't Millie on my porch.

CHAPTER ONE

FORD

"Welcome aboard, Coach."

I set my pen on the contract I'd just signed. "Glad to be here."

Kurt Howard, athletics director and my new boss, stretched an arm across his desk.

As I shook his hand, I hoped like hell this hadn't been a mistake.

One year. I'd agreed to be the head football coach for the Treasure State Wildcats for one year. If after this season I realized Mission wasn't the right place for Joey and me, then we'd pack our bags and find somewhere new. As long as it wasn't Seattle, I was game for just about anywhere.

"How'd the move go?" Kurt asked as he stood, leading the way out of his office.

"Not bad," I lied. "Moving company made it easy."

They'd packed everything from my house in Seattle and loaded it onto a truck. While Joey and I had been on a plane destined for Montana, they'd hauled our belongings and my new Silverado over the interstate.

Getting to Montana had been relatively simple. The hard part was going to be settling in now that we were here.

The moving crew had arrived one day after us to unload the semi. Unload, but not unpack. That job was on me, which meant my house was full of boxes and randomly placed pieces of furniture.

This morning, I'd spent an hour searching for coffee cups. Finding a single, white ceramic mug had required me to riffle through five boxes full of kitchen shit I hadn't used in years.

It was tempting to only unpack the necessities. Part of me wondered if it would be smarter to stick with the essentials only, at least until the season got underway. After some practices and a game or two, I'd have a better idea if this could become a long-term gig.

If not, well . . . less stuff to repack if I just kept the boxes.

"How's your daughter?" Kurt asked. "Is she excited to be in Montana?"

"Definitely," I lied again, following him down the hallway of the administrative section of the fieldhouse.

Joey didn't want to be in Montana. On the flight out, she'd refused to speak to me. She'd been sweet as pie to the flight attendants, but other than the occasional glare, I might as well have been a stranger in seat 2B.

She was only nine, but her mother had taught her how to deliver one hell of a cold shoulder.

Joey's room was the only one I'd fully unpacked—it hadn't scored me any points. Even though her things were there, it wasn't home. Not yet. We just needed time. Time on our own. Time in the new house. Time in Mission.

Maybe after a few weeks, we'd find a new normal. And maybe one day, Joey would realize why I'd taken this job.

It was a chance for a fresh start. A chance for a new adventure. A chance to get some distance from her mother. But Joey was just a kid, and I'd made a decision that had moved her away from her friends, her school and the only home she'd ever known.

I checked my watch as I followed Kurt. Now that my contract was signed, hopefully this meeting would wrap up soon. It would do Joey and me both some good to cut loose on a Friday afternoon, get some ice cream, find a park and blow off some steam. Throw a ball around or something. There couldn't be much more to cover today, right?

As Kurt and I passed a row of cubicles, heads popped up from behind the short walls. I nodded and smiled at the few people who waved. New faces to go with remodeled spaces.

I'd spent a lot of time in this building as a student athlete, back when I'd called myself a Wildcat. In those days, the coaches' offices had been up here and the administration had been in an entirely different building.

But since, the place had undergone a major facelift. The floor was open, cubicles at its center. Along the exterior walls were private offices, like Kurt's, that overlooked the parking lot behind the fieldhouse and, beyond that, the football stadium.

Desks were crowded with laptops and monitors and Wildcat water bottles. A few cubes had the school's pennant pinned to the wall. And being it was Friday, everyone was decked out in royal blue and silver.

Go Big Blue.

How many times had the team chanted that in the locker room before a game? Now I got to call myself a Wildcat again. Pride surged, just being here where my football career had started.

"Right this way." Kurt stopped by a door, shoving it open to a stairwell.

My hand skimmed over the blue iron railing as we made our way to the first floor. I checked my watch again. Maybe I'd have time to swing by the bookstore in the student union to pick up some apparel. Gray slacks and a navy button-down had been my only options when I'd packed my travel bag in Seattle. I owned a lot of blue, except everything had the Seahawks logo.

Maybe a new Wildcat sweatshirt and tee for Joey would buy me a smile.

"Your office is on this floor in the coaches' wing," Kurt said as we rounded a landing, jogged down another flight of stairs and pushed through the exit on the first floor. "We remodeled this place about five years ago. Built new men's and women's locker rooms. Relocated the weight room and added a state-of-the-art fitness facility. We also created a designated place for coaches so you're not as far removed from the players."

"It looks great." Clean. Open. The once dark, tunneled hallways had been expanded. Bright-white lights illuminated the concrete floors and light gray walls.

"Normally we'd have given you the full tour during the interview process, but . . ."

But last-minute exceptions had been made, by both parties.

My interviews with Kurt had been done over the phone and through video conferences. The first had been just twenty days ago.

This past winter, the previous head football coach was let go after a scandal hit the front page of every major sports media outlet in the country. The minor ones too.

Kurt and the athletic department spent months attempting to repair their reputation and recruit a new head coach. They found a good guy—I'd actually met him once at a charity fundraiser years ago. Experienced. Professional. Highly in demand.

Apparently, TSU extended a verbal agreement. They thought he accepted, pending a draft contract from their legal team. But wires got crossed, and three days after the alleged verbal agreement, their new coach showed up on SportsCenter, having accepted a position at Kansas State.

With the season approaching fast, Kurt was forced to scramble for a new coach. But few were willing to come here knowing there was a mess to clean up. When rejection followed rejection, Kurt asked for suggestions from the coaching staff. My buddy Toren—the defensive coordinator for the Cats—tossed out my name.

Toren knew I didn't mind a mess, especially since this one paled in comparison to the cluster that was my personal life. And he'd also known that I was looking to leave Seattle.

Now, less than a month later, here I was.

The hiring process had been a whirlwind, on both sides. Kurt's desperation had come across loud and clear. Maybe I could have exploited that, but getting out of Seattle had been more important than scoring the perfect contract.

One year.

We'd give this one year.

My annual salary was a fraction of what I was used to with the Seahawks, but I'd saved enough money for a lifetime. What was important about this job wasn't the bonus provisions or the automatic extension clauses, but the location.

Mission was tucked into a valley beside the Mission

9

Mountains in western Montana. It had grown in the past decade to a city with a decent-sized airport and plenty of commerce. The university was still the cornerstone of the economy, but I suspected before too long, that would change as more businesses in the area flourished. But despite its growth, Mission still had small-town roots.

Joey would have space to breathe here. We wouldn't go out to dinner and get mobbed by fans wanting autographs and pictures. And Sienna, for the time being, was two states away.

For me, that was bonus provision enough.

"You're the last spot down this hall, with the biggest space and a great view." Kurt led me past a line of offices. Each had their door open, and as we passed, faces lifted from screens to watch me walk by.

The air smelled like bleach and concrete and rubber. The faint sound of weights lifting and crashing echoed in the background.

I knew these smells. I knew these sounds. They meant Wildcat football.

This was happening. This was actually happening. I was the head football coach for the Treasure State Wildcats. My alma mater.

There hadn't been time to let that reality settle in. There hadn't been time to ride the high of accepting this job. Until now.

I was the head football coach for the Treasure State Wildcats.

Fuck yeah. I fist pumped at my side.

"Well, look who the cat dragged in." Toren came walking down the hallway, headed our direction with a grin on his face. "Kurt, I'm surprised. I didn't think you'd actually convince Ford to leave the big city."

I held out my hand, smiling at my oldest friend. "Didn't take much. He promised I got to be your boss, and I couldn't resist the chance to torture you."

"Like old times." He pulled me in for a hug, slapping me on the back. At six four, we were the same height and build. "I know you're just getting settled in, but let's meet for a beer or something soon. Be great to catch up."

I nodded. "You're on."

"Good to have you back on Montana soil, man." He clapped me on the shoulder, then disappeared into the office next to the only dark one in the row.

Mine.

"Here we are." Kurt waved me through the office's open door and flipped on the lights behind me. "I was hoping to have time to introduce you to the other coaches and tour the facility, but we've got a meeting with President Cruz in ten minutes."

"No problem."

"On Monday, we'll do the full tour and introductions. We'll get you through the Human Resources checklist too. You probably noticed but our website is under construction for some rebranding."

"Yeah, I saw that." Except for a few high-level pages, there hadn't been much to glean about the department.

"Once we get the staff directory up again, we'll arrange for headshots. Have Marketing get with you to draft a bio."

"Whatever you need." I did a quick turn around my office, taking it all in. The desk was positioned in front of the windows. Beyond them, the sun glittered like a jewel in the cloudless azure sky.

God, I'd missed Montana. There was a reason they called it Big Sky Country. I'd forgotten just how beautiful Mission was with mountain peaks to greet you at every turn.

"I'll give you a minute alone," Kurt said. "Restrooms are down the hall on your right, just past the door to the stairwell. We'll be meeting in the Missouri conference room. Keep on going past the bathrooms to the last door that direction. Can't miss it."

"I'll be right behind you."

Kurt stretched his hand out for another shake, his brown eyes softening and crinkling around the edges. "Really glad you're here, Ford."

"So am I." And that was the damn truth.

Kurt left me to breathe, and I walked to the desk, taking a seat in the chair. It didn't fit quite right. It was a bit small for my large frame, but I didn't plan on sitting here much.

My office was on the field.

I pulled my phone from my pocket, checking to make sure there wasn't a text from Joey's babysitter. Her last message was from after lunch, saying all was going well. She'd sent a picture of the two of them having a peanut butter and grape jelly picnic in the backyard. There'd actually been a smile on Joey's face.

Bless those college kids. At least the babysitter could make Joey happy.

Kurt had sent me this sitter's contact info because she was on the ski team. A local nanny agency was in the process of narrowing down full-time candidates, but until I hired one, my plan was to leverage any student looking to make a few extra bucks this summer.

I tucked my phone away and stood, pushing my chair into the desk. Then, not wanting to be late to my first meeting with the university president, I headed down the hall, waving at Toren as I passed his office for the conference room.

Kurt was seated at the head of the table, his fingers tapping on the wood as he stared out the window. Sunlight streamed inside and made his short, gray hair nearly white.

"You found it." He sat straighter as I walked inside.

"Sure did."

He smiled, still tapping, as I took a chair. His eyes kept darting toward the door.

The stiffness of his shoulders and that constant tapping —his nerves were palpable and made the hairs on the back of my neck stand on end.

Uh . . . "This is just an introductory meeting, isn't it?"

"Yep." His voice was too bright.

Why was he nervous? Was he always like this around the university's president? Maybe I should be worried too, but it took more than a meeting to make me sweat these days.

I'd spent years playing against men who wanted nothing more than to smash my body into the turf. I'd faced countless reporters who loved to make any player look the fool on camera. I'd been summoned to the general manager's office one too many times to be nervous today.

This was only a job. A job I'd give my all to for one year. But still, it was only a job.

I wasn't here for the money or the prestige. I'd coach this team to the best of my ability and either that would be good enough, or it wouldn't. End of story.

Hell, most of the reason I'd even taken this job was to accelerate a move away from Seattle. That, and as a coach, I could stay connected to the game.

Besides my daughter, there wasn't anything I loved more

than football. When playing had no longer been an option, coaching had been the next logical step.

Heels clicked down the hall before a woman in her fifties strolled into the room wearing a navy pantsuit, silver-rimmed glasses and a wide smile.

I stood, waiting to be introduced.

"President Cruz." Kurt burst from his chair, holding it out for her to take his place. "Thanks for fitting us into your schedule."

"Hi, Kurt. I'm a little early. I hope that's okay." She smiled at him, ignored his offered chair and came right up to me.

She was a little thing. Five feet tall, even in her heels, with sharp-cut bangs and a dark bob that hit her at the chin. Short and petite, but this woman had presence. She was in charge, full stop. Only an idiot would cross her.

"Coach Ellis. Welcome."

I shook her outstretched hand. "Honored to be here, ma'am."

"Pfft. Call me Carly."

"Carly." I nodded and pulled out the chair directly beside mine.

Kurt's smile faltered as she took the seat. He recovered quickly, sitting down and opening his mouth, but President Cruz spoke first.

"We're lucky to find someone with your experience on short notice," she said.

Experience? I'd only coached—as an assistant with the Seahawks—for a year. Though I had been a player in the NFL for nine. "Timing worked out for us both. And it will be great to wear Wildcat colors again. Though after driving through campus, I'm not sure this is the same school."

Buildings occupied the once open lawns. The dorm where I'd lived my freshman year had undergone a complete transformation, and if the name hadn't been out front, I wouldn't have thought it was the same place.

"We're growing," she said. "We need a football program to keep pace." *And bring in the dollars.*

I grinned at the subtle warning in her tone. This lady wasn't fucking around. "Understood."

"I'll count this year a win if we can beat the Grizzlies," Kurt said.

I chuckled. "Glad to see that hasn't changed."

The Treasure State Wildcats versus the University of Montana Grizzlies was a rivalry that dated to long before my time on this earth. It was great when we beat the Montana State Bobcats too, but winning against the Griz had always been the ultimate test of a season.

We could finish the year with a losing record and no hope of making the playoffs, but as long as we beat the Grizzlies, the fans and alumni would call it a victory.

"Yes, we do love beating the Grizzlies." President Cruz nodded. "But mostly, I'd love to avoid another scandal."

Kurt stiffened at my side, and when President Cruz looked his way, this time there was nothing subtle about the warning.

The former coach had been fired, but I suspected Kurt was on notice as well, likely the cause of his nerves.

Another set of footsteps came from the hallway, interrupting our conversation. Who else had Kurt invited to our meeting?

A woman appeared in the doorway, her head bent and her face hidden behind a long sweep of silky chocolate hair curled into loose waves. She wore a starched white shirt tucked into pressed khaki slacks, both of which fit her lean frame to perfection.

The moment she looked up, my mouth went dry. Rosy cheekbones. Soft, pink lips. A cute nose and vibrant hazel eyes.

Eyes I'd memorized years ago.

Millie.

The air rushed from my lungs.

What. The. Fuck. What was Millie doing here?

"Am I late?" She swept into the room and took the seat across from mine.

"We started early," President Cruz said. "Have you two had the chance to meet?"

I opened my mouth but no words came out. Because Millie—*my Millie*—was staring at me like I was just an old acquaintance. A familiar face and nothing more.

"We have, actually." Her smile widened but it wasn't her real smile. It didn't reach those beautiful eyes. "Hi, Ford."

I cleared my throat. "Hi, Millie."

Her name was one I hadn't spoken in years. It had rolled through my mind countless times, but I hadn't let myself say it aloud. With it came too much regret. Too many *what if*s.

"Millie is an assistant AD," Kurt said.

Hold up.

Did that make her my boss?

CHAPTER TWO

MILLIE

Stay cool.
Breathe.
Just. Act. Normal.

That would be a lot easier to do if Ford didn't look so good. Damn him. Damn his blue eyes. Damn that sharp jaw. Damn those broad shoulders.

Just . . . *damn him.*

I'd known for the past twenty-four hours that he was coming here. Somehow, unbeknownst to me, Kurt had hired Ford as the head football coach. Apparently I was the last staff member in the athletics department to hear the news. The whiplash from that announcement had sent me home early yesterday afternoon. I'd made a pit stop at the grocery store to load up on wine.

Then I'd had a private pity party last night, polishing off a bottle of cabernet while wallowing in the past. But when I'd woken up this morning, slightly hungover, I'd put all of those feelings away and gone on a five-mile run.

My history with Ford was just that. History. Nothing more. So what if he was working here? The Treasure State Athletics Program was big enough for us both, right?

Right.

"I'm going to let you all talk." President Cruz stood from her chair and held out a hand to Ford.

He stood too, towering over her. Most people did, but I'd forgotten just how big he was. Even I felt small standing by his side, and I was taller than most women at five eight. And his height was amplified by this energy he created. This allure. People gravitated toward Ford.

"Pleasure to meet you, President Cruz."

"Carly," she corrected.

He dipped his chin. "Carly."

"Welcome to Treasure State." She nodded at Kurt, then gave me a smile. "Love the nail polish, Millie."

The pearly white was new as of last night, before I'd been too tipsy to hold the brush steady. "Thanks, President Cruz."

She didn't tell me to call her Carly. She used to, for the entire first year of my employment, but had finally given up. I wouldn't call her Carly, not because I didn't want to, but because Kurt had instructed me not to.

It's unprofessional.

I doubted he'd tell Ford the same.

As President Cruz walked out of the conference room, the air lightened. I didn't find her intimidating, maybe because she'd been nothing but kind and genuine to me in my tenure at TSU. Kurt, on the other hand, became this jittery, anxious mess whenever she was around.

Granted, she was his boss, and he was on thin ice. If I were in his position, I'd be sweating too.

Ford resumed his seat, eyes locking on my face.

Oh boy. I'd forgotten just how potent his gaze could be. Twenty-four hours hadn't been enough time to prepare for this, but I forced a smile, tucked my hands underneath my thighs to hide their trembling and turned to Kurt. This was his meeting, after all.

Kurt relaxed, folding his hands together on the table. It was blissfully quiet now that the freaking tapping had stopped. "You'll have to forgive me if you already know this, Ford. I thought I'd just cover some basics. It's probably not all that different from the Seahawks hierarchy, or how things were done when you were an athlete here."

"That was a long time ago." Ford's gaze darted to me, but I kept mine firmly fixed on Kurt.

It *had* been a long time ago. Ten years and three months.

But who was counting?

"The team is yours to manage. I'll do my best to stay out of the way. Mostly, I like to work behind the scenes. Scheduling. Budgets. Facilities, that sort of thing. My job is to put you guys in a position to win."

I swallowed a scoff. Kurt didn't understand the meaning of *behind the scenes.* Part of his job was to schmooze donors and wealthy alums during the games. Except on game days, as long as the weather was nice, he'd be on the sidelines, stepping on everyone's toes. Anything to stand in the limelight.

Though unlike his predecessor, Ford was the type of man who'd tell Kurt to get off his field, even if Kurt was his boss. I actually hoped to see that one of these Saturdays.

"Millie is the assistant AD of internal operations. She serves as the administrator for most of the sports programs. Track and field. Skiing. Rodeo. Golf. Tennis. Cross country. Volleyball. Women's basketball."

Ford cast me another glance, probably because Kurt had listed every sport except the two most popular.

Each women's sport fell into my area of responsibility, along with the other programs that didn't draw in major donor dollars or massive crowds. But considering that those programs were the most decorated in the department, it was a point of pride to manage them. The women's basketball team had been crushing it in the NCAA tournament these past few years.

It wasn't that I didn't have the capacity to take on every sport. I *wanted* the opportunity. Except no matter how many trophies my coaches and teams won, no matter how efficient and effective I proved to be, Kurt kept the men's football and basketball programs to manage himself.

Bandwidth. That had been his reason. Because they were so high profile, he'd been concerned that I didn't have the bandwidth to manage them too.

It was utter bullshit. He just liked the prestige.

"The football and men's basketball programs are the exceptions," Kurt continued. "I'll coordinate with you just like I do with Coach Kincaid of the basketball team. But the reason I invited Millie here today is because strength and conditioning fall within her downline, so there will be some overlap."

Ford nodded. "All right."

"The rest of my team you'll meet next week," Kurt said. "There are a lot of shared duties, but if you ever can't find me for a question, Millie's the best resource. She knows every-thing there is to know about our department."

I sat a little taller. It was rare that Kurt gave me compli-ments, but this one, especially in front of Ford, I'd gladly take.

"We've got a general rule around here. No matter your position, we all pitch in when it comes to fundraising. Over the weekend I'll be sending you the schedule of upcoming donor events for the summer and fall. There aren't many, but I'd like you to be there. I know you just got here, but we're playing catch-up. And everyone's going to want to meet you."

Ford simply nodded again. His gaze dropped to the table and a crease formed between his eyebrows, like maybe he hadn't expected the hectic schedule.

"To be frank with you, Ford, we're in reputation-management mode."

"If we're being honest, I'd probably classify it as *repair* mode," I said. There was no point sugarcoating the situation.

"Yes, I suppose you're right." Kurt sighed. "The former coach smeared our school's name with horseshit. Because of it, we're down thirty-three percent of our annual donations. The boosters are, um . . . cautious."

If cautious meant angry.

"I get it," Ford said. "I'll make nice with the donors and do my best to generate some positive PR."

"Great." Kurt blew out a long breath. "Like I said, I'll email you the list of upcoming events. Monday, we'll get you set up with an official TSU email and phone. And I'll send you a list of more kids in the program who offered to babysit too."

The babysitters. Of course. The list I'd been compiling was for Ford.

Kurt had come to me earlier this week to ask if there were any students who needed some additional income. I'd known one off the top of my head, so I'd given him her name, but he'd wanted a whole list.

Since most of the athletes had access to the weight room and gym over the summer, I'd stopped by during a busy time and collected names and numbers. Most had been from girls on the track and golf teams who weren't on full-ride scholarships.

With school and practice, none of them had the time to get part-time jobs, especially given the busy competition travel schedule. Many took on babysitting to help pay rent.

And Ford needed child care. For his daughter.

Sienna's daughter.

The reality of this whole situation pinched harder than I'd expected it to, and I looked to the table, enduring the twinge of pain.

Breathe. It was fine. Everything would be fine.

I'd seen pictures of Ford's daughter from a year ago. He'd taken her as his date to a charity event. Ford had stunned in a black tux, but the girl had stolen the show with her blond hair and frilly pink dress.

I hadn't let myself look at Ford's Instagram after that night.

"There's a lot to cover come Monday morning, but if you think of anything over the weekend, you've got my number," Kurt said.

"I do," Ford said. "Thanks."

"Here." Kurt dug out his phone from his pocket. "I'll text you Millie's number in case I'm unavailable."

What? No. Ford didn't need my number. He'd want to talk.

I was not about the talking.

Despite my silent protest, Kurt's fingers flew across the screen.

Damn it. *Don't kill your boss. Do not kill your boss.*

Ford's phone dinged.

I cringed.

"Well, I've got another meeting to get to," I lied, standing from the table. "Good to see you again, Ford."

That lie came out as smoothly as the first, and before either man could stop me, I was out of the conference room and down the hallway, pushing through the door to the stairwell. I couldn't take the stairs two at a time in my heels, but I jogged, hitting the administration floor and marching past cubicles.

"Hey, Millie," someone called.

I raised a hand to wave but didn't stop walking until I reached the safety of my office. With the door closed, I sagged against its frame. "Shit."

Okay, that was harder than I'd thought it would be. A lot harder. If Ford hadn't been so goddamn handsome . . .

I shoved off the door, pulling it open. I'd always had an open-door policy with the staff and athletes. This office wasn't closed unless I was having a confidential meeting and needed privacy.

"I'm not changing for Ford Ellis, no matter what he looks like," I muttered as I took a seat at my desk, shuffling through some papers scattered on the surface. "Why can't he be one of those football guys who gets a bulging belly and receding hairline?"

"Still talking to yourself, I see."

My heart jumped into my throat.

There he was, filling the threshold with that muscular frame.

Damn him.

That gorgeous face shouldn't have taken me so off guard. It wasn't like I hadn't seen him these past ten years. I'd watched his Seahawks games on TV. I'd seen the memes from adoring female fans. Some had proposed marriage. Some had offered to have his baby. The man was utterly irresistible on the jumbotron. Up close?

Oh, I was in trouble.

It was in the quiet moments that I'd always appreciated Ford's features. During the times when it had just been the two of us. When his smile had been unguarded. When his smooth voice had been a regular part of my dreams.

Years ago.

Before he'd left me humiliated and brokenhearted.

"Can I help you with something?" I asked, shaking the mouse to wake up my computer.

The brilliant plan I'd devised last night over my bottle of wine was to act aloof. Ford and I would be coworkers, nothing more. I'd do my job. He'd do his. I hadn't interacted much with the previous football coach, and I saw no reason to change that.

Except my hands started trembling again.

Ford came into my office, making the space too small. He pulled out the chair on the other side of my desk and took a seat. A whiff of his cologne carried my way. Spice, leather, cedar and masculine as hell. It hadn't changed.

I'd use up all of my future birthday wishes if it meant I could forget that scent. If I could forget all things Ford Ellis.

My fingers splayed across the keyboard, and I willed them to keep still. My eyes stayed trained on the monitor and my inbox.

Aloof. I was aloof.

Ford leaned back in his chair, his hands resting in his lap. I caught the gold glint on one of his fingers. A ring.

A Super Bowl ring.

Ford had been a star wide receiver, treasured by Seahawks fans, but when he'd caught a nearly impossible catch to win the Super Bowl, he'd made history.

His picture had been splashed everywhere. I hadn't been able to turn on the TV without seeing an interview of him post game or a replay of the catch. He'd been voted one of *People* magazine's Sexiest Men Alive.

Then during a game the following season, a cornerback had taken a cheap shot. Ford had torn his ACL, and the damage had been irreparable.

I'd cried for him the night he'd announced his retirement. I'd sobbed for a lost career and the heartache I'd felt all the way from Seattle. When the Seahawks franchise had taken him on as a coach, I'd thought it was kismet.

Ford had always been good at lifting up his teammates. He was a natural leader.

I'd thought it would be easier to forget him if he wasn't on ESPN. I could finally let go of the past if I didn't see his face on Monday Night Football.

The joke was on me.

This was karma's way of punishing me for the lip gloss I'd stolen from Target when I was fifteen, wasn't it?

"Are you going to talk to me?"

Nope. "Of course," I said, my eyes on the screen as I pretended to read an email. "What can I help you with?"

"Are you going to look at me?"

Not if I can help it. But that was a dare if I'd ever heard one, so I tore my eyes from the screen and found those brilliant blues waiting.

"Hey, Mills."

I swallowed hard. He was the only person in the world who called me Mills. "Hey, Ford."

"Long time."

Ten years and three months.

But who's counting?

CHAPTER THREE

FORD

W ell, she wasn't my boss. That was one less complication. But considering the way she was staring through me, not at me, simply being coworkers would be difficult enough.

Maybe this job had been a bad idea.

I couldn't believe it. I couldn't stop staring at her. Millie. *My* Millie.

She was more beautiful than I remembered. Her hair was longer than it had been in college. Her features were more elegant and refined. I supposed we'd both lost that youthful look from our twenties.

A sweet, citrus scent clung to the air, like tangerines and fresh cut flowers. Millie's perfume hadn't changed.

Her hazel gaze darted past my shoulder, then to the door, then to her desk, then back to her computer screen. She looked everywhere but at my face.

She had to have known I was coming on as head coach. As one of Kurt's assistant ADs, she had to have known I was being interviewed. Was she okay with that?

Was I?

Maybe I would have thought twice about accepting Kurt's offer had I known she was here. Not that it wasn't damn good to see her face. But I'd come to Montana to simplify life.

Nothing about Millie and me had ever been simple.

This was the problem with interviewing for and accepting a job within a twenty-day span. I'd poked around the website, not finding much information. But otherwise, I hadn't spent any time researching the department. My focus had been on the actual move—buying a house and traveling across three states. Relocating my child.

Except Toren would have known about Millie. That bastard. I was going to fucking murder him for not giving me a warning about this. He knew our history. And he'd been there when it had all fallen apart.

Goddamn. *Millie.*

There was no ring on her left hand. Another complication.

"You look good."

She pulled her lower lip between her teeth, a nervous habit that had always been adorable. "Thanks."

Why wouldn't she look at me? "Millie."

Her eyes closed, and for a minute, I thought maybe I'd broken through. But then she squared her shoulders, put on the same professional, sterile smile she'd worn in the conference room downstairs and faced me with her hands folded on the desk. "It's good to have you back with the Wildcats, Ford."

Was it? Because that was the most practiced line I'd heard in ages. "It's good to be here."

"Kurt mentioned that the hiring process was . . . accelerated. Have you had a chance to look around the fieldhouse?"

"Not yet." Christ, she sounded like a stranger. *Aloof.* I fucking hated aloof.

"Definitely have Kurt take you on a tour next week. You'll hardly recognize the place."

The building? I was more concerned about recognizing her.

The Millie I'd known hadn't owned a poker face. She hadn't faked a thing. Sometime over the past ten years, she'd gotten good at both.

I'd heard what she'd said as she'd walked into her office. She hadn't realized I'd been right behind her—that I'd left that conference room in a rush and taken the stairs two at a time to catch her. Millie was flustered that I was here and doing her best to smother it.

But at least she'd known I was coming. Meanwhile, seeing her had given me whiplash.

She glanced at the door again, a not-so-subtle hint that I was excused.

I relaxed deeper into the chair. Maybe if I sat here long enough, I'd catch a glimpse of the woman I'd once known. "How long have you worked here?"

"Nine years," she clipped with another glance at the door. "I started here after graduation."

"You always talked about working for a university program."

Her smile tightened. "I did."

Clearly, she didn't want to talk about the past. There'd be no stroll down memory lane. Yet. Eventually, there were things to say, apologies to make, but before we opened that wound, I needed to get my head on straight about exactly what I had to say.

Maybe we could meet for dinner, somewhere quiet.

"Look, Mills. We should talk—"

"You'll have a good team this year," she blurted. "I don't know how much time you've spent learning about the players. The former head coach might have been a disgrace to the Wildcat program, but your coaching staff is solid."

Football. She wanted to talk about football?

I guess football was better than being shot down for a dinner invite.

"Toren and I kept in touch over the years," I told her. "He wasn't a fan of my predecessor either and had a lot of frustrations. But he said the other guys were good. It's part of the reason I agreed to this. I trust him. It'll be nice to meet everyone next week."

I should be downstairs right now, introducing myself. But Millie always had a way of stealing my focus.

She wore more makeup than she used to. Lipstick instead of lip balm. There was a shimmer on her eyelids that made the vibrant hazel pop beneath her long, dark eyelashes.

Millie. Her name kept looping through my mind on instant replay.

So much had changed in our years apart, and yet when I stared at her, I was twenty-three again, sitting at her side in the philosophy class we'd both needed for core credits.

I'd been a fifth-year senior. She'd been a junior. Both of us had barely passed the course because instead of listening to the professor, we'd sat in the back of the lecture hall, filling spiral notebooks with notes to one another.

A lifetime had passed since those days.

Yeah, we really needed to talk.

"How much do you know about the scandal?" she asked, seemingly intent on keeping the conversation about work and only work.

"Not much. Kurt brushed over the details in most of our conversations."

"No surprise," she muttered.

"I read what was reported publicly. I caught a headline one day as I was walking past a newsstand." Seeing Treasure State in the news wasn't common, and I'd done a double take at the lead story.

"It was ugly," she said. "Our general counsel did her best to keep as many details as possible away from the media. But in a nutshell, one of the red-shirt freshmen was brought to the ER last spring. He had alcohol poisoning from a party and a bag of Adderall in his pocket."

"The party was at the coach's house, right?"

Millie nodded. "The coach wasn't there when the cops arrived. He claimed to have been camping that night and had left the house unlocked. He blamed the players for breaking in."

"Camping?"

"Without a tent, sleeping bag or coat in his vehicle. In late April."

April in Montana often meant snow, not sunny and seventy degrees.

"No one bought his story," she said. "When the players started coming forward and saying that he'd invited them over, the details fell into place. Somehow he'd gotten word that the cops were on the way and bolted."

"Why would he throw parties?" That was an easy way to get fired.

"Apparently he'd been doing it for years. Maybe it was

31

his way of bonding with the younger players. Most of the upperclassmen knew about them but didn't attend. They said it was . . . awkward. Coach always asked the guys to bring girls along."

"Shit," I muttered.

"Pretty much. Only one girl came forward and admitted to sleeping with him. She was a sophomore on the golf team. She's already transferred to Eastern Washington."

"That's quite the mess."

From the picture I'd seen in the paper, the coach had to have been in his fifties. He had the former-football-player look Millie had been muttering about—the bulging belly and receding hairline.

"You've got your work cut out for you," she said. "Most of the players and staff seem glad to have him gone, but they won't be overly trusting."

"Good to know. I'll sync up with the coaching staff and get their take too. Then I'll make it a point to spend some extra time with the kids in the weight room."

Sometimes the best way to build a rapport with the players was on their turf, not in my office. At least, that was what my favorite high-school coach had always done.

"Thanks for the heads-up, Millie."

"You're welcome. This is a good program, Ford. We work hard, and it's not fair that the actions of one person have tarnished our reputation. Please keep that in mind." There was an edge to her voice. A thinly veiled accusation.

"What are you implying?" Did she think I'd do something to hurt this school or these kids?

"I don't know why you're here." She raised her chin. "It can't be for the money. Even as an assistant coach with the

Seahawks, you had to be making more than you will here. Is it for the fame?"

I scoffed. "I've had enough fame to last two lifetimes." And though I was sure that being the head coach for TSU meant I'd be recognized, the *fame* in Mission would be nothing compared to what I'd endured in Seattle.

Division I FCS football was a far cry from the NFL.

"Then why?" she asked.

"It was time for a change of scenery." And that was the explanation she'd get for now. Because anything else meant delving into the past and this was not the time.

Millie studied me like she knew there was more to my answer—she'd always been good at reading me—but she didn't push it. She simply gave me another polite smile and ambivalent stare.

She'd always been good at getting right under my skin too. Clearly, that hadn't changed.

I opened my mouth, not exactly sure what to say but . . . something. Except my phone vibrated in my pocket. It was a text from Joey's babysitter, asking if they could walk to the park in our neighborhood. I typed a quick reply, then tucked my phone away.

"Sorry. Just Joey's sitter checking in."

Something flashed in Millie's gaze. Pain? Anger? She covered it before I could decide and those eyes once again flicked to the door. "I'm sure you've got plenty to do. I'm about to sign off for the weekend myself."

And with that, I was dismissed. The temperature in the room dropped ten degrees. Her fingers flew across the keyboard and not even the warm summer sunshine could compete with her icy indifference.

I sighed and pushed out of her chair, heading for the door.

"Ford." She stopped me before I reached the threshold.

"Yeah?" I glanced back and the look on her face rocked me on my heels.

Gone was the tight smile. Gone was the cool stare. She looked . . . sad. "I'm sorry about your knee."

There she is. There was my Millie. The one who looked like she was about to cry because she knew what an injury like that meant to me. "Thank you."

"I was watching your game. When it happened . . ." She closed her eyes and shook her head. "It was awful."

"Not the best night." Though the months afterward had been worse.

The surgery to repair my torn ACL had been considered a success by the doctors, but I'd known during the first stages of physical therapy that things weren't the same. No matter how hard I'd worked, how careful I'd been, I'd realized after my first practice back with the team that my knee wouldn't be *normal* again.

How many guys pushed it too far for just one more game? In the end, I'd decided that walking without a limp was more important than football. I wanted to be able to hike with Joey. To chase her around the yard. To walk her down the aisle one day without a cane.

"It worked out in the end. I like coaching. And I always said I'd end my career on a high." I thumbed the ring on my hand.

This ring was the only valuable piece of jewelry I owned, and my movers wouldn't put it on the truck, so I'd worn it on the plane. I rarely wore it, but today when I'd been getting dressed, I'd put it on. Maybe to give myself a boost of confidence. While I was fairly certain I was failing as a father, I might make it as a decent Wildcat coach.

"You definitely reached the high." A ghost of a proud smile graced her soft lips. "It was a great Super Bowl game."

"It was." Damn, but I loved that she'd watched. I wouldn't let myself hope that she'd rooted for me, but the fact that she'd watched was enough.

There was a sparkle in her eyes and for the briefest moment, she stared at me like she had once a long time ago. But that glint was gone too soon. Millie dropped her hazel gaze and when she looked back up, it was to the door. "Good luck with the team, Ford."

"See you around, Millie."

My Millie.

Except she wasn't mine anymore, was she? I'd lost her a long time ago when I'd walked away.

When I'd made the wrong choice for myself.

And the right one for my daughter.

CHAPTER FOUR

MILLIE

Autumn looked me up and down, then shook her head. "You can't wear that."

"Why?" I glanced at my gray pants and matching gray blouse. "I look fine, don't I?"

"Yes, you look *fine*. But we can do better than fine."

"Autumn, I don't want to change." My shoulders slumped. Were all best friends this pushy when it came to their counterparts' wardrobes? "I need to go, or I'll be late."

She ignored me and marched into my walk-in closet. "I know you love your monochromatic ensembles, but tonight is not the night to be dull."

"It's just a fundraiser. Dull is the dress code."

"Black. Gray. White. Cream. Navy. Would it kill you to buy something red?" The hangers scraped against the rod as she rifled through my closet.

"Red is the color of the enemy." You wouldn't catch me in anything that might be misconstrued as a Grizzly shade.

"You take your job too seriously."

"I like to take my job too seriously." I walked to my bed,

slumping on the edge. Without work, what did I have? A modest two-bedroom home with a mortgage and a Kia Telluride with thirty thousand miles.

"Ford is going to be there tonight, right?"

"Yes," I muttered.

"So don't you want to look hot?"

"I don't know." I plucked at my white duvet. I'd chosen my outfit tonight because it was simple and plain and maybe if I blended in with the crowd, I'd be able to avoid Ford.

"Here." Autumn walked out of my closet with two dresses, holding one up. "This is my first choice."

"Absolutely not." It was a strapless black cocktail dress with a short skirt. "This is a work function."

She frowned and held up the other option. "Then this one."

It was another black dress, but one that wouldn't get me fired. The neckline was high, close to a mock turtleneck. It had cap sleeves and hit me just below the knee. Boring on the hanger, but sexy on my body because of the snug fit. As a lifelong runner, I didn't have a lot of curves to work with, and this dress gave me the illusion of a figure.

"It's boring enough for work and tight enough to drive Ford wild," Autumn said.

"That's not the goal."

"It has to be the goal. You're going to walk into this party wearing this sexy dress, and every time he looks at you, it will be his punishment."

Did I want to punish Ford?

Yes.

Did I have the guts to do it?

Probably not.

Which was why my tactic when dealing with our new coach had been avoidance.

In the past two weeks, I'd made sure to stay as far away from Ford as possible. If I saw him walking down the hallway, I turned and walked the other way. I'd filled my calendar with meeting after meeting so that when I was in my office, the door was closed. But mostly, I'd avoided my office entirely, not wanting a repeat of Ford's first day.

Luckily, he'd been busy getting settled into his new role.

Kurt was in full-fledged bragger mode. Whenever we crossed paths, he'd drone on and on about Ford.

The coaching staff loves him. They've gelled in just two weeks.

The players are already idolizing Ford. Isn't that amazing?

This was the best hiring decision I've made in my career.

Always nice to hear that from your boss.

Dismissing Kurt's opinions would have been easier if he'd been wrong. But I'd walked by the coach's conference room a few times in the past two weeks, Ford seated at the head of the table surrounded by his crew. The assistant coaches had been hanging on Ford's every word.

I was just grateful that since he was so busy, I'd been given a reprieve. With him reviewing player stats, the practice schedule and the lineup of this season's games, I'd almost had a normal two weeks.

Almost.

There was simply no dodging the presence that was Ford Ellis, even in a collegiate fieldhouse.

I had hope for this situation yet. Next week marked the first full week of August, and with the players starting practice on Monday, I might actually be able to avoid Ford until November. Longer if the Wildcats made the playoffs.

But first, I needed to make it through tonight's fundraiser.

"I'm just going to wear this." I gestured to my gray on gray. "I'll blend."

"No." Autumn tossed the dresses on the bed beside me and reached for the button on my blouse.

"What are you doing?" I swatted at her hand but she was determined, opening two before I was able to shove her away. "You're surprisingly good at unbuttoning shirts."

She laughed. "It was that lawyer I dated last year. Remember him? Tall, dark and—"

"Douchey. Oh, I remember." The asshole had cheated on her four months into their relationship.

"That's him. He was always in these button-down shirts, and although douchey, he had a great body and was *really* good in bed. Maybe I should call him."

"Absolutely not." She'd cried for a week after their breakup.

"Wear this dress, and I promise not to call him."

I groaned. "Blackmail? Really?"

"It works." She shrugged and picked up the dress, shaking it in my face. "Time to change or you're going to be late."

Not only did she get her way about my outfit, but she also managed to convince me to take down my hair and wear a darker shade of lipstick.

Autumn and I had been friends for years. We'd met at a wine tasting downtown, and after three flights, we'd shared a cab home and been friends ever since.

I didn't have a lot of friends, mostly because I worked all

the time. But Autumn hadn't let my demanding schedule get in the way of our time together. I was closer to her than I was my own sister, Macie. And Autumn was one of the few people I'd trusted with my story about Ford.

Not many hated that man, but Autumn did.

For me.

And I loved her for it. Even if she'd convinced me to wear four-inch stiletto heels.

"Shit," I muttered as I pulled into the stadium's parking lot, already filled with vehicles. I was late.

Hurrying from my car to the entrance, I rushed past the student manning the check-in station and hit the button at the elevators. The fundraiser tonight was for a select group of local boosters who each had a sky suite at the stadium. They were here to meet Ford and chat with the other coaches.

My attendance wasn't really necessary, but per Kurt's requirement, we all showed up for these events. Maybe after a little mingling, I'd be free to escape.

"Two hours. Three, tops," I told myself as I rode the elevator to the Stadium Club on the third floor.

Saturdays in the fall were spent here at the stadium, stationed in the club or in the endzone with special guests or ticketholders who'd paid for premium access. On the weekends when there were other events, like volleyball games, I pulled double duty.

Meanwhile, Kurt only worked the club when it was either too hot or too cold outside. When the weather was perfect, he'd be crowding the sidelines and getting in everyone's way. If there was a home football game, not a chance he'd stop by the fieldhouse to cheer on the volleyball players even though they deserved the attention.

The hum of chatter welcomed me as the elevator doors slid open. I stepped onto the floor, smiled at a student on the catering staff and swiped a glass of champagne from her tray.

"Millie, there you are. Thank God." Drew, the assistant AD of fan development, rushed over. This was his party, and from the flush of his cheeks, he'd already lost control. "Ford just got mobbed. Literally mobbed. I don't know what to do. I've never seen anything like it before. I'm afraid someone is going to get trampled in a stampede."

I glanced past him to the center of the room. Sure enough, Ford was surrounded by an island of people. Had he not stood head and shoulders above them all, he might have been swallowed whole.

There was a smile on his face and anyone else might have thought he was handling the crowd fine. But there was a stiffness to his shoulders. A tension to his jaw.

Ford didn't deserve my rescue, but to the rescue I would go. *Damn him.*

"You go peel people away from the left side, and I'll tackle the right," I told Drew, then flicked a wrist toward the other coaches clustered together by a cocktail table. "Tell those guys to break up the huddle and mingle."

"Thanks, Millie," Drew said before rushing away to follow my orders.

No surprise, Kurt was standing right beside Ford with a smug grin on his face. He'd be no help tonight.

After a long sip of my champagne, I plastered on a smile and did my job. I helped separate the mob, creating smaller conversation groups by introducing donors to each other. I steered people toward cocktail tables and waved over the catering staff to keep them fed.

Fifteen minutes later, when I glanced over my shoulder at Ford, he actually had breathing room.

His piercing blue gaze met mine, and my heart skipped as his gaze trailed over my shoulders and down the length of my dress. His jaw clenched before he turned away.

Punishment. Autumn would gloat for weeks.

It took concentrated effort not to look at him throughout the party. The other coaches drifted around the room, each standing taller than most of the guests.

When Toren spotted me, he winked.

I shot him my fiercest glare.

He'd suggested Ford for the head coach position, something I'd learned in the past two weeks. The jerkface. Toren was the only guy on the coaching team or in the department who knew my history with Ford. Besides Autumn, he was probably the only other person in Mission who knew about our past.

As far as I was concerned, it was going to stay that way.

Ford Ellis was my coworker. Period.

A caterer was coming my way carrying another tray of champagne. I was about to wave the kid over and snatch another glass when one magically appeared in front of me.

"Thank—" The large hand connected to the flute belonged to Ford.

"Hi, Mills." His rugged, deep voice, which had somehow gotten sexier in the past decade, sent tingles down my spine.

I took the drink and tipped it to my lips, taking a long pull before breathing again. It was a mistake. One breath and his spicy cologne filled my nose and weakened my knees.

"How are you?" he asked. "Haven't seen you around."

"It's a busy time of year, Coach."

He was as breathtaking tonight as he'd been two weeks

ago. Still no bulging belly or receding hairline. Instead, he was a pillar of honed muscle. Ford had been strong in college, having spent hours in the weight room, but years in the NFL had transformed him into the perfect male athlete. He was mouthwatering.

Damn him.

He wore a pair of charcoal slacks and a royal-blue Wildcat quarter-zip. The material clung to his strong chest, and with the sleeves pushed up, the black tattoos on his right forearm were on display.

There were more than I'd remembered. Part of me wanted to ask what they meant. Ford had a story for all the ink on his skin.

But those tattoos were none of my business. Not anymore.

"How are things going tonight?" I asked. Maybe if I focused on business, I wouldn't get distracted by those arms or that flat stomach. During our encounter two weeks ago, I'd managed to keep the discussion purely professional. It had worked for me then, so I was sticking with that strategy tonight.

"So far so good, I hope." He took a sip of beer from his pint glass. "Kurt's become my shadow."

"Get used to that," I said, looking past him for my boss.

"He went to the bathroom."

"Ah." That explained why he wasn't clinging to Ford's side like he had been all night.

"Look, Mills. Before the seasons starts, I'd like to talk about—"

"Can I have cake, Daddy?" A girl appeared at his side, interrupting our conversation.

My heart twisted.

This was her. This was his daughter.

I took in her sweet face. The blue eyes she'd inherited from her father. The long, blond hair from her mother. The button nose and the smudge of chocolate at the corner of her mouth that told me she'd already had cake and was campaigning for seconds.

Like I'd seen on Ford's Instagram, she was a miniature Sienna. There was a bit of Ford in her face, but mostly when I stared at her, I saw her mother.

I'd spent the better part of ten years forgetting that face. This little girl's smile was threatening to undo that hard work.

"Where's Emma?" Ford asked her.

Emma—one of the girls on the ski team and someone on my babysitting list.

"She's talking to somebody."

I searched the room and found Emma standing with an older couple, probably making polite conversation. Most of the alumni loved chatting with students as much as they loved talking to staff.

"We had a little mix-up," Ford said, raking a hand through the waves in his light brown hair. "Emma thought this only went until six, so she made plans. I figured I'd never get out of here by then, so Joey's tagging along. And eating cake." He wiped chocolate from the corner of her mouth with his thumb.

It was precious. The way he gazed at her, like she was his entire world, was adorable.

I dropped my eyes to the floor.

"Who are you?" Joey asked, and I blinked, bringing my eyes back to her face.

"Manners," Ford scolded.

"Sorry," she mumbled.

"This is my daughter, Josalynn. We call her Joey."

Joey. God, she was cute. There was a gap between her front teeth. She was wearing a navy dress with sheer half sleeves. The fabric was dotted with tiny gold stars, the same color as her ballet flats.

"Hi, Joey." I forced a smile. "I'm Millie."

"We work together," Ford added.

She looked me up and down. "Are you a coach?"

"No. I work in the office doing boring stuff."

"Oh." She studied my face, tilting her own to the side. Her eyes narrowed. Then something dawned and her attention swung to her father. "Daddy, isn't this the lady in that picture on your bookshelf?"

CHAPTER FIVE

FORD

I loved my daughter wholeheartedly. But for fuck's sake, I needed to buy her a filter. Why, of all the things to bring up, did she have to mention the picture?

Millie's eyes widened.

I opened my mouth, ready to explain, but was halted by Kurt and his impeccably bad timing.

"Hey, Ford. There's a few people I'd like you to meet."

I'd heard that sentence a hundred times tonight.

"Sure." I gave him a tight smile, then looked at Millie. "We need to talk."

"About what?" Kurt asked, looking between the two of us.

"Personal history," I answered at the same time Millie blurted, "Nothing."

I shot her a frown.

She gave me that irritating, polite smile. "I'll let you guys get back to work and do the same myself. Nice to meet you, Joey."

Before Joey could respond, Millie spun on a heel and

strode toward a group of people, giving me a perfect view of her ass in that sexy-as-fuck black dress.

I tore my eyes away before Kurt and Joey caught me drooling. This was not the place for an erection.

"Can I have cake?" Joey asked.

"You mean more cake."

She gave me that devilish grin she'd made famous by six. "Yeah."

"Go ahead." I jerked my chin in her sitter's direction. "But find Emma first and stay with her."

"Okay." Joey raced away, leaving me in Kurt's clutches.

Kurt hadn't seemed too happy to see my daughter in tow when I'd stepped off the elevator. He'd quickly hidden his disapproval and told me it was fine. That this was a family event. Except Joey was the only kid here under eighteen.

Whatever. He'd have to deal with her tagging along from time to time. I was a single dad, and my kid was my priority.

"Ready?" he asked.

"Lead the way." I cast a glance over my shoulder at Millie as I followed my new boss.

She was talking to a couple in matching Wildcat shirts, but her gaze was over their shoulders to where my daughter was dragging Emma toward the dessert table. There was hurt in Millie's expression as she stared at Joey. The last thing I wanted was to cause her more pain, and damn it, we needed to talk.

"Here we are." Kurt addressed an older gentleman with a handlebar mustache and a belt buckle the size of a softball. "Ford Ellis, meet John Jones."

I zoned out as he rattled off the man's profession and affiliation to TSU. I'd met so many people tonight that there wasn't a hope in hell I'd remember every name. Especially not with my focus pulled in different directions.

I'd been keeping an eye on Joey, even with the sitter here. Then Millie had walked into the room wearing that outfit, and she'd drawn my attention too. Did she have to wear a dress that tight? If she'd intended to punish me, it was working. She was the most beautiful woman in the room, and I wasn't the only man who struggled to keep his eyes away.

One shithead had leered so blatantly that I'd interrupted the conversation to stand in front of him, blocking his view of her ass.

If I could just pull her aside for another minute, maybe I could convince her to meet me for dinner or a drink. Except every time I tried to get closer to her, she'd see me coming and find someone, anyone, else to talk to.

So I was forced to make pleasantries for another hour, smiling and shaking hands while my coaching staff did the same.

They'd all shown up like soldiers tonight, knowing we were on a mission to fix our program's tarnished reputation. Most of the guys seemed to carry some guilt because they'd worked under the former coach's command. It wasn't their fault but I appreciated the extra dedication to our cause.

I'd expected some direct questions about the scandal tonight, yet no one had brought it up to me personally. There'd only been a few murmurs in passing. Hopefully that was the case for my staff too. They deserved a reprieve.

In the past two weeks, I'd sat down with each of the coaches for a one-on-one conversation. From what I could tell, not a single member of my staff had known about the parties. If I'd misjudged and found out later that one of them had known, it would mean an immediate termination. But mostly, my impression was that the coaches had been embarrassed by their former boss and frustrated that none of the players had told them what was happening.

As far as I was concerned, the scandal was behind us. We were moving forward, and at yesterday's team meeting, I'd instructed them on our priorities.

Number one, we needed to get the kids to talk to us. A player who didn't confide in his coach might be a good player but there'd always be a lack of trust. If those kids had personal problems, academic problems, financial problems, I wanted a coach to be the first person they thought to go to.

If I'd had that type of relationship with a coach of mine in college, well . . . maybe I would have made different decisions, especially where Sienna was concerned. What I'd lacked then as a mentor, I wanted to provide to this team now.

Our second priority was showing up for the fans. They needed to see that the actions of one man didn't define Wildcat football. Not a single coach had grumbled about attending this event tonight. It might not be fun, none of us were born to charm donors, but it was necessary. So we'd shown up with our game faces on.

The third priority was pulling off a successful season. We had the talent, both on the field and on the sidelines. As part of my individual meetings, I'd gone through every coach's résumé and discussed with them their strengths and limitations. There were a few roles I'd be shifting after practices started. Otherwise, we were going to do the best with our current lineup. I needed their tenure here. I needed a few familiar faces on staff.

Toren had vouched for the other coaches when he'd come over to my place last weekend. We'd sat on my living room couch and had a couple of beers while he'd given me his take on the staff.

The only guy he didn't trust in the department was Kurt. He had no proof, but he said that the general feeling around the fieldhouse was that when the former coach had been busted, Kurt hadn't been surprised.

So I was keeping one eye on my boss and the other on the prize. Win as many games as possible. Avoid any scandals. Beat the Grizzlies. If we made it to the playoffs, I'd be ecstatic.

The job was important. But Joey was getting the majority of my energy and attention. I was focused on getting her settled. Maybe seeing more smiles than scowls on her face.

Beyond that, I wanted to make peace with Millie.

She'd been on my mind constantly these past two weeks. That office door of hers had been closed every time I'd stopped by. No surprise, she'd been avoiding me. And I'd given her the time to do it.

Except we couldn't avoid the past forever, and if we were going to be working together, it was time to clear the air. It was time to say the things I should have said ten years ago.

"Coach Ellis, I've got to go." Emma came rushing over during a break in conversation with Joey at her side.

"Thanks, Emma." I reached into my rear pocket for my wallet, fishing out some cash. "Still on for next week?"

"I'll be there." She nodded, then held out a fist to Joey. "See ya, Jo."

"Bye." My daughter knocked her knuckles against Emma's, then leaned into my leg. "Can we go now?"

"Soon." I put a hand on her shoulder. "Thanks for sticking it out."

"I'm bored."

Yeah, me too. "Want to play a game on my phone?"

Joey shrugged. "I guess."

"Just keep the volume low," I said, handing it over.

She leaned against me, playing her game, while Kurt kept pulling people in my direction. I did my best to keep Joey content and quiet while I visited about the season and my time with the Seahawks.

I lost track of the number of times people recounted my Super Bowl winning play. I fought yawn after yawn, the lack of sleep catching up to me.

Every evening since the move, I'd spent my time entertaining Joey, playing games, exploring Mission, whatever she wanted. Then after she crashed, I'd work for a few hours to unpack boxes. I hadn't had a solid eight hours sleep in, well . . . weeks. But I smiled through the exhaustion, stifling yawns, and kept my pulse on Millie in the room.

Her smile was unwavering. It dazzled. Her musical laugh caught my ear from time to time, causing warmth to spread through my chest. As much as people gravitated toward me, they were equally drawn in her direction. She had a bigger group clustered around her than any of the coaches.

Millie fit here effortlessly. She was a natural at making small talk and would never forget a name. After ten minutes in her company, you felt like you'd known her for years. She just had that way about her. People confided in her because they knew their secrets would be safe.

But she guarded her own secrets too.

From what I could tell, she hadn't told a soul about our past. Whenever I brought her name up with the other coaches, they'd smile and boast about how awesome she was, how knowledgeable she was about sports. The only person at the university who seemed to know Millie and I had a history was Toren.

"Can I get you another beer?" Kurt asked when he noticed that my glass was empty. It had been for an hour.

"No, thanks."

"I'm going to grab one for myself. Be back." He leaned in closer. "You're doing great."

Why did he sound surprised? I'd spent plenty of time around wealthy donors. Hell, I was one.

Kurt must not know about the money I'd gifted to Treasure State a few years ago when they'd been going through an extensive capital campaign to fund the fieldhouse's remodel.

I'd given them a quarter of a million dollars, though I'd done it in Joey's name. It wasn't a huge amount in the grand scheme, but enough that I'd gotten my daughter's name on a hallway plaque. I'd have to hunt it down one of these days and show her.

"How's it going, princess?" I asked Joey.

She looked up at me with pleading eyes. "This sucks. Can we go now?"

"Don't say sucks." I checked my watch. "And we'll go soon."

The crowd was beginning to thin, but it was still bright outside, which didn't hurry people home like a dark night would have. These long Montana summer days made it easy to stay up late. Too late. Last night I hadn't crashed until one. And when the sun had streamed through my bedroom window around six this morning, I'd gotten up to unpack a few more boxes.

The house was still a mess, but the kitchen was set up. I

could actually cook a meal for us. Toren's visit had motivated me to put the living room and my office together, including the bookshelf with Millie's picture.

I scanned the room, finding her just as she stepped into the elevator. *Shit.*

"How's it going?" Toren came over, following my gaze to the elevator.

"Would you mind hanging with Joey for just a minute? I was hoping to catch Millie before she left."

"Sure, man." He plucked my phone from Joey's hands.

"Hey!" She shot him a scowl that quickly turned into a smile because Joey loved Toren. When he'd come over last weekend, he'd spent a solid hour in her room, letting her paint his fingernails blue and silver. Though he'd picked most of it off, the colors still lingered along his cuticles.

"Want to do something fun?" he asked, bending close and lowering his voice.

"Like what?"

He nodded to the glass windows that overlooked the stadium. "Sneak onto the field."

"Yes." She fist pumped.

"I'll find you," I told him, then raced for the elevators.

They opened for me the moment I pushed the button, but the ride to the first floor was agonizing. When it stopped, I flew out the door and jogged out of the stadium to the parking lot.

Millie moved with grace and elegance toward the parked cars, like she was on a runway, not black asphalt. Her legs were a mile long with those stiletto heels, and the dress molded to her hips and thighs.

"Millie," I called as she strode toward a silver Kia SUV.

She glanced over her shoulder, keys in hand, but didn't stop.

"Millie, hold up."

She ignored me and kept walking.

Her legs were long, but not as long as mine. And she couldn't outpace me in those shoes.

"Millie." I touched her elbow when I caught up.

She jerked it away and turned, frown in place. "What do you want, Ford?"

"To talk."

"No." She shook her head. "I don't want to talk."

"There are things to say."

"Why? It's unnecessary. It's in the past."

Like hell it was. "It's been ten years. At the very least, let's catch up."

"Yeah, sure. Maybe sometime."

Liar.

She turned away, her strides faster and each accentuated by the click of a heel.

"Mills."

Click. Click. "Ford."

"Dinner. Or lunch."

Click. Click.

"Breakfast?" She'd always liked pancakes.

"What picture?" She whirled on me so fast I nearly ran into her. "On your bookshelf. What picture?"

"Oh." I'd forgotten Joey's overshare. "One from college."

"Which one?"

The only one of her I'd let myself keep. The only photo of Millie I'd let myself look at in all this time. Ten years and I hadn't searched for her on Facebook or Instagram. I hadn't asked Toren if he stayed in touch with her.

Not that I hadn't been curious. Not that I hadn't wondered.

But I'd been married. Unhappily, but married. And Millie was a temptation like no other.

I knew that if I started thinking about Millie, well . . . I wouldn't have stopped.

That picture on my bookshelf was the only exception. I'd tucked it away at the back of a World War II book that I'd known Sienna would never touch. Because had she found that picture, she would have shredded it instantly.

"It's from my last season here," I told her. "After the Griz game."

We'd been standing on the field. She'd asked a random guy to take a picture. I'd been sweaty and smiling from a victory over the Grizzlies. She'd been tucked into my side, my arm around her shoulders and my pads making me look like a giant compared to her lean frame.

She'd been in a blue parka and matching beanie. Her nose and cheeks had been rosy because there'd been a ton of snow and it had been well below zero. But her smile had chased away any of the cold.

Toren had been on my other side, grinning at someone out of the shot.

Most people, Joey included, saw three friends laughing and smiling after a victory.

Me, I saw what I'd lost.

"Why would you put it on your bookshelf?" she asked.

Damn good question. Seeing that photo always hurt. "Joey hasn't taken the divorce well. For a while, she thought it was just temporary. I thought maybe if I took away the family pictures, it would help."

It had been a year since the divorce. Eighteen months

since Sienna and I had separated. Joey knew now it was permanent, but it had taken almost that entire time to get her there.

And that photo, for better or worse, was a favorite of mine.

Millie swallowed hard. "That doesn't really answer my question. Why me?"

"I like that picture."

Millie had gotten it printed and given me a copy. Did she still have hers? Did she ever think about me? Did she know how much I regretted what had happened?

These unanswered questions would drive me mad.

"An hour, Mills. Just an hour to talk."

"It's unnecessary."

Twice she'd said that word and twice it rubbed me the wrong way. Nothing about us had ever been unnecessary.

"Monday," I said. "After work, we can grab a drink."

"No."

"Great. See you then." Without another word, I turned and walked away.

"Ford," she called to my back.

I stole a page from her playbook and just kept walking.

CHAPTER SIX

MILLIE

"I have to go," I told Autumn for the third time. My phone was sandwiched between my shoulder and a cheek as I rushed to shut down my computer and get out of the office.

Ford hadn't let me reject him at the fundraiser, but there was no way I was meeting him for an afternoon drink to *talk*.

"Hold on," she said. "I'm almost done. So we finished eating and then he took me home and—"

"You had sex. You told me that already."

"I did?"

"Yes. That was the first thing you said when I answered the phone. You said, 'I had sex last night.'" It had been a while since I'd told her the same. Thirteen months. I'd been counting.

"It was just okay." She sighed. "I only had one orgasm."

"Well, you've got me beat." The only orgasms I'd had lately were courtesy of my vibrator. "I'm hanging up now. I'm trying to get out of here early. I'll call you later."

"Okay, fine. Bye."

"Bye." I ended the call, yanked my purse from my desk's

bottom drawer, then shoved my phone inside before slinging it over my shoulder. It felt heavier than it had this morning, even though I hadn't touched it since I'd stowed it around six thirty.

I'd come in early this morning to work through some emails. Then I'd slogged through meeting after meeting. Most had been in fieldhouse conference rooms, but two had been held in the student union building and another in the library, forcing me to traipse across campus.

Not only was my brain fried but my feet were killing me. I'd made the mistake of wearing heels instead of tennis shoes and now I was paying for it.

The second I got in my car, these shoes were history. I'd drive home barefoot. Then I'd slip into some sweats and spend the rest of my evening reading a book. With any luck, I could get my mind off Ford.

Why was he pushing this so hard? It wasn't like he'd been the one humiliated ten years ago. No, that had been me. And if I didn't want to relive those awful memories, who was he to force them upon me?

Nope. Not happening.

Unless he needed to discuss the weight room schedule, we had nothing else to talk about. Whatever had happened in the past was no longer relevant. We'd have to find a way to coexist here because I wasn't going to leave. And I wasn't going to bend.

My job wasn't just a job, this was my career. This was my livelihood. Working for a university, working with student athletes, was my dream.

I loved sports. I loved competition. And I loved cheering for a victory, even if it wasn't my own.

For years, I'd competed as a distance runner, first in high

school and then here at TSU. Some of my fondest memories were from competition events or bus rides to meets. My friends had been my teammates. And during my senior year, after Ford had left, running had given me a purpose. An outlet.

My scholarship had helped me pay tuition because otherwise I wouldn't have been able to afford college. Even so, I'd only just finished paying off my student loans.

Collegiate track and field had been the pinnacle of my running days. I still enjoyed doing it recreationally. Just yesterday, I'd knocked out ten miles. But I wasn't destined for the Olympics and had no desire to pursue a professional career.

Sports administration had been the obvious choice after graduation. I wasn't interested in becoming a trainer. I didn't want to teach high school health and wellness. But this, the inner workings of a college program, was the perfect fit. Even better, I was still a Wildcat.

Ford Ellis wasn't going to screw this up. We'd get past this awkward phase, and eventually, he'd realize what needed to be said had been said already. Why dredge up ancient history?

Still, Ford was as stubborn as he was gorgeous. He'd insist on a conversation, and if I refused, I wouldn't put it past him to barricade me in my office. The man had left me no choice but to take the coward's way out and leave early.

I was digging through my purse for my keys when I stepped into the hallway and ran into the solid wall of a man's chest.

"Whoa." Adrian's hands came to my shoulders, steadying me as I teetered on my heels.

"Oh, you scared me." I pressed a hand to my racing heart.

"Sorry. And hi." He dropped a kiss to my forehead.

"Adrian," I scolded and took a step away.

"Sorry." He held up his hands. "Habit."

A habit he needed to break. Thirteen months ago.

Adrian and I had dated for two years. We'd started out slow, taking our time getting to know each other. Since he didn't work for the athletics department, a relationship wasn't against the rules. He'd been new to the alumni foundation, and we'd crossed paths a few times at campus events before he'd asked me out on a first date.

The next couple of years had gone quickly, and when he'd asked me to move in with him, I'd considered it. I'd really, honestly considered it.

But I didn't love Adrian. I'd said the words—a mistake—when I hadn't truly felt them.

There was only one man who'd melted into the corners of my heart. Who'd tucked himself so deeply beneath my skin that his name had become like invisible ink. Part of me wished, especially these past two weeks, that name had been Adrian. It would have been so much easier to dismiss Ford if I were in love with another man.

The breakup with Adrian had been messy. After two years together, we'd had mutual friends who'd ended up choosing sides—his. We hadn't officially lived together but our lives had been intertwined. We were both TSU employees. We might not work together daily, but our paths crossed often enough that the first six months after the split had been excruciating.

Thankfully, he'd started dating someone around that six-month mark. The woman had been a middle-school teacher in town and though they hadn't dated long, it had been the reset Adrian and I had needed.

I'd foolishly thought we could be friends who shared conversation and the occasional lunch. We'd had one such lunch a month ago, and ever since, Adrian had acted like we were on the road to reconciliation.

The late-night *good night, babe* texts. The impromptu visits to my office. The forehead kisses.

"What are you doing here?" I asked.

"Wanted to see what you were doing for dinner."

"She's got plans." A deep, resonant voice sent a shiver racing down my spine.

Shit. So much for an early escape.

Ford came up from behind Adrian, stopping at my side.

I craned my neck, daring a quick glance at Ford's clear, blue eyes. Eyes currently locked on my forehead, glaring at the spot Adrian had kissed.

"What plans?" Adrian looked between Ford and me, his forehead furrowing. He was tall and broad, a former student athlete himself. He'd played baseball at Wake Forest, but he had nothing on Ford's six-four frame, rippled with cut muscle.

"Drinks," Ford answered as I said, "No plans."

God, I didn't have the energy for this.

"Mills." Ford's hands fisted on his narrow hips.

"Mills?" Adrian blinked. He'd called me Mills a few times while we'd dated. I'd lied and told him I hated that nickname.

The truth was, Ford had claimed it first.

"Adrian Allen, meet Coach Ford Ellis." I wagged a finger between them. "Ford, meet Adrian."

"The new coach." Adrian sized up Ford with a scowl,

then gave him a tight smile and extended a hand. Like it or not, Adrian would be working with Ford too. "Nice to meet you. I work for the alumni foundation across the street."

Ford simply nodded as he shook Adrian's hand.

There was a fundraiser at the alumni foundation on the calendar. This introduction between Adrian and Ford had been inevitable. But what should have been two colleagues meeting for the first time now felt more like high school boys puffing up their chests.

And I was stuck in the middle.

"If you'll both excuse me, it's been a long day, and I'm headed home." I slipped past them, hoping I could disappear.

But Adrian's voice stopped me. "Millie?"

My shoulders slumped as I turned. "Yeah?"

"I'll call you later."

I should tell him not to bother. I should reestablish our boundaries. But I wouldn't reject him like that in front of Ford. I might not be in love with Adrian, but I cared about his heart. "Okay."

Ford's hands fisted at his sides.

I ignored it and headed for the stairwell. I would have jogged, but my feet hurt too bad to hustle. Through the door and down the first flight of stairs, my chest lightened. I was home free. But then the door above me opened and the heavy thud of footsteps told me exactly who was following.

My heels clicked on the concrete as I kept on walking.

"Where do you want to go for drinks?" Ford asked.

"Home."

"Then I'll follow you."

I huffed. "Alone. I'm going home alone."

"I told you there were things to say."

"And I told you it was unnecessary."

Ford was right behind me as we reached the ground level. He stood close, too close, as I pushed through the exit that opened to the parking lot. The summer sunshine was blinding, so I dug through my purse for a pair of sunglasses and slid them on.

"Have a good night."

"Millie." His voice was a snare, halting my feet. "Who was that?"

"Who? Adrian?"

"Are you together?" His jaw clenched as envy coated his timbre.

Oh, hell no. Ford didn't get to be jealous. It was sexy that he was, but no. Just . . . no.

Part of me wanted to lie about Adrian. To make Ford squirm. I considered it for a split second, but university staff gossiped worse than teenage girls. The last thing I needed was Adrian hearing that we were getting back together when we most definitely were not.

"No," I said. "We broke up."

"How long?"

"How long what?"

"How long were you together?"

"That's none of your business." Just like his marriage was none of mine.

His jaw clenched even tighter, but he didn't push on the Adrian topic. "Want to go downtown?"

"No."

"Then I'll follow you home."

A dry laugh bubbled free. "Damn, but you are stubborn."

"Someone once told me it was my best trait."

Me. Ford was the most determined person I'd ever met.

On the field. In life. When he put his mind to something, he accepted nothing less than a win. He never gave up.

Except for me.

He'd given up on me.

In my heart, I knew he'd made the right choice. He'd chosen to give his daughter the best possible life, and our friendship would have only caused trouble. I truly hoped that he'd succeeded where Joey was concerned. That the heartache I'd endured had meant his little girl was happy.

"Come on, Millie. Please."

"No."

He growled. "Why?"

"Because you left." My admission came out in a rush, rocking Ford on his heels. Sometimes the only thing that cut through his stubborn streak was a slap of the hard truth. "We were friends. Best friends. And then you left."

His eyes softened. "Which is why we should talk. Please, Millicent."

Damn him. How dare he use those old tricks? How dare he say my full name?

No one called me Millicent, not even my family. I was Millie to the world, but for Ford, that had never been good enough. He'd shorten my name to Mills most of the time, but when he really wanted to get his point across, I was Millicent. And I caved. Every. Single. Time.

"Downtown or your place?" he asked.

There was no chance I was letting him invade my house. It was hard enough keeping him from my mind as it was, I didn't need his heady scent invading my living room or the image of his large frame on my couch. I'd wind up having inappropriate dreams about him tonight—I probably would anyway.

"Ugh. Fine. You win." I tossed up a hand.

The corner of his mouth turned up.

"Parking downtown is a mess in the summer and it will be busy." That, and there was a higher chance we'd bump into someone from the university downtown. I wasn't willing to risk anyone overhearing our conversation. "But there's a brewery off Second Avenue that's quiet. Craft Six."

His grin widened into a full-blown smirk. "Meet you there."

"Don't be smug about it." I pointed a finger at his nose.

"Never."

Stubborn. Confident. That combination had always been my weakness.

Or maybe my weakness had always been Ford.

CHAPTER SEVEN

FORD

Millie sat in a tall-backed booth, her eyes aimed out the glass window next to the table. Her lower lip was worried between her teeth.

At least I wasn't the only one nervous for this conversation. My heart had been pounding since the moment she'd agreed to meet me at this brewery.

No way this was going to be a casual catch-up with an old friend.

This was going to fucking hurt.

But we couldn't put this discussion off any longer.

Millie had to get to the place where she didn't run the other way when she spotted me in the hallways. And I had to get to the point where I could look at her and not have this crippling urge to apologize profusely while pulling her into my arms.

We needed to lay it all on the field and have the talk I'd avoided a decade ago. Maybe then it would be easier to tuck away the past and move on.

I blew out a deep breath and crossed the room, taking in the cement floors and corrugated steel walls. The open ceilings showcased the exposed duct work, and the tangy scent of hops clung to the air.

Millie's shoulders tensed when I slid into the opposite side of the booth. On the table in front of her were two beers, each the color of wheat with a layer of white foam.

"I ordered you their signature IPA," she said, looking anywhere but at my face.

God, I hated that she was uncomfortable. Because in my entire life, there wasn't a person who'd made me more at ease than Millie. With her, I'd always been able to be myself. To be honest without hesitation.

"I like IPAs." I lifted my glass and took a sip, the cold, bitter flavor bursting on my tongue. "Not bad."

She traced a fingertip around the rim of her glass before lifting it to her pink lips.

Maybe she couldn't look my direction, but for me, it was impossible not to stare.

She'd twisted her hair into a knot at the nape of her neck since leaving the fieldhouse. The sleeveless white blouse she wore was loose in contrast to her fitted slacks, which showcased her toned legs. Simple diamond studs decorated her delicate earlobes.

Had *Adrian* given her those earrings? Had he stripped her out of that blouse to suck on her rosy nipples?

I swallowed down a surge of envy with another gulp of beer.

Maybe this would be easier if she didn't spark an old flame. If she could walk into a room and not steal my attention. If I could look at Millie and not see *my Millie*.

But she wasn't mine, not anymore. Yet the idea of her with another man made my skin crawl. *Fucking Adrian.*

How long had they been together? How serious had they been? If he was kissing her forehead, were they getting back together?

Did she love him?

The pit in my gut doubled in depth. I tried to fill it with another gulp of beer. Did I really want answers about Adrian and Millie? *Probably not.*

"Are you still running?" I asked.

"Almost every day." She nodded, toying with the smart watch on her wrist.

"Any races?"

"I usually do the Mission half marathon in September. Otherwise, no."

"Just you and the pavement." She'd always said that was her happy place.

"Yeah." Millie gave me a small smile, but otherwise, her attention was locked on that damn pint glass, her finger in constant motion as it traced the rim.

The brewery wasn't quiet. The hum of conversation drifted from table to table, filling the open space. The clink of glasses drifted from the bar. But the silence at our table was as thick and solid as a brick wall.

It took effort for me to keep my mouth shut, but I waited, knowing that I'd pushed hard to even get her here. If I kept pushing, I'd end up shoving her out the door.

"Where's Joey?" she finally asked.

"With a babysitter." Today's was on the golf team. "My parents are visiting from Vegas next week. They'll hang with Joey while I'm working, then the week after, our nanny starts. Just in time for school."

"What grade?"

"Fourth."

"How are your parents?" she asked.

"They're good. Annoyed I didn't move to Vegas."

"Why didn't you?" Her eyes flicked to mine.

Progress. "I considered it. Mostly because then I'd have help with Joey. But . . . it's not home."

When I was fourteen, my parents had moved us from San Diego to Las Vegas. I hadn't spent enough time there for it to feel like my own. And since I had no ties to California either, I wasn't exactly sure where home was. It wasn't Seattle, not anymore.

But Montana had potential.

"Where is . . . Sienna?" Millie's voice was laced with irritation.

I spoke Sienna's name the same way these days. "Seattle."

Her eyebrows lifted. "But Joey is here with you."

"Exactly." I took another drink of my beer, buying myself another moment. Then I said what I'd come here to say. "Millie, I'm sorry."

"I know." Her eyes were on that glass again.

"Do you?"

She lifted a shoulder. "It was a hard situation. You did what you thought was best."

"I never meant to hurt you."

"It's been a long time, Ford." She flicked her wrist. "We can just leave it in the past."

No, we couldn't. I wanted a friendship with Millie. Once upon a time, she'd been my best friend too. If there was even a chance at winning that back, I was taking it.

"When Sienna told me she was pregnant, I freaked," I said. "I shut down. I shut everyone out. You included."

Millie lifted her glass, her hand shaking slightly as she raised it to her lips and took a huge gulp. When she set the glass down, she'd drained it by a third.

Fuck. "I should have talked to someone. Anyone." Instead, I'd let my fears take control of the wheel and drive me off a cliff.

"You could have talked to me." Her gaze lifted and there was fire in those hazel irises.

"I'm sorry that I didn't."

She turned to the window at our side, her posture relaxing just a bit.

"I'm not here to make excuses."

Millie faced me again. "Then why are you here?" It was a genuine question. "Why do this? It's been years."

"Because like you said . . . we were friends. Best friends." And more. Even if it had only been a kiss.

Her throat bobbed. "You cut me out of the most important decision in your life. And silly me, I'd thought I was important."

"You were."

She scoffed. "And that was how you treated me? You didn't even call me to tell me Sienna was pregnant. I found out from another girl on the team."

I winced. "Not my finest moment."

Sienna had gotten pregnant right before we'd broken up. We'd always used condoms, but before I'd called our relationship quits, one must have broken.

Millie was the reason I'd ended it with Sienna.

We'd been friends for years. Then one day, I'd taken a look at Millie and wanted to kiss her. I hadn't, and even

70

though Millie and I had been nothing but platonic up to that point, it had felt a lot like cheating. So I'd ended it with Sienna.

The breakup had been a shitshow. My ex was nothing if not dramatic. She'd screamed from the top of her lungs how much she hated me. I hadn't given a damn. I'd been free to be with my Millie.

Then it had all fallen apart.

At least I'd gotten Joey.

"When Sienna handed me that positive pregnancy test, I freaked," I said. "I talked to no one, Millie. I blocked out the world because the noise in my head was crippling. I know I should have told you. I just . . . I froze. I choked."

"You should have told me."

"I should have told you. But I was terrified." Of becoming a father. Of losing my child before I'd even had the chance to meet her. "No excuses. I fucked up."

"I would have supported you." Her teeth clenched. "Through all of it."

"Like I said, I fucked up." First by pushing Millie away. Then by marrying Sienna. Our marriage had been doomed from *I do*.

After the paternity test results had come through, Sienna had used her tears as a weapon. She'd manipulated my fears and capitalized on my panic. She'd cried on my shoulder and told me how frightened she was to be a single mother. When she'd tossed out the idea of an adoption, I'd lost my mind.

The idea of someone else raising my child . . .

Fuck no.

So I'd solved Sienna's problem. I'd offered to marry her, and she hadn't even blinked.

My life had turned upside down in a matter of a week.

Sienna and I had gone to the courthouse for a quick wedding. A few days later, I'd been drafted to the NFL. I'd gone in the fifth round to the Seahawks and had been lucky enough to stick with their franchise for my entire professional career.

I'd been stupid enough to stick with Sienna too.

Maybe I was just jaded after years of living with her poison. Maybe in the beginning, she'd been genuinely scared, and her pregnancy, our marriage, hadn't been a trap.

Did it matter? We were over now.

Sienna had gotten exactly what she'd wanted—an NFL husband's paycheck and the chance to shove Millie out of my life. At least I'd gotten exactly what I'd wanted too.

Joey.

"What do you want me to say to this, Ford?" Millie asked.

"Nothing." I gave her a sad smile. "I wish I'd made a hundred decisions differently. For the pain I caused you, I'm sorry. Bottom of my heart, I'm sorry."

She picked up her glass, raising it for a drink, but set it on the table before the rim could touch her lips. "I kissed you. I thought you two were broken up, so I kissed you. Was that cheating?"

"No."

Millie swallowed hard. "But did you still love her?"

"Not even after we got married."

"I thought . . ." A hint of relief crossed Millie's face. "I kissed you and I thought . . ."

"You thought I didn't like you that way."

She nodded. "I thought maybe you regretted it. That you wanted to just be friends and I crossed a line."

"No, Mills. I have never regretted that kiss."

Yeah, it had taken me off guard, but I'd kissed her too. For her to doubt that, for her to feel ashamed by that . . . goddamn, I was such an asshole. All these years, all these feelings she'd suffered because I'd been such a fucking coward.

Instead of talking to Millie, I'd shut her out. The moment Sienna had handed me that pregnancy test, I'd put distance between Millie and me. I'd stopped returning her texts. I'd skipped our philosophy class to avoid her. Coincidently, it had been just after our kiss.

No wonder Millie thought that kiss was the reason I'd ghosted her. In reality, I'd been drowning. My ex-girlfriend, a woman who hated Millie with every fiber of her being, had been pregnant with my child, threatening to give up our baby. At the time, the only choice I'd seen was to sacrifice my friendship with Millie and let her go.

"I should have talked to you. But I was trying to do the right thing for Joey. It was never about Sienna. It was always for my daughter."

Millie turned to the glass again, her finger circling the rim once more.

"I don't want to hurt you. I had no idea you were working at TSU, let alone in the athletics department. Otherwise, I would have reached out first."

She nodded, still avoiding eye contact. "You never looked me up?"

"No," I admitted. "But not because I didn't think of you." She stayed quiet.

"I'm here," I said. "I want to be here. I want to do a good job and give Joey some normal for once in her life."

Another nod.

This was the point when I should shut up. When I

should be satisfied that I'd been able to speak to her at all and that she'd listened. But did I get my ass out of this booth? Did I leave her alone to move on?

No. Because when it came to Millicent Cunningham, I wasn't willing to admit the game was over. Not yet.

"I'd like to start again."

That got her attention. Her face whipped to mine, those hazel eyes wide. "Start what?"

Us. "A friendship. That was where we started. Think you could be my friend again?"

"Maybe," she whispered.

It wasn't a no. And for today, I'd take it as a win. "Fair enough."

I fished my wallet from my pocket and put a hundred-dollar bill on the table. Then I slid out of the booth, ready to head home to my kid, when Millie stopped me.

"Ford?"

"Yeah?"

"Joey is lucky to have you as her dad. To have you fight for her."

"I'll always fight for her."

"Good." She nodded, then turned away to hide the tears swimming in her eyes.

Millie's father had died when she was in eighth grade. He'd been a pilot and was killed in a car accident on his way to the airport. From all she'd told me about him, he'd been the type of dad who would have kicked my ass for hurting his daughter's heart.

I would have let him.

If any man hurt Joey like that, he'd be dead. I fought for my girl.

But maybe it was time I fought for someone else too.

Me.

Maybe it was time to fight for what I wanted.

At the moment, what I wanted had beautiful hazel eyes and soft chocolate hair.

"See you at work, Millie."

CHAPTER EIGHT

MILLIE

"Where have you been?" Autumn asked.

I couldn't remember the last time she'd answered one of my phone calls with a *hello*, but that was Autumn. She was unapologetically direct and considered most pleasantries a waste of time, especially for her closest friends.

I laughed as I walked across the parking lot at the grocery store. "Work. Home. The same places I always go."

"You've been avoiding me. I called you three times this week."

"Work has been super busy." It wasn't a complete lie.

With the fall semester starting soon, everyone was gearing up for another school year and work had been busy. But yes, I had been avoiding her. I'd been avoiding everyone.

In the week since Ford and I had met at the brewery, I'd spent most of my time alone.

Contemplating. Remembering. Healing.

I was glad Ford had pushed our discussion. I'd needed to hear his explanation, to know why he'd cut me out so abruptly. For a week, I'd let our conversation roll around in my mind. I'd let it sink in and stitch some of the wounds I'd ignored for a decade.

Those last few weeks of my junior year had been brutal. Ford had avoided me. I'd avoided Ford. Every time I'd crossed paths with Sienna, she'd given me a snide grin and rubbed her flat stomach.

I'd felt duped. Used. Humiliated. When it came to boys, brave I was not. But for the first time in my life, I'd initiated a kiss and the next day, Ford had shut me out of his life.

All I'd wanted was to finish the semester and escape Ford. Except he'd just been drafted to the NFL and his success had been a constant topic around campus and the fieldhouse.

It had been impossible, wanting to celebrate my friend, yet feeling so bitter at the same time.

Maybe it would have been better if I'd never kissed him in the first place. We would have just stayed friends. Maybe he would have told me about Sienna and the baby instead of vanishing from my life.

For a decade, I'd thought that kiss had been our demise. That he'd kissed me back out of pity. That he hadn't wanted to reject me outright. That he hadn't wanted to admit he was still in love with Sienna.

But after our discussion at the brewery, well . . .

The past ten years looked a lot different than they had a week ago.

Except a week hadn't been long enough, and I was still wrestling with my emotions, trying to make sense of the tangled mess in my heart. I would tell Autumn about my conversation with Ford. Eventually. But not today.

So I was sticking with my white lie.

I'd been super busy.

"Busy," she deadpanned. "That's the excuse you're going with? Don't forget who you're talking to, Millie."

"It's true. You know how it goes this time of year. My schedule has been nuts. Oh, but Adrian stopped by my office yesterday. Again."

His visit yesterday marked the fourth since his introduction to Ford.

Autumn groaned. "Oh, Adrian."

"I don't want to be harsh. I know I hurt him when we broke up."

"Yeah, but he has got to move on. We're bordering on pathetic now."

She wasn't wrong.

"What are you doing today?" she asked.

"Hitting the grocery store," I said, snagging a cart past the double doors. "Doing some laundry. Just chilling. You?"

"Working until seven. I had a client call for a last-minute cut and color, and like a sucker, I agreed to fit her in late. Want to meet up for a drink or something when I'm done?"

"Um . . ." I'd gone for a seven-mile run this morning before it had gotten too hot, and now all I wanted to do was laze around the house. Maybe bake cookies. I'd earned some sugar calories today.

And as soon as school started, a weekend at home would be rare until Christmas break. My Saturdays were about to be consumed with sports.

"Maybe," I told her.

"Your maybe means no."

I smiled. "Not always."

"Yes, always. Whatever. I'll just go have fun by myself."

"By yourself? Yeah, right. You're never alone."

78

Autumn thrived when she was surrounded by other people. She drew energy from social interactions, and it was why she made such an amazing hairdresser. Biased as I was, I doubted anyone could sit in her chair and not have a good time.

"Call me when you get off," I said. "I might change my mind."

"Okay." She made a smooching noise. "Bye."

"Bye." I ended the call and tucked it into my purse in the cart. Then I started for the baking aisle.

I was standing in front of the flour when my phone rang again. "Hi, Mom," I answered.

"Hello, sweetie. What are you doing?"

"Shopping. You?"

"Just heading over to Macie's house. We're baking cookies."

"I was thinking about doing the same today."

"Great minds." She laughed. "Listen, the reason I was calling was to see if you wanted to come here for Thanksgiving. Macie really wants to host."

"I thought I was getting to host this time." Last year, we'd agreed to swap back and forth. Macie's house, then mine. That way my sister wasn't always responsible for cooking on the holidays. But the last time either Macie or Mom had visited me had been two years ago for my birthday.

If I wanted to see my family, I had to get in my car and make the trek across the state to Billings.

"I know that's what we talked about, Millie, but with Macie and the kids, having them in their own house just makes it easier."

"Okay." I sighed, knowing there was no point in arguing. It would be easier for the kids. And Mom took Macie's side in all things. If this was what Macie wanted, this was what Macie would get.

"It will be great to see you," Mom said. "I'd better let you go. I'm just pulling up to your sister's house. Bye."

She didn't even let me say goodbye before she ended the call.

Her favoritism screamed louder than an air horn. It had during every single conversation we'd had in, well . . . forever.

It wasn't that we had a bad relationship. It just paled in comparison to hers with Macie. The three of us had banded together after Dad died. We'd all been devastated by his loss. But Macie, two years my senior, had spiraled into a severe depression.

Mom had made the choice any parent would probably make. She'd given Macie her fullest, doing everything in her power to get my sister to the other side of her grief. I didn't blame either of them, I just knew I was second choice.

Mostly, I missed my dad. I'd always miss my dad. Where Macie had Mom, Dad had been mine. Maybe today, because I missed him, I'd make his favorite cookies.

Brushing the phone call aside, I hefted a bag of flour into my cart, then continued on, heading for the milk and eggs, when a familiar figure rounded the end of the baking aisle. His hair was trapped beneath a baseball hat, but I'd recognize that broad frame and sexy swagger anywhere.

Ford. *Shit.*

We hadn't seen each other since the brewery. I really had been busy and he'd given me space.

But this was the problem with Mission. Even though there'd been an influx of residents in recent years, it was still a small town at heart. Bumping into people at the grocery store was inevitable, especially for TSU employees. Going to Costco on a Sunday was like attending a weekly staff meeting.

Ford's large frame stretched a gray T-shirt to the max across his shoulders and chest. A pair of faded jeans hung from his narrow hips, draping to a pair of tennis shoes. The hat shielded his eyes but couldn't hide his straight, white smile.

A smile aimed at his daughter as they walked hand in hand my direction.

Joey spotted me first, tugging on Ford's hand before she pointed down the aisle.

He followed her finger, and when it landed on me, that smile faltered. His steps slowed, and he mouthed, "Sorry."

For coming to the store on a Saturday?

Ford Ellis was making it difficult for me to stay aloof.

"Oh boy," I whispered, then took a fortifying inhale and continued on, pushing my cart their direction.

Ford's gaze raked over the gray leggings and black tank top I'd pulled on after my shower. There was a lot of appreciation in that gaze, much like the fundraiser event when I'd felt his eyes on my ass in that black dress more than once.

I'd been checked out by plenty of men in my day, but when Ford looked a woman up and down, only a fool's heart wouldn't skip.

"Hey, Mills." His gravelly voice gave me goose bumps.

"Hi." My voice was too breathy. *Ugh. Just. Act. Normal. Millie.* "Uh, hey, Joey."

"Hi." She smiled, swinging her dad's hand back and forth between them.

"What are you guys shopping for today?"

"Cake." Ford raised his empty basket and jerked his chin to the frosting section at my side.

"Daddy bet me I couldn't eat all of my green beans last night at dinner, and I did, so I get to pick out a cake."

"Yeah, she really showed me." Ford winked.

"Ah." I smiled, doing my best not to let that wink turn me into a puddle. "Well, good luck. I'm doing some baking of my own."

"What are you making?" Joey asked, pointing to my cart.

"Monster cookies."

"I want monster cookies." Joey's eyes shot to Ford. "Can we make those instead?"

"Uh . . ." Panic flashed across his face. "Sorry, princess. I don't know how to make monster cookies."

"Oh." Joey's shoulders slumped. "I wish Nana was still here. She can make cookies."

Ford's panic turned to disappointment and regret as he stared at his daughter. And at the moment, he looked like all he wanted in the world was to give his girl a batch of monster cookies. He really would do anything to make her happy, wouldn't he?

He was a good dad.

I'd had a good dad too.

It was hard, acting aloof. Avoiding Ford. What if I just . . . stopped?

Yes, it had hurt. Yes, it had been humiliating. But ten years . . .

It was time to move on.

"I can send you my recipe," I told him. "And we can make sure you've got all of the ingredients."

"Yes." Joey's face lit up.

No wonder he'd do anything for her. Joey's blond hair

was pulled into a high ponytail, much like my own. She was dressed in a hot pink romper with matching sandals. The kid was stinking adorable.

"Thanks." Ford's entire frame sagged. "Lead the way."

I whirled my cart around and returned to the flour and sugars. "Do you have flour?"

"No."

I pulled it off the shelf and handed it over. "Sugar?"

He shook his head. "No."

"Brown sugar? Baking soda? Chocolate chips?"

Another no, followed by another no, followed by another no.

"What exactly do you have?" I asked when his basket was so full that his bicep bulged as he held it.

"I'm not exactly known for my baking." He grimaced. "I stick to the grill and microwave."

"Have you ever made cookies before?"

"Nope."

"But you can make a cake, right? That's not very different."

"No cake either. We were going to buy one from the bakery. Joey was going to pick out frosting to decorate it her own way."

Except now she wanted cookies and those he'd have to bake.

"Oh." The smirk that tugged at my mouth was evil. Call it retribution, but the mental image of Ford in the kitchen, flour dusting every surface as he muddled through a recipe, was a tiny victory.

"I do not see this ending well," Ford mumbled.

"This will be good for you. Besides, cookies are easy. Do you own a cookie sheet?"

"I'm scared of the oven, Mills."

"You could come over and help us," Joey said. "Teach Daddy how to make 'em."

My smirk dropped. "Oh, uh . . ."

"Great idea, princess." Now it was Ford's turn to be smug. "You were going to make cookies anyway, right?"

Yes, I had been planning to make cookies. In *my* kitchen.

"Please?" Joey's plea came with doe eyes and clasped hands. It was the most pathetic, endearing look I'd ever seen.

Oh, hell. "How do you say no to that face?" I asked Ford.

"He doesn't," Joey answered for him.

Ford chuckled. "It's true. She usually gets her way."

"I don't think—"

"Please." He looked just as pathetic and endearing as his daughter. Add to that the desperation in his eyes . . .

Damn him. I was doomed.

"Please?" Joey begged again, clasping her hands in front of her chest.

Gah. "Okay." God, I was weak.

"Yes!" Joey fist pumped and danced in the center of the aisle.

But it was the victorious glint in Ford's eyes that made my heart stop.

It was a look I'd seen before, in person and on ESPN. It was the look Ford got whenever he won.

And I had the sinking feeling that it had nothing to do with monster cookies.

CHAPTER NINE

FORD

This was a horrible idea.

"What are you doing?" Joey asked as I raced around the kitchen, rinsing the cereal bowls I'd left in the sink after breakfast, then shoving them into the dishwasher.

"Cleaning. Go make your bed."

She groaned. "Do I have to?"

"If you want monster cookies, yes."

"Fine." She spun and stomped to her room. She'd deployed that move countless times since we'd come to Mission, along with her snotty eye roll.

Normally, I'd call her back and scold her for the attitude. But today, I was letting it go.

Either Joey and I were laughing and smiling, like we had been at the grocery store, or we were at each other's throats. We'd been fighting constantly since the move—since before the move—and today, with Millie coming over, I didn't want to be in an argument with my daughter.

So I let her storm to her room while I busted my butt to

clean up the kitchen. I had no idea how long it would take Millie to finish shopping and drop her own groceries at home before coming here, but I moved like I was running a forty-yard dash.

With the dishes done, I wiped the countertops and shoved the growing stack of mail I'd been ignoring into a drawer. Then I hit the living room, picking up the glass I'd left on the end table and wiping the crumbs from Joey's latest snack.

I wasn't a slob, but damn, when had the house gotten so messy? Okay, so maybe I'd gotten a little too comfortable in Seattle because Joey's nanny had kept everything spotless. She hadn't minded light cleaning and doing the occasional load of laundry. Whatever she hadn't tackled, my house-keeper had covered.

Except I didn't have a housekeeper yet. The nanny I'd hired to work here was starting Monday, and I wasn't sure how she'd feel about cleaning. For now, I was on my own, and Millie's approval felt important.

I didn't want her to see I was struggling.

I didn't want her friendship out of pity.

Joey's bathroom was next to clean since it was closest. I washed her teal toothpaste from the sink basin and hung a fresh hand towel on the hook. Then I made another mental note to text Mom later and thank her for scrubbing the toilet before they'd flown home to Vegas last week.

Mom had reminded me no less than ten times on their visit that she'd happily clean for me if I lived in Nevada. My parents had both dished out a ration of shit that I'd moved to Montana, but they'd only been teasing. They knew how much I loved coaching and football. They knew how much I loved Treasure State. And they'd made sure on more than one occasion to tell me I was doing a good job with Joey.

Was I? At the moment, I felt like I was failing at every turn. The dirty dishes. The unpacked boxes. The piles of laundry. Where the hell had Mom hidden the vacuum?

It was just a messy house. I told myself that every evening when I walked through the door. It was just a messy house, and neither my babysitters nor Joey seemed to mind. Millie probably wouldn't either, yet . . . I cleaned.

Never in my life had I attempted to bake. The extent of my time with the oven was to cook frozen pizzas or tater tots. In Seattle, I'd had a chef on staff. Should I hire a chef here? Or figure out how to cook? Maybe teach Joey along the way.

"Joey, is your bed made?" I called as I hustled out of her bathroom.

"Yes," she yelled back.

"Good, now put your jammies in the hamper and pick up any toys."

She grumbled as I rushed to my own bedroom, hiding the basket of clean clothes in the closet. The bed was unmade, the sheets rumpled. The playbook I'd been reviewing last night was open on my nightstand. I just shut the door and hoped Millie wouldn't want a house tour.

In the living room, four boxes were stacked beside the gas fireplace, each containing books and trophies and whatever other trinkets I'd collected over the years. I hefted one from the stack and hauled it to the office.

Millie might want to see the photo Joey had mentioned at the alumni fundraiser, and I didn't want her to know that, at the moment, that photo was the *only* item on my bookshelf.

I carted the box to the office, snagging a pair of scissors off my desk to cut the packing tape. Then I pulled out trophies and plaques, each wrapped in paper, and put them on the shelf.

"Where are the books?" I reached the bottom of the box and gritted my teeth.

Well, at least the bookshelf didn't look bare. But now it might as well have been a shrine to my career. The whole thing oozed arrogance. I was about to rewrap everything, including the photo, when the doorbell rang.

"She's here!" Joey shouted, her footsteps pounding out of her room.

"Joey, don't—" I raced after her, almost tripping over my own damn feet in an attempt to catch her before she opened the door.

In Seattle, we'd lived in a gated community with a security guard stationed at the entrance. There'd been no such thing as random visitors.

"Hold up." I stopped her just as her hand touched the knob. "You can't be opening the door to people, Josalynn. Even if you think you know who it is."

"Why?" Joey's favorite question these days.

"Because it's not safe. Wait for a grown-up, okay?"

She stared at me like I'd grown another arm, then pointed to the sidelight. "I can *see* Millie."

"It's not—" Why was arguing with a nine-year-old so difficult? "Just . . . don't open the door."

"Maybe someone could open the door," Millie said, her voice muffled. "These bags are heavy."

Joey shot me a frown before turning the knob.

"Thanks." Millie shuffled inside from the stoop, her arms looped with plastic sacks.

"Here." I snagged them all, slipping them off her wrists and peeking inside. Hadn't I bought the ingredients at the store earlier? "What's—"

"I'll show you to the kitchen." Joey grabbed Millie's hand and started to pull.

"Oh, okay." Millie glanced to the door, like she was contemplating an escape, but Joey was strong and her grip fierce.

My gaze tracked down Millie's body as they walked through the entryway, taking in her slender shoulders and slim waist. She was in the same gray leggings and tank from the grocery store, and the outfit left nothing to the imagination. Her legs were just as toned as they'd been in college. Her hips had the perfect curve, slightly fuller than they'd been and even more enticing.

My cock twitched behind my jeans. "Fuck."

"Daddy!" Joey called. "Bring the stuff."

"Coming." I found Joey and Millie in the kitchen, my daughter opening and closing every drawer and cabinet, giving Millie an extensive tour. With the bags deposited on the island, I scrubbed a hand over my face. Was two o'clock on a Saturday afternoon too early for a beer?

"And that's the fridge." Joey pointed to it across the room, then giggled when she realized it was obvious.

"What's all this?" I asked, touching one of the bags I'd hauled in.

A pretty flush crept up Millie's cheeks. "Stuff for a cake too."

My Millie. This was the Millie I knew. Thoughtful. Caring. A little bit shy.

"Both?" Joey's jaw dropped, then she fist pumped. "Yes."

"We'd better get started." Millie walked to the oven,

punching buttons to the correct temperature. Then she baked.

I couldn't keep my eyes off her as she moved around the kitchen, working like she'd been here a thousand times. She moved with grace, effortlessly mixing and measuring and scooping and stirring.

Joey hauled in a chair from the dining room, positioning it at Millie's side, her attention as rapt as my own. And the wonder on my daughter's face . . .

Something in my chest pinched as I watched them together. Joey had baked cookies with my mother before.

Just not her own.

Sienna wouldn't have been caught dead in the kitchen unless she was faking a cooking video for her social media accounts. The reality was that our chef had prepared her no-carb, no-dairy, no-gluten, no-sugar, no-taste meals. A cookie? She would have called a priest to perform an exorcism.

That was why Joey loved sweets. It hadn't been until after the divorce that treats had been a regular part of our life. Maybe it was foolish to indulge her, but I was doing it anyway.

With the first batch of cookies in the oven, Millie washed her hands, then leaned against the counter. "Think you can do it on your own next time, Coach?"

"Maybe." *Not in a million years.* I hadn't paid a lick of attention to the baking, too busy watching her the entire time.

"Want to see my room?" Joey asked, hopping off the chair.

"Sure." Millie glanced at the timer on the oven. "We have thirteen minutes."

Joey raced from the kitchen, her blond ponytail swishing as she ran.

Ponytails. Braids. Space buns. I couldn't bake cookies, but I'd been doing Joey's hair since she was a toddler. That counted for something, right?

Millie followed, her own ponytail hanging sleek and straight down her spine. Like a damn arrow straight to the ass I couldn't stop drooling over. Blood rushed to my groin. Again.

"Get it together, Ellis," I muttered when she was out of earshot, then unstuck my feet and followed.

Joey's voice carried down the hallway from her bedroom. Just like she'd done in the kitchen, she showed Millie everything, from the books on her shelf to her favorite unicorn stuffie she kept on her nightstand to the collection of purses she'd amassed in her walk-in closet.

"My dad said we can paint my room pink." Joey flopped on her bed and patted the quilt. "But not this kind of pink. A pale pink. Like . . . a super light color. Do you like pink?"

"I like pink." Millie took a seat beside Joey. "But my favorite color is blue."

"What kind of blue? Light blue? Or dark blue?"

Millie stared into my daughter's eyes. "Bright blue, like the color of your eyes."

The color of my eyes.

I leaned against the doorframe, enduring another twisting in my chest. They sure made a good picture, Millie and my daughter.

"Do you like nail polish?" Joey asked.

"I do." Millie spread out her fingers, holding them in front of her and inspecting her bare nails. "I just took off the polish I had on this week."

Joey's face lit up. "Want me to paint your nails? I have lots and lots of colors."

Millie glanced my way. "Uh, sure?"

I chuckled. "It's either your nails or mine."

"He lets me paint his nails sometimes." Joey walked to her closet to haul out the plastic tub full of her polishes.

Along with hairstyles, I'd become an expert at nail polish remover too. At least once a week Joey would paint my nails, then I'd wait for her to go to bed and take it off so I wasn't ridiculed at work.

"You can sit at my desk," Joey said.

"Okay." Millie stood from the bed and went to the desk, pulling out the rose velvet chair.

Joey's eyes danced as she gave me a beautiful, toothy smile before popping the top on the tub. "What color? Blue?"

"How about pink?" Millie splayed her hand on the desk's surface. "You pick the shade."

Joey went for her favorite neon. One that I knew from experience was a pain in the ass to remove because it clung to the cuticles. With her tongue poking out one corner of her mouth, something she did whenever she was concentrating, Joey went to work.

Her focus was entirely on her task, so she missed the way Millie stared at her. When I'd introduced them at the fundraiser, there'd been a flash of pain on Millie's face. But today, it was more like curiosity.

The oven's timer dinged.

Joey froze, nail brush midair.

Millie's face whipped to the door and kitchen beyond.

"I'll get it." I shoved off the door.

"Just swap out the pan we already set out for the next one," Millie said. "Thirteen minutes."

"Got it." The scent of sugar greeted me when I got to the oven. I rummaged through the drawers until I found an oven mitt, then did as Millie had instructed, swapping out one cookie sheet for the next.

With the new batch baking and another thirteen minutes on the timer, I found my way to Joey's bedroom again.

Except it was empty.

"Joey?" I called.

"In here," she yelled from down the hall. From the office.

"Great," I muttered. They'd gone to look at the photo.

Joey was holding it up when I reached the door.

"Seems like a lifetime ago." Millie took it from Joey's hand, her eyebrows knitted together as she peered at the picture. She studied it so hard it was like the rest of us had faded away.

"Millie," I said.

She startled, looking up with unshed tears in her eyes. Then she handed the photo back to Joey. "Would you, um . . . excuse me for a minute?"

It was too much, wasn't it? Too much at once. I'd stormed into Millie's life, raining buckets of old emotions over her shoulders and had barely given her time to find a damn umbrella.

Joey's smile faded as Millie dashed from the room. "Is she okay?"

"Yeah." I walked closer, taking the photo and putting it back on the shelf. "Once these cookies are done, we'll let Millie go home, okay? I'm sure she had other plans today."

"Oh." Her forehead furrowed. "But do you think she's having fun?"

"Absolutely. Are you having fun?"

She nodded. "Yeah. I like Millie."

"Me too, princess." *Me too.*

CHAPTER TEN

FORD

"Can you crack the eggs so I don't wreck my nails?" Millie asked Joey.

"Okay, sure!" She beamed as she lifted an egg from the carton.

Joey and I had left the office and found Millie in the kitchen, hauling out everything she'd brought over, careful not to smudge her neon pink polish. She'd pretended that everything was fine, that whatever had happened in the office was a distant memory. And while Joey hadn't noticed anything amiss, I had.

Millie's smile was too polite. Too practiced. It was the smile she'd given me the day I'd signed my contract. Beautiful but hesitant.

Joey cracked the egg on the side of the bowl, then winced. "Oops."

Millie peered into the batter. "That's okay. It's just a little shell."

"How do I get that out?"

"Just scoop it out with part of the shell. Or you can use a spoon."

Joey nodded, doing as instructed. "Got it."

"Good job." Millie put her hand on my daughter's shoulder. "Toss them in the sink and then I'll stir while you wash your hands."

"'Kay."

Like with the cookies, I stood off to the side of my wide kitchen, the silent observer as they mixed and poured the chocolate batter into a pan before sliding it into the oven.

"That's it." Millie patted her hands with a towel, and even though her polish was probably set, she made sure to be careful not to touch the color. "Easy, right?"

"Super easy." Joey gave her a sure nod.

"Think you can help your dad next time?"

"Yep."

"Awesome." Millie held out her hand for a fist bump. "Thanks for helping me today. This was fun."

"So fun." Joey tapped her knuckles. "Can I have a cookie?"

"One," I said, moving in closer.

Joey snatched the largest from the plate where they were cooling. "Now what?"

"Now, I've got to get going," Millie said. "I have a mountain of laundry waiting for me at home."

Joey pouted. "But the cake's not even done."

"I think you guys can take it from here." Millie pointed to the last plastic bag on the counter. "There's frosting in there. As soon as the cake is cool, you can decorate it however you'd like."

"But—"

"Joey." I put my hand on my daughter's shoulder. "How about we say thanks to Millie?"

"Thanks, Millie."

"You can go play," I told her. "I'll walk Millie out."

Joey chomped a bite of her cookie before skulking past the island. She was about out of the kitchen when she paused, throwing an arm in the air. "Yuuuum. These cookies are soooo good."

Millie laughed. "I'm glad you like them. And thanks for doing my nails."

"Can you come back next weekend?"

"Oh, uh—"

"Next weekend we're busy," I told Joey.

"We are? With what?" Her shoulders slumped as she frowned. "Wait. Don't tell me. Football stuff?"

I nodded. "Football stuff."

The coaches were coming over for a barbeque. I'd found a caterer to do the heavy lifting. The point of the barbeque was for my staff to see my home. To relax in my company. So far, our meetings had been good and practice was off to a nice start. But there was still this underlying tension among the coaches, like they were all walking on eggshells.

It was no different than with the players. If they didn't trust me, there was no way I'd be able to lead this team.

"Football stuff is so boring." Joey groaned.

"You don't like football?" Millie asked.

"Not really."

"Bummer. I love football. It was my dad's favorite sport, and we used to sit on the couch every Sunday with loads of snacks and cookies and junk food to eat while we watched game after game."

Millie knew the rules better than most of my college teammates. Which had been one hell of a turn-on.

"I actually love all sports," she told Joey. "But football is special."

"I mean, football isn't *that* bad." Joey waved her hand in the air, like she could erase her previous statement. "It's just, like, all the time around here. It's never ending."

"Not as much as it was in Seattle though," I said. "Right?"

"Yeah." She shrugged. "I guess."

I'd still have to travel for away games. Joey would still spend plenty of time with a nanny. But the season was shorter than in the NFL and the trips weren't as long or demanding.

"Maybe, if it's okay with your dad, you can come to a game with me," Millie said. "As long as you promise to cheer really loud."

"Can I?" Joey's eyes flew to mine. "Please?"

No way I'd shut down that sort of excitement, especially for football. "Sure."

"Yes." She chomped another bite of her cookie, then skipped away, heading for her room.

"She's never shown much interest in sports," I told Millie. "Thanks for that."

"You're welcome. I'm always looking for the opportunity to create a Wildcat fan."

"Still get a little crazy at the games?"

Millie blushed and dropped her gaze to the floor. "Maybe."

The Millie I remembered was the loudest person in the stadium. When we scored, she'd scream like she'd run the ball into the endzone herself. When the refs made a bad call, she'd go ballistic. And when we won, her cheers could be heard across the field.

That, or I'd just always listened for Millie.

"I don't get to watch many from the stands these days," she said. "I'm usually working. But I'll make sure to find a game when I can sit with Joey or take her on the sidelines."

"Appreciate it," I said, following her toward the front door.

"You have a lovely home."

"It's a work in progress. We're still getting settled in." There was some furniture from our Seattle house that didn't quite fit this space. And Millie hadn't seen the plethora of boxes stashed behind closed doors.

But even if it wasn't exactly how I wanted it, the foundation was here for the future. And God, it was nice not to see so much goddamn white. Sienna had decorated our modern Seattle house in shades of white and cream. I'd spilled a bottle of orange Gatorade on the couch once, and she'd spent a week not talking to me.

Actually, that had been a nice week.

There was some white in this house, but otherwise, it had a rustic vibe. And if Joey wanted a pink bedroom, she'd have a pink bedroom.

The tall ceilings and open spaces were just right for a guy my size so I didn't feel cramped. The warm wooden floors, the hewn beams and the stone fireplace made it cozy. Home. The far wall of the living room was made entirely of windows that looked out on the golf course beyond our backyard. In the distance, the indigo mountains stretched to the blue sky with an evergreen forest at their feet.

"This is a nice golf course," Millie said as she opened the

door. "We do an annual fundraiser here in the spring. Have you played it yet?"

"No. My membership to the club hasn't been officially approved yet."

She raised her eyebrows. "They won't approve *the* Ford Ellis? Don't you have to be a member to live in this neighborhood?"

"Yes." I chuckled. "They gave me a little exception as they wait for the next membership board meeting. It's just logistics, and I haven't pushed. At this point, I'm just glad I have an address. I took a gamble after my first meeting with Kurt."

"A gamble?"

"He hadn't offered me the job yet, but I was counting on his desperation. So I asked Toren for the name of a good realtor. I called her up and asked her to find me a nice house in the best school district. A construction company she often works with was in the middle of building this place. We did a FaceTime tour. I told her I wanted it, and she called in a favor so they could rush construction. Finished it the day before we arrived."

"You bought this house sight unseen? Before it was even finished?" Millie's eyes widened. "What if Kurt hadn't offered you the job?"

Not offered me the job? "Millie."

She rolled her eyes. "I see that winning all those trophies and awards in your office did not shrink your ego."

I laughed. "Not in the slightest."

"Do you miss playing?"

"Every day. But I love coaching too." It was second best, but it came with the bonus of time with my daughter.

"Why didn't you just stay with the Seahawks?"

"I was ready to get out of Seattle."

Millie didn't ask why. She didn't need to. Sienna's name hung in the air like the stench of a rotten egg.

"About that picture in the office—"

"Don't worry about it." She waved it off. "Just . . . memories, you know?"

"Yeah." I had a lot of memories with Millie.

The best, the most bittersweet, was that night she'd kissed me out of the blue while we'd been studying. Not that I hadn't wanted it. It had just taken me by surprise.

In another life, I would have kissed her with every sunrise. Every sunset. She would have been the woman cheering me on at the Super Bowl. The woman I'd gone home to every night. But that future wasn't the one we'd been dealt.

And I couldn't regret the past ten years. I'd never regret my daughter.

"Thanks for doing this today."

"You're welcome." She opened the door and stepped onto the stoop. "Good luck with the cake."

"Hold up." I wanted one more minute with her. If I was lucky, maybe she'd give me two. Millie had spent the entire afternoon in my kitchen but that time had been for Joey. Now that it was just us, I wanted to drag it out, so I held up a finger. "Forgot something. Hang tight."

Before she could argue, I spun and jogged through the house, weaving past the living room as I hustled to the kitchen. I yanked three paper towels from the holder and used them to wrap up a stack of monster cookies, then jogged them back.

"You earned cookies."

The corner of her mouth turned up as she took them from my hand. "Bye, Ford."

"Bye, Mills." I watched as she crossed to the driveway, rounding the front of her Kia.

Her hand touched the door's handle but she paused, staring at me from over the hood. "Thank you."

"For what? The cookies? You made them."

"No." She shook her head. "For closure."

Hold up. Closure? What the hell was she talking about? And why did that word sound a lot like a goodbye?

"See you around, Coach."

I took a step, lifting a hand to stop her, but she was already behind the wheel. Then she was gone, reversing out of my driveway and pulling onto the street.

Closure?

That was not what our discussion at the brewery had been about. We'd needed to clear the air. I'd needed to tell her my side of the story and hear hers. Yeah, I'd wanted to mend the past. But closure?

"Fuck no."

This wasn't over.

The game hadn't even started yet.

CHAPTER ELEVEN

MILLIE

There was a lightness to my step as I crossed the parking lot at the fieldhouse. Most of my coworkers trudged into the office on Monday mornings, but I always enjoyed the start of a new week.

That sentiment was heightened today mostly because, for the first time since Ford had arrived in Mission nearly a month ago, I wasn't dreading an encounter. There'd be no avoiding him in the halls. No closed office door. No hiding when I heard his husky voice.

Ford had been right to force a discussion about the past. But it hadn't been that conversation or the monster cookies or the cake that had finally given my heart some closure. It hadn't even been his apology.

It had been that photo in his office.

I remembered that day like it was yesterday. We'd been standing on the football field after a game. It had been so freaking cold and my toes had been numb, but I hadn't cared a bit because the Wildcats had beaten the Grizzlies.

I'd given my phone to a random stranger in the crowd to

take a picture of me, Ford and Toren. My cheeks had been red in the picture, not just from the cold but because Ford had put his arm around me. Those were the days when I'd pretended not to be in love with Sienna's boyfriend.

But I'd been so in love with Ford.

His hair had been sweaty and steaming from wearing his helmet. He'd stood like Goliath, his broad frame made even bigger with his pads.

Toren had been on his other side, and right as the photo had been taken, he'd been smiling to someone out of the shot —probably a girl. If I hadn't been in love with Ford, I probably would have had a major crush on Toren Greely.

He was a total playboy, always had been. In college, he'd always had girls swooning over his devilish smirk and sparkling, gray-green eyes. It was Toren's undeniable charm that was so irresistible.

Well, to most women. Toren had only ever been my friend. Always kind. Always there to make me laugh. Always willing to place a silly bet on something trivial because we loved to compete with each other.

It hadn't been a secret that Toren had stayed in touch with Ford over the years, but he'd never thrown that in my face. Toren knew Ford was a sore subject—or had been.

Now, it didn't sting. Ten years, and the pain was just . . . gone. Forgotten.

When I'd looked at that photo in Ford's office, what I'd seen above all else had been friendship.

Letting go of the resentment, the embarrassment I'd clutched so tightly for years had been surprisingly easy, if not slightly emotional. That was why I'd needed a minute alone on Saturday. Not because looking at the photo hurt.

But because it hadn't.

Ford and I had never been destined for a fairy-tale romance.

Though, once upon a time, we'd been great friends. Maybe, like Ford had suggested, we could be friends again.

Smiling, I opened the fieldhouse door and headed for the stairs. Beneath my arm, my purse bulged with a bottle of water and my lunch bag. I'd brought my last monster cookie to eat later, having saved it over the weekend. Hopefully Joey hadn't eaten too many and given herself a stomachache.

When I looked at her face, it was still hard not to see Sienna, but by the time I'd left on Saturday, I'd seen more glimpses of Ford in her too. Mostly in her personality. She was her father's daughter. Smart. Confident. Bold. And the girl had a steady hand with a polish brush.

My neon-pink nails skimmed the navy railing while I climbed the stairs to the next floor. The manicure was flawless, and the shade was the only pop of color in my otherwise gray outfit of charcoal slacks and a graphite sleeveless blouse. My tennis shoes, also gray, were new and the soles plush.

Maybe when this manicure began to chip, I'd beg Joey for another. And I'd meant what I'd told Ford, that it would be fun to take her to a game.

The office was quiet as I shoved through the stairwell door, most cubicles empty. But the smell of coffee lingered in the air, so someone had beat me in this morning.

"Hey, Millie." Drew came walking out of the break room with a steaming mug.

"Good morning. How was your weekend?"

"Went to the lake. It was nice to get away, enjoy a weekend while we still have them."

"Two more weeks to go." Then we'd be swamped until, well . . . June.

Most of the upperclassmen were already in town. But in two weeks, the freshmen would be moving into the dorms. They always brought a new level of excitement and energy to campus. Classes would start and then the football season would be underway.

Personally, I couldn't wait. Every year, it was like my own first year in college all over again. Only this time, without Sienna's drama.

My freshman year had started off well. It had been an exciting time. Or, I'd thought so. Looking back, that entire year had been tainted by Sienna.

But in the beginning, we'd had fun as new roommates. As quick friends.

That had been the year before she'd met Ford, when she'd been different. Sweet. Or maybe I'd just been naïve. Maybe she'd always been a snake, and I'd overlooked her true nature because I'd been so happy to have a friend.

Friends had been hard in high school. Especially girls. Everyone had pitied me after Dad's death. It had been hard to know if people actually liked me for me, or were only being kind because their parents had told them to be nice.

But when I came to Mission for school, no one knew I was Jack Cunningham's daughter. It was a fresh start. A new beginning. And Sienna chose *me*.

She was gorgeous and clever. She loved the spotlight, and even as a freshman, she became the popular girl on the track and field team. Apparently, that wasn't enough.

We each competed in the 800 meters, and while Sienna was fast, she wasn't faster than me. She started to get short and snippy with me any time I beat her in practice. By spring semester, when we were in the thick of competitions and meets, she barely spoke to me.

Then one afternoon, I came back to our dorm room early from class only to overhear her talking trash about me. How she only pretended to be my friend because we were living together. How she couldn't wait to move out. How I was sad and mopey and it was annoying her.

Yeah, I had been sad. I had been moping. The week before had marked the anniversary of my dad's death.

From that moment on, I decided I didn't want Sienna as a friend, that maybe I didn't want any friends who were girls. Period.

When I came back after summer break to start my sophomore year, I kept my distance from Sienna. I lived on campus because it was easier to get it covered by financial aid and my partial scholarship, while she moved into an apartment with some of the other girls on the team.

I crossed paths with her at practice and at the occasional party. It was at one of those parties that I met Ford. My crush on him was instant. Sienna had been at the party too.

A week later, they'd started dating.

Maybe she'd chased him because my crush had been obvious. Maybe I was giving myself too much credit and she hadn't given a damn about me. Ford was, well . . . Ford. The star player on the football team. The hottest guy on campus. The guy every girl wanted.

And Sienna won.

She beat me.

Her victory had always left a bitter taste in my mouth. Though it wasn't as sour this morning, not with Joey's cute face in mind. Not with her neon-pink polish decorating my nails.

There was a smile on my face as I turned into my office—

and froze. A sky-blue gift bag teeming with white tissue paper, topped with a card, sat on my desk.

"Oh no." I groaned, coming into the office and stowing my purse in a drawer. "Adrian, this has to stop."

I plucked the card from the bag, expecting his neat handwriting and a dinner invitation. Instead, it was a mess of chicken scratch.

Ford.

And Joey. Her name was scrawled beneath his.

Ten years and his scribble hadn't changed. It was just as messy as it had been when we'd passed notes back and forth in class and he'd had to read his to me because I couldn't make out half the words.

The tissue paper crinkled as I tore into the gift bag and lifted out a plastic food container with a red lid and a plastic fork. There was a piece of chocolate cake inside and a bag of Swedish fish.

I giggled. "I'm so eating this cake for breakfast."

"I heard that." Ford appeared in the doorway, his frame filling the threshold.

"Your handwriting is as messy as ever." I waved the note card. "I'm glad Joey's is legible."

He chuckled. "She's in charge of the grocery list because if I make it, neither of us can read it by the time we go shopping."

A blush crept into my cheeks like I was twenty again, not thirty-one. I normally didn't blush. But Ford seemed to be the exception to everything.

I lifted the bag of Swedish fish. "These were always your favorite, not mine."

"I know." He smirked, shoving off the door to close the distance between us. Then he sat on the edge of my desk, stealing the candy from my hand and tearing open the bag. "With the cookies and cake at home, I wouldn't let Joey buy candy. But I wanted some for myself."

"So you put it in my gift as a ruse. Seems like cheating, Coach."

He popped a fish in his mouth, grinning as he chewed.

My gaze dropped to his mouth, drawn to the way his lips moved and his jaw flexed. The way his Adam's apple bobbed as he swallowed. That blush seemed to spread through my whole body, a rush of warmth flooding my veins.

"It's easier, isn't it?"

"Huh?" I tore my gaze from his mouth, meeting those stunning blue eyes.

"Talking about the past. It's easier."

"It is." *Thank you, closure.* Maybe that had been my problem all along. Instead of sorting through my feelings when it came to Ford, I'd just blocked them out.

"Thanks again for this weekend," he said. "You made Joey's Saturday. And mine."

"You're welcome."

Wow, he smelled delicious. Better than any cake or candy. That masculine scent of cedar and leather was mixed with the freshness of soap from this morning's shower. The mental image of a dripping-wet, naked Ford popped into my mind. A pulse bloomed in my core and my mouth went dry.

"Coffee. I need some coffee." Except I didn't make a move to leave.

Even seated on the edge of my desk, Ford was so tall that we were nearly eye level. It would be so easy to lean in, to kiss his mouth.

Oh, jeez. What was wrong with me? Hadn't that exact thought gotten me into trouble in the first place? Besides, I'd just gotten closure with Ford. We were friends, sort of. We were working toward being friends.

We were, however, most definitely coworkers.

I shouldn't be thinking about kissing him. I shouldn't be thinking about him naked.

Pick up your feet, Millie.

My toes didn't so much as wiggle.

Ford leaned in closer, just an inch.

My eyes dropped to his mouth again. "Coffee."

"You said that already, Mills."

"I did?"

Did he want to kiss me? Did I want to kiss him? *Yep.*

Oh, hell. I was in trouble.

The world got fuzzy at the edges. Anything outside of this office faded away. Until a throat cleared.

I jerked away from Ford.

"What's going on here?"

Kurt. My boss. *Our* boss.

He stood in the threshold of my office, where Ford had been. His fists were planted on his hips.

Yep. Trouble. So much trouble.

CHAPTER TWELVE

FORD

M illie looked like she was about to faint. Or puke. Hopefully the reason that the color had drained from her face had everything to do with Kurt standing in her doorway, not the fact that I'd been seconds away from kissing her pretty mouth.

"Morning, Kurt." I lifted the hand with my bag of candy.

"Hi, Ford." He looked between Millie and me, his gray eyebrows pulled together.

The fact that he did not greet Millie irked me immediately.

I bit back a snarky comment and faced Millie again, leaning in close like I was studying her eyeball. "Well, I can't see anything in there, but maybe you got an eyelash stuck in there or a hair or something."

"Uh . . ." She blinked. But the confusion on her face only lasted a split second before she realized what I was doing. Then she leaned away, poking and prodding at her eye. "Gah. Well, thanks for checking. But there's definitely something in there."

"Think I've got some eye drops in my office. Want some?"

"No, that's okay. I'm sure it will get better soon." She stepped back, facing Kurt with that polite, cool smile. She kept her eye halfway closed, keeping up the ruse. "Hey, Kurt. Did you have a nice weekend?"

"Yeah." That muttered, one-word reply was all Kurt gave her. Then he focused his attention on me again, his smile going a bit too wide. Too forced. "How was your weekend? Do anything fun with Joey?"

"It was good. We did some shopping and made cookies."

"Ah. Sounds nice."

Did it? Because his tone said otherwise.

Kurt had spent the better part of the past three weeks kissing my ass. We'd talked about football. He'd praised me for hitting the ground running. And he'd always made sure to ask about Joey.

Anything related to the team, our conversations felt genuine. But when it came to my daughter, there was a shallow feel to his questions. Like he felt obligated to ask because Joey was important to me, but he didn't really give a shit about my answer.

Would he give Millie more than a passing glance if he knew she was important to me too?

One of these days, I'd have to ask her how she really felt about our boss.

"Do I have any candy in my teeth?" I pulled my lips away from my teeth, showing Millie as many of my pearly whites as possible.

She fought a smile. "All clear, Coach."

"Thanks." I smacked my knee, standing from the edge of her desk. "I've got a meeting with President Cruz this morning. Probably shouldn't show up with red candy in my teeth."

Kurt's forehead furrowed. "You have a meeting with President Cruz?"

"At eight thirty." I nodded, and from the shock on his face, I guess he hadn't been invited.

"That's, uh . . . super." He puffed up his chest, like this meeting had been his idea. "It's good you're getting to know her. She's a real supporter of our programs."

"Yeah, she seems great." I stuffed the candy in my pocket for later as Millie shuffled behind her desk to take a chair. "See ya, Millie."

"Bye, Ford. Thanks for your help with the, uh . . . eyelash thing." Millie pointed to her face as she clicked her mouse.

"No problem. Glad I was walking by and could help out."

"Lucky timing," she said, relief written all over her face.

Kurt shifted out of the threshold so I could walk past, then he joined me in the hallway. "If you've got a minute, maybe swing by my office after your meeting with Carly."

I checked my watch. "I'll try. Today is hectic. But I've got a few minutes now if you want to catch up?"

"No, that's all right. We'll talk later."

Later, because he wanted a recap of my meeting with President Cruz.

"Have a good day, Kurt." I raised a hand, then headed for the stairwell.

It was still early. I doubted anyone from my staff had made it to work yet so I'd likely have the coaches' wing to myself. I'd come in early this morning to give Millie her cake, but the quiet wouldn't last long. Within the next hour, my day would be off to a dead sprint. By the time five o'clock rolled around, my head would be spinning.

Then I'd head home, giving Joey the last of my energy and, hopefully, getting a bit more unpacking done. With the coaches' barbeque this next weekend, it was time to get motivated and finish. That, and if by some miracle I could get Millie to come over again, I didn't want to be hiding boxes behind closed doors.

The stairwell door opened above me as I rounded the landing.

Kurt poked his face out. "Practice is at one?"

"Yep." Every day this week, we'd be having a full-team practice. Then the guys would get to rest, and this evening, they'd come back when it wasn't so hot, around seven, to meet with my assistant coaches and run position drills.

Tonight, I'd be skipping the second practice, but I'd be here the rest of the week with Joey in tow.

Though she'd probably prefer to have a babysitter than accompany me to a practice, I selfishly wanted to spend a little time with my kid, even if that meant we were at football. I'd bribe her with ice cream or a new Nintendo Switch game.

"I'll see you out there," Kurt said.

I nodded, clamping my teeth together before I could tell him to back off.

The last thing my coaches and players needed right now was Kurt playing helicopter at practice. He'd come out to the field last week too, hovering close and asking stupid questions. By Friday, I'd been ready to strangle him.

Whatever. If I was the only person who Kurt annoyed, I'd deal. As long as he didn't interfere with my staff or players, I'd let him step all over my damn toes.

When I reached the first floor, the sound of laughter carried from around a corner. Toren and two other coaches were lingering outside my dark office. Guess I'd been wrong to assume I'd beat everyone in.

"Morning, guys," I said.

"Ford." Toren waved me into their huddle. "I need you to settle something."

"Okay." It was nice to see happy, relaxed faces in this hallway for a change.

"Remember that time in college when Millie bet me that she could beat me at the forty?"

I nodded. "Yeah."

Toren had been talking shit about how she was fast but only at a middle distance race, that she had endurance and speed but not short-range sprint speed. So Millie had bet him fifty bucks that she'd beat him at a forty-yard dash.

"Who was faster?" he asked. "Me or Millie?"

"Millie."

Parks O'Haire, my offensive coordinator and quarterbacks coach, burst out laughing. "I knew it."

"Hold up." Toren put a hand in the air. "She did not beat me."

I chuckled. "Then you have selective memory."

Yes, Toren had won. The first race. He'd beat her by a hair.

Millie had challenged him again, double or nothing.

And she'd smoked him.

When he'd asked for a third match, she'd smoked him again.

"Maybe having you here wasn't such a good idea," he muttered. "You know too much."

"Probably." I grinned. "What brought this discussion on?"

"Oh, Parks was asking me how much money I owed Millie."

"You owe Millie money?"

Toren grimaced.

"They bet on everything, Ford," Parks said. "Just last week they bet who could eat a cheeseburger from Five Guys faster. Per usual, she won."

It took effort to keep my smile in place as a sour taste spread over my tongue. The taste of jealousy.

Millie and Toren had been friends for ages too. Of course they'd eaten lunch together.

Toren had never had his sights on the NFL. He was a talented player, but he'd always wanted to be a coach. So he'd gone to Oregon to coach for the Ducks out of college. But when a spot had opened up at TSU a few years ago, he'd jumped at the chance to come home to Montana.

He'd had years working alongside Millie. Of making bets and sharing lunches. It shouldn't have surprised me or bothered me, yet here I was, both surprised and bothered.

Why hadn't this occurred to me by now?

Probably because not once since I'd left Mission had Toren mentioned Millie. Not during phone calls. Not during the few visits he'd made to Seattle to watch a Seahawks game. Certainly not when I'd been interviewing for the head coach position.

Not once.

Why? Was he protecting her? From me?

Fuck, that idea burned.

"So how much, Toren?" one of the guys asked. "Or should I head upstairs and ask Millie?"

"Let's just say it's more than zero and less than a million dollars." Toren shook his head. "And on that note, time for me to get to work."

"I'm asking Millie." Parks shot Toren a smirk and, before anyone could stop him, took off jogging for the stairwell door.

They were all friends with Millie, weren't they? I'd been so preoccupied by my own life that I hadn't considered that, not until today. But it was probably just like it had been in college. There hadn't been a single guy on the football team who hadn't considered Mills a friend. The only person I'd ever known not to like Millie had been Sienna.

That should have been enough of a red flag.

Millie had always joked that she was just one of the guys. But she'd had no goddamn clue.

Half the guys on the team had been in love with her. She'd show up to a party, and I'd spend the first hour shooting pointed glares around the room, reminding everyone that she was not to be touched.

My Millie. Even when we'd just been friends, she'd always been mine.

If she had actually wanted to date one of them, I probably would have lost my mind. Luckily, she'd never shown any interest. The only dates I remembered her going on had been with guys she'd met in class, not through athletics. No one had gotten past a third date, thank fuck.

Sienna had never come out and told me why she'd disliked Millie so much. She hadn't needed to. Sienna's jealousy had been obvious. But I'd dismissed it, hoping one day my girlfriend could reconcile with my best friend and we could all get along.

Clearly, I'd been fucking delusional.

Toward the end of our relationship, Sienna's nasty attitude toward Millie had been the cause of most of our fights. Sienna had let it slip once that the reason Millie went to all the football parties was because of her "pathetic crush" on me.

Well, surprise, surprise, Sienna. I'd had a crush on Millie too.

It had just taken me too damn long to figure it out.

"What drills are you going to run today?" Toren asked another one of the coaches.

As the conversation between them steered toward this afternoon's practice, I should have paid attention. Normally, when it came to football, I was all in. Except my head was on the next floor up, stuck in Millie's office.

Parks had seemed awfully eager to go talk to her. What was that about? Was he interested in her? Was she interested in him? Or was she still stuck on that Adrian?

The stairwell door flew open and Parks came striding out with a knowing smirk. "She said you owe her five hundred and fifteen dollars."

Toren scoffed. "No way."

"I trust Millie's math more than yours," Parks said. "Better bust out that checkbook, Tor. Before she starts charging interest."

"There's no way that number is correct," Toren muttered before his mouth flattened into a thin line and he disappeared into his office.

The huddle disbanded, everyone retreating to their own desks to start the day. Except when I picked up my feet, it wasn't to walk into my office. It was to march straight into Toren's.

"What's up?" he asked as I closed the door behind me.

This was fucking ridiculous. I had no right to be jealous. Yet I couldn't leave without knowing the truth.

"You and Millie." The words were sticky. "Have you, um . . ." Hold up. What if he said yes? Maybe I didn't really want to know the answer, after all.

Understanding softened his expression. "Nah, man. It's never been like that."

The air rushed out of my lungs. *Thank fuck.* "Before I moved, you didn't tell me she was here. Why?"

"I didn't want Millie being here to keep you from coming."

It wouldn't have. But I could see why Toren might think otherwise. He'd watched me walk away from Millie the first time, seemingly without a backward glance.

"All right." I turned, about to leave and get ready for the day, but Toren stopped me.

"You and I have always been friends." He stood a little taller, pinning back his shoulders. "Millie's my friend too. Do right by her this time around."

I knew what was at stake. I wasn't a twenty-something kid, scared and stuck in a difficult position. Everything was different this time around. Toren's warning was—to steal Millie's word—unnecessary.

But I didn't tell him that. I simply gave him a nod before leaving his office for my own. If I hadn't been here to watch out for Millie these past few years, at least she'd had Toren.

I walked to my desk, taking a seat and firing up my computer. I opened up my inbox and its few unread emails, except I couldn't seem to focus on the screen.

If Kurt hadn't interrupted us, I would have kissed Millie. Would she have kissed me back?

I couldn't remember what she tasted like. We'd only kissed the once and it had been too long ago. Was she sweet? What sound did she make when a man sealed his mouth over hers?

"Fuck it." I had to know.

So I shoved away from my desk, lengthening my strides as I walked down the hallway. Then I took the stairs two at a time, hoping Millie hadn't left her office yet.

A few people waved as I walked past their cubicles. It was busier than it had been earlier, people settling in for a Monday. Conversation drifted from the break room and the scent of coffee clung to the air.

Millie was still there when I strode into her office, closing the door behind me. "Oh, hi. What's up?"

I rounded her desk, taking her chair and spinning it so she had to face me. Then I bent, my hands on the armrests, and did what I should have done earlier this morning. What I should have done a decade ago. What I should have done every day for the past ten years.

I kissed my Millie.

CHAPTER THIRTEEN

MILLIE

Ford was kissing me. That, or I'd fallen asleep at my desk and was dreaming.

His tongue swept against mine in a lazy swirl. He sucked my lower lip between his teeth.

God, he tasted good. Sweet, like his candy, and masculine, all Ford. His cologne wrapped around me like a curl of smoke, filling my lungs. His tongue fluttered against mine, drawing out a mewl. Desire coiled in my core, twisting tighter and tighter with every press of his soft lips.

This was no dream.

My imagination wasn't rich enough to afford this kiss.

It put the kiss we'd had in college to utter shame.

Not even Adrian, who was a good kisser, could compete. With every single stroke of his tongue, Ford was ruining me for anyone else.

If it had taken me all those years to recover from our first kiss, how was I going to walk away from this one? That thought was like throwing a bucket of ice water over my head in the dead of winter.

I tore my mouth away, pulling out of Ford's grasp. Then I inched away, the backs of my knees hitting my chair. Wait. When had I stood up?

Ford's lips were wet. Mine probably were too.

"Oh my God. What are we doing?" My hands came to my cheeks, my skin feeling too hot.

"Millie." His eyes searched mine. "Breathe."

"Why did you kiss me?"

"Because I wanted to." He reached out and tucked a lock of hair behind my ear. "Because you wanted me to."

Yes. Yes, I had. Despite my better judgment.

Except where did we go from here? Where did I even want to go?

We had enough history between us to fill a textbook. There was too much heartache—mine. There were too many personal complications—his. Plus, we were coworkers.

We. Were. Coworkers.

That kiss could get me fired.

After last year's scandal, Kurt had begun enforcing the department's no-fraternization policy and code of conduct mercilessly. He'd just terminated our financial aid coordinator because she'd started dating our sports dietitian.

"I don't—" *know what I'm saying.* "We—" *are freaking out. No, not we. Me. I'm freaking out.* "This. I think—" *Gah!*

I couldn't form a coherent thought, let alone a whole sentence.

My calendar came to my rescue. A ding from my phone, a meeting reminder, filled the office. I swept it up from my desk, clutching it against my chest like it was a shield. Then, after sucking in some oxygen, I stood taller, squaring my shoulders. And looked Ford in the eye.

He was grinning. It was sexy.

My eyes dropped straight to his mouth. I wanted to kiss it again. *Oh, shit. Don't look there.* My gaze fell to his chest.

It was broad and wide. Did he have chest hair now? I couldn't remember if he'd had chest hair in college. Strange, considering I remembered everything else about Ford Ellis. I liked chest hair.

Why am I thinking about chest hair? Right. Because I was staring at his chest.

I lifted my phone, swiping the screen to unlock it. Since it was the safest place to look, I glued my eyes to the screen. "I need to go."

"Mills—" he said as I skirted around him with a "See you later."

I needed my laptop for this next meeting, but it was left behind, with Ford, as I hurried for the door. With my chin ducked, my hair formed a curtain around my face, a shelter as I rushed for the stairs.

The minute I stepped into the stairwell, I loosened a breath and touched my lips. They burned. Ford's kiss was like a brand searing my skin.

I closed my eyes, taking a long inhale, then I started down the stairs. My ankle rolled on the first step, but luckily, my hand shot out for the railing. "Ugh. Get a grip, Millie. It was just a kiss."

The best kiss of my life but . . . whatever. Later, tonight, with a bottle of wine, I'd decide how I felt about it. This morning, right now, I had a job to do.

So I swallowed hard, made sure my footing was solid, then marched, stair by stair to the first floor for my meeting.

Aspen Quinn, the women's volleyball coach, was waiting for me in the Jefferson conference room. "Hi, Millie."

"Morning." My cheeks still felt hot. Aspen couldn't tell

that I'd been kissed, right? "I, um—" I shook my head, clearing the Ford haze. "How was your weekend?"

"Good. I went on a long hike and got a sunburn." She nodded to her angry red shoulder. "Did you have a good weekend?"

"Yeah, it was nice. I, uh, baked." With Ford. And his daughter.

Then he'd kissed me two minutes ago, and now I had the urge to crawl under this table and hide. Or rock in the corner. One of the two.

Ten years ago, I would have been dancing through the hallways and telling anyone who would listen that Ford Ellis had a great tongue. Oh, how times had changed.

I'd changed. Ford had changed too.

What happened to him wanting friendship, anyway? And wait a minute, I'd told him I needed time. Barging into my office and kissing me wasn't exactly him giving me space, was it?

"Millie?"

I blinked. *Shit.* "Oh, sorry, Aspen."

"Are you okay?"

"Yes." I sighed. "It's a Monday, and I'm all over the place this morning." Shoving all thoughts of Ford aside, I folded my hands on the table. "How's everything going?"

"So far so good. The girls are all starting to filter back into the gym. The freshmen are here and getting settled into their dorm rooms."

Most of the incoming freshmen recruits were able to get into their rooms well ahead of the official campus move-in day. The athletes would get settled, join the upperclassmen on the team for practices and spend a couple weeks with quiet halls. Then the madness of the fall semester would begin.

Aspen gave me the rest of her short update, the meeting only lasting thirty minutes. Normally, our weekly meetings took a whole hour, but at the moment, we were relatively drama-free. It was a glorious time in the athletics department, like a honeymoon, when everyone was happy, students and coaches alike.

It wouldn't last, but for now, I was enjoying the levity.

Part of my job was mediating any disputes between athletes and coaches—or more commonly, coaches and other coaches. Though Aspen rarely had an issue with anyone. She was a favorite, sweet and smart. She loved sports and was always willing to compromise. Her athletes adored her and the other coaches respected her. So without much official business to discuss, we chatted about a new restaurant downtown instead.

"Thanks for the recommendation, Millie," she said, leaving the conference room.

"Anytime. Let me know if you need anything."

"I will." She smiled, then headed for her office.

I aimed my feet for the stairwell, checking my phone to see what meeting was up next. Too focused on my schedule, I rounded a corner and nearly collided with President Cruz. "Oh, my goodness. I'm so sorry."

She laughed, raising her phone in the air. "My fault. I was texting and walking."

"Guilty." I lifted my phone too. "You must be on your way to meet with Ford."

"I am." She nodded. "I figured I'd get out of my office for a change. Spend a little time wandering around campus. I do love it when the students are here, but there's something special about it right now, don't you think?"

"It's the anticipation." I smiled. "It's electric."

"Yes, exactly." She pointed to my nose. "That's the perfect way to describe it."

"Describe what?" a male voice asked.

Kurt walked up to my side, inserting himself into the conversation. Was he just going to barge in on me all day?

"Oh, um, campus," I said. "We were just talking about how there's an electricity in the air this time of year."

"Ah." He gave me a tight smile, then practically shouldered me out of the way to talk to Carly. "Good morning, President Cruz."

"Kurt." It was her turn for a tight smile.

"You're meeting with Ford?" he asked.

"Apparently everyone knows my schedule this morning."

His fingers began tapping on his leg at his side. "I'll walk you to his office."

"Oh, that's all right. I'm sure I can find it." There was an edge to her tone, a reminder that this was her university. That she knew her way around. Maybe I wouldn't have noticed that edge except it was such a sharp contrast to the warmth she had when talking to me. "Good to see you, Millie."

"You too, President Cruz."

Frustration rolled off Kurt in waves as she disappeared.

"Well, I'd better—"

Kurt stopped me with a scowl. "You need to let me handle communications with Carly."

Don't roll your eyes. Do not roll your eyes. "I was just saying hello."

"And with Ford?"

Oh, shit. Maybe Kurt hadn't bought that whole eyelash-in-my-eyeball ploy after all. "Um. I, uh—"

"This season is critical."

"I know the season is critical," I said.

"You never told me you knew Ford."

"You never asked." Instead, he'd hired Ford without a word to the rest of the freaking department. "We just went to college together."

And he'd just kissed me but . . . details.

Kurt's lips pursed. "I need Ford coming to me if there's a problem. We can't have another problematic year."

He couldn't have another problematic year. "I'm not trying to interfe—"

"Just stay away from him, Millie." Kurt's voice rose.

I tensed. What the hell? Had he just . . . verbally slapped my hand?

Yep. I'd just been scolded by my boss. Never, ever, ever in my entire life had I been reprimanded at work. Granted, I hadn't had many bosses other than Kurt. But still.

I'd just gotten in trouble. An imaginary pink slip might as well have appeared out of thin air.

My nose stung. My throat burned at the threat of tears.

"You have plenty on your own plate," Kurt said. "Focus on your programs."

"Understood." I nodded, then pointed toward the stairs, needing to get out of here before he saw me cry. "I've got to get to another meeting."

Without another word, I walked past him, skipping every other step as I run-walked. Then I flew up the stairs, seeking the sanctuary of my office. The moment I was inside, I closed myself in, sagging against the door.

"Ouch." I sniffled, my eyes flooding.

How long had it taken me to get this office instead of a cubicle? Years. I'd worked my ass off for this room with a window and a desk and an actual door. I'd worked my ass off to establish myself as a leader on this team.

I'd worked my ass off for nine years.

Ford had been in Mission for less than a month.

There wasn't a doubt in my mind that where Kurt was concerned, in a contest between Ford and me, I'd come out the loser.

Millie Cunningham, assistant athletics director, was easily replaceable.

Ford Ellis was not.

I wouldn't lose my job, not for Ford. Not for a kiss, no matter how good. So I shoved off the door, standing tall. Then I walked to the plastic container on my desk, taking a long look at the half-eaten piece of chocolate cake inside.

Then I tossed the whole thing in the trash.

CHAPTER FOURTEEN

FORD

I was late to practice.

Are you going to ignore me forever?

I'd sent that text at 7:13 this morning. Considering it was noon and Millie hadn't replied, I guess I had my answer.

It had been a week since our kiss. A week of nothing. Millie had become a ghost.

And I was fucking sick of it.

I dragged a hand over my jaw, the stubble I hadn't shaved this morning scraping against my palm. Was I bad at kissing? Had it been an epic disappointment and that was the reason she was ignoring me?

No. No fucking way.

Goddamn it, that had been a great kiss. So what was her problem?

Sure, maybe I'd come on a little strong. Call it desperation. Sienna had been the only woman in my life for years, and even then, our sex life hadn't exactly been active.

Well . . . hers had been.

I, on the other hand, hadn't touched a woman in years.

There had been no temptation. My fist and I had gotten on just fine. Except just the thought of Millie's mouth made me hard. And no matter how many cold showers I'd suffered through this week, jacking off to the mental image of her face, it hadn't been enough.

She'd flipped a switch.

Like hell I was going to let her ignore me.

"I'm not suffering alone," I muttered, shoving away from my desk.

The first practice of the day had started fifteen minutes ago. Millie probably thought I was on the field. Maybe she'd have her guard down. Maybe she'd be in her office, thinking it was safe.

Instead of walking out the door and into the sunshine, I let my long strides eat up the hallway to the stairwell. I was just about to shove through the door when I heard my name.

"Ford." Parks rushed my way. The look on his face said I wasn't going to make it to Millie's office. *Damn.*

"What's up?"

"Got a problem. Rush is missing."

"Missing?" I blinked. "What do you mean *missing?*" I doubted anyone would try to kidnap a twenty-one-year-old man standing six three and weighing 220 pounds.

"No one has seen him today. And he's not answering his phone."

Fuck. "Okay," I drawled. "But he was at practice yesterday. Has anyone seen him since?"

"Nope. His roommate said he never came home last night."

"Hell." I dragged a hand through my hair. This was not something I needed today. "Who does he live with?"

"Maverick Houston. Punter. He's the one who told me Rush was missing."

"What's Rush's number?" I dug my phone from my pocket, unlocking the screen, just as footsteps pounded behind Parks.

"Coach." Houston jogged to us, his chest heaving as he breathed. His brown hair was sweaty.

Maybe we needed to double up on conditioning for special teams.

"Find him?" Parks asked.

Houston shook his head, still panting. "No, but his car is parked at the stadium. It's empty. Ran back as soon as I saw it. Maybe he's somewhere in the building?"

I grumbled, not in the mood to track down a missing quarterback. "Any idea why he wouldn't show up to practice or go home last night? Was he partying or something?"

It was the preseason, but we'd implemented some rules already with the team, including a curfew of midnight. No drinking. No time downtown at the bars. Anyone caught breaking those rules was benched. Indefinitely.

This year, I'd drawn a hard line, and no one had better cross me.

"I doubt it, Coach," Houston said. "Rush isn't really the partying type."

Well, that was something. "Was he acting off yesterday?"

Both Houston and Parks shook their heads.

Rush had seemed fine to me too, but I also didn't know the kid well. Not yet. He was a senior but he had another year of eligibility left so I'd have another season with him. So far, I'd only interacted with him at practice and in the weight room the few times I'd gone to work out. I'd wanted to make an appearance with the guys. From everything I'd seen, Rush was extremely focused and dedicated.

Not much more a coach could ask from his starting quarterback.

Except to show up for fucking practice.

"You guys hit the field," I said. "I'll see if I can track him down. Text me his phone number?"

Parks nodded, then jerked his chin for Houston to follow him outside.

I gave the door to the stairwell a longing glance, then turned around and trudged toward the locker room.

It smelled of metal lockers, sweaty cleats and sharp cologne. But there was an undercurrent of fresh paint and bleach. Whoever had designed the remodel had given it bright lighting and a spacious layout. It was a hell of a lot nicer than the locker room we'd had during my days as a Wildcat player.

"Rush?" I called.

No answer. Not that I'd expected one.

I checked the bathroom next, then the showers. Every corner of the locker room was empty, so I pushed through the door that led to the weight room.

The space was huge, three times the size of what I remembered from my college years. There were universities where the football team had their own, private weight room and gym space. At TSU, we shared these facilities with the other teams. But given how big they were, how there were separate spaces to divide students, I doubted we'd ever have an issue feeling crowded. And it was good for our players to interact with athletes from other sports. It broadened the comradery throughout athletics as a whole.

I scanned the room. *Empty.* My phone vibrated in my

pocket and I dug it out. Parks had texted Rush's number so I saved it into my contacts, then tapped his name. The phone rang in my ear.

And another chimed in the background.

"What the . . ." I pulled my phone from my ear, listening for the other ring. Then I started walking, weaving past machines and benches, toward the farthest corner of the room.

And the guy sitting in a corner, hiding behind a weight rack.

"Rush."

He held his phone, the device small compared to his grip. It kept ringing and ringing. He just stared at the screen.

I ended the call and dropped to my haunches. "Rush."

"Coach." His voice was hoarse. He blinked, his bloodshot eyes flicking up to mine.

"Tell me what's going on." A demand, not an ask.

Rush swallowed hard, turning to give me his profile. His jaw was covered in stubble. His dirty blond hair was sticking up all over the place, like he'd been running his hands through it for hours.

"Are you in trouble?" I asked.

He nodded.

"Scale of one to ten, how bad is it?"

His Adam's apple bobbed. "Eleven."

Fuck. I sat on the mat, mirroring his posture with my forearms draped over my knees.

"Aren't you going to scream at me?" he asked. "Tell me to get off my ass and get to practice?"

"Not really a fan of screaming." On or off the field. But given that he'd even asked me that question, I now knew more about the previous head coach. Maybe Rush's high school coaches too.

He kept staring at the wall, at some invisible spot in the concrete.

So I waited, giving him time, hoping that he'd open up. It took so long that my ass started to go numb, but I didn't shift. I didn't move. I just waited.

Then finally, he shifted his gaze to his phone once more and began tapping the screen. His eyes flooded. He sniffled. Then he handed it over so I could read the text he'd pulled up.

I'm pregnant.

Two words that dragged me ten years into the past. It was a damn good thing that I was sitting.

Maybe I did feel like screaming after all.

———

I MISSED PRACTICE. So did Rush.

Instead, we sat on the floor of the weight room.

And I told him a story.

Turns out, Rush Ramsey and I weren't so different. Though instead of knocking up his girlfriend, the text that had sent him into a spiral had been from a one-night stand.

"My life is over."

"Your life is different," I corrected. "Not over. Just different."

Rush opened his mouth, like he was going to argue, except then his gaze snagged on my shirt.

I hadn't done laundry this weekend. We'd had the coaches over for a barbeque, then the rest of the time I'd spent it with Joey. Laundry was on tonight's agenda since my hamper was overflowing. When I'd gone to get dressed this morning, each of my Treasure State shirts had been dirty. So I'd chosen this shirt because it was white and lightweight, good for hot afternoons spent on the practice field.

It was a Super Bowl championship T-shirt.

Maybe exactly the shirt that Rush needed to see. Dads made it to the Super Bowl too.

"It'll be all right." I stood, reaching out a hand to help Rush to his feet. "Call her. Talk it through."

He took it, no hesitation, and stood. "Thanks, Coach."

"Welcome. You have my number. I'm here, day or night."

Rush's face was still pale, his eyes too wide. But the hopelessness had faded, just a little. "Sorry about practice. I'll make it up to you."

I believed he would. "We'll talk tomorrow, yeah?"

"Yeah."

I clapped him on the shoulder, then steered him for the door. "Your car is at the stadium. Houston found it."

"I, uh . . ." Rush ducked his chin. "Sometimes I come to the field. To think. Sorry. That's probably breaking the rules."

If football was his safe haven, I sure as hell wasn't going to punish him for it. It had been mine too. That, and Millie.

I escorted Rush to the door, watching as he started across the fieldhouse parking lot and to the stadium beyond. Then when he vanished from sight, I retreated to my office, feeling like someone had shaken each and every one of my bones.

Had I helped Rush? Had I made it worse? I'd been honest about my life. About Sienna. About the years of misery we'd spent together simply because of Joey. Maybe I shouldn't have shared that much. Maybe I shouldn't have shared at all.

My stomach knotted, and before I even made it to my chair, I spun around, returning to the hallway. My legs carried me to the second floor. I followed the faint scent of tangerines and flowers, finding Millie in her office.

Her eyes went wide when I strode in, closing the door behind me. She shot up from her chair, taking a step back and holding up a hand. "Um, what are you doing?"

I walked right into her space, brushing that hand aside as I trapped her in the corner. "Stop ignoring me."

"I'm—"

Before she could lie, I bent and sealed my mouth over hers.

The knot in my gut untied. The rattling in my bones stopped.

My tongue swept inside, tangling with hers. A whimper, sexy and subtle, escaped her throat. Damn, but she tasted good. Sweet. Warm. Just a swirl, just a taste, that was all I let myself take before I pulled away.

Her eyelids fluttered open.

My gaze searched hers, soaking in every striation of green and gold and brown and gray in those pretty hazel irises.

"Ford." She placed a hand over my heart, like she was about to push me away, but there wasn't any force behind the touch.

So I covered it with my palm. "Millie."

She stared at my knuckles, her shoulders sagging as she blew out a long breath. "You have to stop kissing me."

I tucked a lock of hair behind her ear. "No."

CHAPTER FIFTEEN

FORD

A knock at my office door startled me out of my staring contest with the window. "Coach Ellis?"

I spun around. Rush lingered in the hall, so I waved him in. "Come on in."

For a guy his size, Rush didn't make a lot of noise when he walked. Light feet, a great skill for a quarterback. Or maybe I'd just been too stuck in my own head to hear him approach. My focus had been as sharp as a spoon the past two days.

Since I'd kissed Millie in her office and she'd asked me to stop.

Why was she so against this? Probably a question I should have asked instead of telling her *no* and marching out of her office. But I wasn't going to argue about this.

I'd endured too many years with a woman I hadn't loved. I'd stayed with Sienna because I'd thought it was best for Joey. Turns out, a shit marriage didn't create a great environment for a child.

Joey's happiness was my utmost priority. Maybe there

was a chance I could have that happiness for us both. And if there was even a slight chance that Millie and I could have something special, something we'd missed the first time around, then damn it, I wasn't going to stop.

What was holding her back? Was she still hung up on the past? Maybe she hadn't forgiven me for what I'd done. I wouldn't blame her. But damn it, if we could get through it, if we could get to the other side . . .

That was the win. The ultimate win.

So no, I wasn't stopping. Not a chance in hell.

But I'd give her some time to catch up. Millie was fast. She'd get there. And in the meantime, I had a football team to coach. And a player to help through the biggest change of his life.

Rush took the chair across from my desk, sitting on its edge with his hands folded in his lap.

"How are you?" I asked.

He lifted a shoulder. "A mess."

This kid's honesty was refreshing. "Understandable. You did good at practice yesterday."

Rush had worked his ass off, running circles around everyone else. He'd pushed himself, he'd pushed his team, and damn, this kid had an arm. "I'm just . . . it's what I can control. Me and the ball."

My heart squeezed. Staring at him was a lot like staring into a mirror. I hadn't voiced those exact words ten years ago, but I'd felt them deep in my soul. Football had been the only steady in the earthquake that had been my life.

"Did you talk to her?" I asked.

"To Faye?" He nodded. "Yeah. She's freaking out too. But, um . . . she wants to keep it. The baby."

"How do you feel about that?"

He swallowed hard. "I don't know."

"Give it time," I said, my gaze drifting to the framed photo on my desk.

The picture was of Joey and me at the Super Bowl. We were each wearing the championship hats they'd passed out after the win. Confetti flittered in the air, mingling with the noise, the deafening cheers and applause. Joey was sitting on my shoulders, her arms raised high.

I had my head tipped back to stare up at her as she smiled.

Sienna had taken that picture. For all her faults, she'd been a good cheerleader for my career. Maybe that was because it had been her way to garner a sliver of attention. Whatever the reason, I'd always just been glad that she'd brought Joey to my games.

"Thanks for the other day," Rush said. "For talking me through it. Telling me your story."

"You're welcome." I'd probably crossed a hundred different professional lines with how much I'd shared with Rush. But if it had helped, I'd do it again.

"I'll let you get back to work." He smacked the arms of the chair, then stood.

"See you at practice." I waved as he headed out the door, then plucked my phone from the desk to call the nanny.

Except Stephanie didn't answer. Joey did.

"Hi, Daddy."

"Hi. Why are you answering Stephanie's phone?"

"It was just sitting here, and I saw your name come up."

I chuckled, shaking my head. "You can't answer other people's phones."

"But didn't you call to talk to me? It seems like a waste of time for Stephanie to answer just for her to hand me the phone."

This kid. She was too smart for my own good. "Yeah, I did call to talk to you. What are you doing?"

She sighed. "Reading."

"Reading is good for you."

"Reading is boring." She groaned. "What are you doing?"

"Working. Where's Stephanie?"

"Cleaning up the kitchen."

Stephanie had been the hire of the century. She was in her midforties and divorced. Her twin sons had just graduated high school and were about to attend TSU as freshmen. She'd been a teacher before she'd quit to stay home with her kids, but with an empty house, she'd decided to go back to work.

The minute the nanny agency had sent me her résumé, I'd requested an interview.

She was willing to stay late and work weekends. Since she'd started, each evening when I'd walked through the door, the house had been clean. And she even let Joey paint her nails a different color every day.

"Can I talk to her?" I asked.

"Sure." A muffled noise and footsteps filled the background. Then Joey's voice, explaining why she'd answered the phone.

"Hello," Stephanie said.

"Sorry about the phone. We'll work on boundaries."

"Or don't worry about it. She misses you. If she jumps to answer your call, let her. Sooner than you can blink she'll be a teenager and you'll be begging for her to pick up."

I wasn't ready for that stage, not yet. If Joey and I fought now, what was it going to be like when she was in her teens?

"How would you feel about an afternoon off?" I asked. "Maybe you could bring Joey over in about an hour. We'll have lunch and she can hang with me the rest of the day."

"That's fine by me. Are you sure?"

"Yeah. I miss her too."

"Then we'll see you in a bit."

"Bye." I ended the call and sagged in my chair. It wouldn't be as easy to concentrate at practice this afternoon with Joey in tow, but school was starting in a week. She'd start making friends and getting involved in her own activities. The football schedule was demanding already but it was about to reach sheer chaos. My window of time with Joey for the fall was closing, so today, I was having a spontaneous *take-your-daughter-to-work* day.

"Ford." Toren knocked on my door, coming in with the latest version of the playbook. "Question."

"Hit me with it."

The hour passed in a blink. Toren's concern over a couple of players and their positions demanded an impromptu meeting with a couple of the other coaches to swap out a few roles. The minute the meeting was over, Joey arrived, running down the hallway at the fieldhouse, her blond hair streaming behind her.

My kid loved to run.

Sort of like Millie.

"Hey, princess." I swept her into my arms, kissing her cheek before putting her down.

Stephanie joined us, giving Joey a quick goodbye before promising to be at our place at 6:45 tomorrow morning. Then she headed out, and I clasped my daughter's hand.

She still let me hold her hand. That would probably end sooner rather than later too, wouldn't it?

"Feel like exploring?" I asked.

Joey shrugged. "Sure."

We set off from the fieldhouse, taking the long way around campus to the student union. We crossed a few of the green lawns, taking in the brick buildings.

"See that building over there?" I pointed to one of the halls. "I had some classes in that building."

"What about that one?" Joey pointed to another.

I shook my head. "No, but your mom had some in there."

Sienna had been a business marketing major, but she'd never earned her degree. When we'd moved to Seattle, after Joey was born, I'd asked if she wanted to finish school, but she hadn't wanted to go back.

"Where else did Mom hang out?"

"That building in front of us was another one."

We strolled around campus for twenty minutes. I pointed out places from the past. She asked questions. But as the walk continued, those questions dwindled. And a familiar look I hated with every fiber of my being fell over her face.

Longing. Disappointment. Rejection.

Joey missed her mother.

Sienna called each day. Sometimes it would be so late that I'd have to wake Joey up so they could say good night. But phone calls weren't enough, not for a nine-year-old girl.

Unfortunately, it had been like this in Seattle too. Joey had lived with me after Sienna had moved out when we'd separated. Then I'd pushed hard for full custody.

The weekends I'd had away games, Sienna would come over to stay with Joey. But otherwise, when I was home, Joey would only get phone calls. And Sienna had lived in the same fucking city.

Sienna had thrown a fit when I'd told her Joey and I were moving to Mission. She'd threatened to sue for partial custody, to make me stay, yet we'd moved regardless, and no surprise, I hadn't heard a peep from her attorney.

What Sienna didn't seem to comprehend was that it wasn't about her. Hell, she didn't understand that I'd basically done her a favor.

Because now Sienna had an actual excuse—five hundred miles—for why she couldn't pick Joey up from school or come to a school holiday concert. No more texts at the last minute canceling plans. No more promises broken.

If Sienna ever decided to visit, not something she'd offered so far, I wasn't going to tell Joey until Sienna's feet were on Montana soil.

It was for the best. But Joey was nine and all she knew was that her mother had basically disappeared from her life when we'd gotten divorced.

Did she blame me for that? *Probably.*

There was nothing I could do but wait until she was older. And hopefully, one day, she'd understand.

"How about some lunch?" I waved a hand to the student union building. "Popcorn chicken and fries?"

"Sure," she mumbled, her feet trudging along the sidewalk. "Why couldn't I just stay home today?"

"You're not having fun?"

"Not really."

Ouch. "Sorry. I thought we could hang today. Spend some time together before school starts."

"We spend time together every day."

"Yeah, but that's just at home."

"So?"

I pinched the bridge of my nose. "Give it a chance."

"Are we going to have to do football stuff?"

"Yes, we'll have to go to practice."

Joey huffed and rolled her eyes. "Can I just sit in your office and play Nintendo?"

"No." It came out too snappy.

Her eyes narrowed. Another familiar look crossed her face. She clamped her mouth shut, and just like that, I was getting the silent treatment.

So maybe bringing her here hadn't been a great idea after all. "Let's just . . . let's just get some lunch."

I ripped open the door to the student union, letting Joey march inside first. Then I headed for the food court, ordering for us both since she refused to speak to the cashier too.

We got our food and took a seat at a nearby table. The building was mostly empty, only a few students roamed the halls, but that would change soon.

Joey had just taken a bite when she glanced up and her glare was gone.

For a brief moment, I thought maybe she'd forgiven me. Then I realized she wasn't looking at me. I twisted in my chair, wanting to see the source of that joy.

Millie walked through the food court.

My heart skipped. I'd missed her beautiful face these past two days.

Before I could stop her, Joey flew out of her chair, racing past the empty tables to where Millie was ordering a sandwich.

Joey skidded to a stop at her side, her arms instantly wrapping around Millie's waist.

Millie smiled down at my daughter, returning the hug before Joey let her go and pointed to where I was sitting.

I lifted a hand.

Millie's smile faded. Then she glanced over her shoulder.

Kurt emerged from around the corner, eyes glued to his phone.

Joey gave Millie a high five before skipping back to our table. "I asked her if she could have lunch with us but she said she has a meeting."

"Millie's a very important person around here," I said.

"More important than you?"

"Yes." Without a doubt. I was just a football coach. Millie was the person who ensured there were actually programs to be coached.

Joey looked to Millie again with a bit of awe in her gaze. I liked that for my daughter. And I liked that for me because Joey was talking to me again. *Thanks, Mills.*

If Joey needed a role model, I couldn't think of a better one than Millie. A woman who worked hard to help others. A woman who didn't crave the spotlight. A woman who didn't put a fucking reality TV show above her child.

As Kurt came to stand beside Millie, she steeled her spine, putting on that professional smile that didn't reach her eyes.

He started talking, glancing around the open room. When he spotted me, he smiled wider, waving. It dimmed when he saw my lunch date.

Idiot.

Millie didn't look my way again, not even when they sat three tables away.

Not a single glance.

Not since Kurt had entered the food court.

Huh.

On Monday, she'd told me that I had to stop kissing her. Not that she wanted me to stop, but that I *had* to stop. Both times I'd kissed her, we'd been at work. Maybe her hesitancy had nothing to do with me. Maybe it had nothing to do with the past.

Maybe it had everything to do with our boss.

Which meant it was time to find a new playing field.

CHAPTER SIXTEEN

MILLIE

Black. Gray. Beige. Cream.

I stared at the neat, folded stacks of laundry on my white bed. Maybe Autumn was onto something with my wardrobe. "Maybe it is a bit, er . . . boring."

When was the last time I'd bought something bright? I turned, staring into my closet. It was organized by color, and in between the spectrum of white to black, there were only a few pieces that popped.

The only exciting thing about my closet was my tennis shoe collection. But even my newest additions tended to be white or gray. It was the older pairs, with their bold and bright shades, that gave my wardrobe any hope of a personality.

"Fine, it's a lot boring." I frowned, then snatched the phone from the mattress, opening up my Nordstrom app. Filtering to the athletic apparel, I picked out a pair of the boldest blue leggings I could find and a hot pink tank, then tapped checkout.

A ding alerted me to a new email in my inbox, an order

summary, then I tossed my phone aside and put away my dull attire.

I returned the empty basket to the laundry room, then put the dress I'd worn to last night's fundraiser into the dry cleaning bag. The event had been at the fieldhouse, a tour and reception for alumni and boosters. With over three hundred guests to greet and entertain, the evening had felt like a marathon.

We'd invited the coaches as well as a few select student athletes to attend. Ford had been there, mingling and shaking hands. Every time I'd passed him, his gaze had flicked up to meet mine. But we hadn't spoken.

Not since I'd told him to stop kissing me on Monday and he'd adamantly refused.

Yet he hadn't approached me last night. He hadn't sought me out in the crowd. Why did that bother me? Wasn't that what I wanted? To put some distance between us and reestablish some professional boundaries?

"Why am I always thinking about Ford?" I huffed, gave myself a decent eye roll, then headed for the kitchen to grab another glass of water.

Sundays were recovery days, so my run this morning had only been two miles, but after racing around the fieldhouse in heels last night, my calves were cramping.

I'd just drained the glass when the doorbell rang. I wasn't expecting any guests, but it would be Autumn. She was notorious for showing up at my house on Sundays, usually with a bottle of prosecco, and considering I'd been avoiding her, well . . . I was actually surprised she'd waited until after lunch.

She'd take one look at my face and know I was hiding something.

Like kissing Ford. Twice.

I walked to the door, turning the knob with an *I'm sorry I suck as a best friend* poised on the tip of my tongue. But it wasn't Autumn on my front porch.

It was Ford.

And Joey.

"Hi." His blue eyes danced as my jaw dropped.

"Hi, Millie." Joey lifted up on her toes as she waved.

"H-hi. Uh . . . what are you doing here?" I infused my voice with false cheer and plastered on a fake smile—for Joey's sake, not Ford's.

"We're going hiking," he said.

"Did you get lost on the way to the mountains?" I pointed over his shoulder to the blue peaks in the distance. "They're that way."

Ford's smile widened, flashing me those white teeth, and *damn him*, my instinct was to smile back.

Don't smile. Do. Not. Smile.

Joey was smiling too. It was the adorable gap between her front teeth that broke my resolve.

The corner of my mouth turned up.

"Get some shoes," Ford ordered.

My gaze dropped to my bare feet. I looked back up and glared. "Did you just order me around?"

"He does it to me all the time," Joey muttered.

Ford chuckled.

A giggle escaped. "What is happening?"

"Hiking." He snapped his fingers. "Let's go, Mills."

"Can I use your bathroom first?" Joey asked.

"Sure." I stepped aside, waving her in. "Just go down the hallway on your right. It's the first door."

It was a mistake to step so far to the side. Because the moment Joey came in, Ford followed.

I didn't have a massive house. My cottage was eighty years old, and though the previous owners had done a renovation, the rooms, albeit charming, were small.

With him inside, it might as well have been a dollhouse. His presence consumed every inch, charging it with the same electricity he brought into my office.

He was in a navy, sleeveless athletic shirt. His arms, ripped with muscle, were on full display. My gaze traced the lines of his biceps, the curves of his triceps down to his sinewed forearms. His black mesh shorts draped over the bulk of his thighs.

And the tattoos on his right arm, *oh my God*, the tattoos. Ford was so focused. So steady. The tattoos gave him a reckless, sexy edge.

I wiped the corner of my mouth. *Yep, that was drool.*

"Millicent."

My face whipped up to his. While I'd been gawking, he'd closed the gap between us.

Ford leaned in, just an inch, like he was going to kiss me.

I put my hand in front of his face. "Do not kiss me again."

There was a challenge in his eyes. I was so busy trying to make sense of it that I didn't notice his hand shoot up to capture my wrist. His fingers were so long he wrapped it easily. Even when I tugged, he had me trapped.

With that smirk on his mouth, he pulled my hand toward his lips, turning it at the last second to place a chaste kiss on the inside of my wrist before loosening his hold.

I yanked my hand free and took a step away, my skin

buzzing from the softness of his mouth. "You listen as well as a brick wall."

His laugh filled every corner of the house.

My taste in home décor was a lot like my choice in clothing. Black. Gray. Beige. Cream.

Ford's laugh was like a burst of color, yellow and orange and neon green. Even with the sun streaming through my windows, that laugh brightened every room.

"Please don't . . ." I squeezed my eyes shut. "What do you want, Ford?"

"To kiss you again." The toilet flushed from down the hallway. "But Joey's not ready to see that."

Joey was always first for him. I loved that for her.

"We're hiking the T," Ford said.

The T was the collegiate symbol made out of white rocks on a nearby mountainside. It was one of the more popular hikes in the area, mostly because it was close to town and the view was incredible. Plus it had an easy rating for kids and families.

"Great. Have fun. Wear sunscreen."

"It's in the truck. Get some shoes," he ordered again. "I've got an extra water bottle, but if you have one you want, grab it too."

"I'm not going—" Wait. "How did you know where I lived?"

Before he could answer, Joey emerged from the hallway, walking slowly as she looked around the living room and entryway. "I like your house, Millie."

"Thanks, Jo." I smiled at her, then shot a glare at Ford, quirking my eyebrow as a silent reminder to answer my question.

"I asked for your address."

"You what?" It came out nearly a shriek. "Who did you ask?" *Please don't say Kurt.*

"Toren."

"Oh." The air rushed from my lungs. *Phew.* Momentary panic attack over.

"Ready?" Joey asked, slipping her hand into his.

"Yeah. If Millie ever puts on some shoes." He held my stare, unwavering.

Trapped. Again. The bastard had trapped me. Because the moment I glanced down to Joey, I saw the hope on her face. It was the same look she'd given me earlier this week when I'd bumped into them in the student union over lunch.

She'd invited me to eat with them, and I'd had to turn her down because of a meeting with Kurt. Her entire face had crumpled. I'd do just about anything not to see that look again.

Ford must have known I wouldn't tell her no. *Jerkface.*

"Give me a minute." I spun on a heel and marched into my bedroom, finding a pair of older running shoes that could get dusty on a trail. With my shoes on my feet, I returned to the living room where Ford and Joey stood waiting.

"Let's go." He headed for the door, holding it open for Joey to go out first.

Maybe once he was outside, I could fake a sudden migraine and lock him out. I'd make Joey cookies as my apology.

"After you." I waved him forward.

Ford shook his head. "I don't trust you not to lock me out."

This was the problem with Ford Ellis. It might have been ten years, but he knew me too well.

"Fine." I walked out first and when I glanced back, his

gaze was locked on my ass, encased in simple black biker shorts. "Eyes up, Coach."

His jaw clenched.

Joey hopped down the porch steps, passing two flower-pots teeming with white petunias.

The exterior of my house was much like the interior. Gray siding. White trim. Brown cedar shakes. Boring. Even the flowers I'd planted this spring were colorless.

Then there was Joey in her lime shorts and matching tank top.

I glanced down at my own tank, a dove gray.

When had my life become so . . . drab?

"Actually, I'm going to grab a water. Be right back." I spun and veered around Ford to dart back in the house. Then I rushed to the kitchen, rifling through my cabinets until I found a hot pink water bottle.

I filled it at the sink and twisted on the lid, about to run to catch up, but when I turned, I slammed into Ford's large frame.

"Whoa." His hands clamped around my arms, steadying me. "Just making sure you weren't making a getaway out the back."

"I'll go hiking. You win. Happy now?"

"Yes." His smile was victorious, like the smiles I remembered from game days when the Wildcats had won.

So lost in that smile, I didn't have a chance to stop him when he closed the gap this time and sealed his mouth over mine.

One dart of his tongue against my lower lip and I opened for him, my body liquifying as he swept inside.

God, this man could kiss. I didn't remember it being like this. I didn't remember any kiss ever being like this. It was like the color he'd brought into my home with his laugh. Ford's kiss was a symphony of blue and green and red and yellow.

A kaleidoscope.

I clung to his arm with my free hand, afraid if I didn't hold on, my knees would buckle.

He moaned, the deep, rich vibration running straight down my throat and settling between my legs. My pulse bloomed, a throb begging for more.

Before I was ready, Ford pulled away. His lips were wet. He swallowed hard, then dropped his hands, using one to wipe his mouth. "Ready?"

I shook my head. "Maybe this hike is a bad idea."

Even to my own ears it sounded weak and pathetic. Like me, any time Ford was in the room.

"I told you to stop kissing me," I whispered.

Ford plucked the water bottle from my grip. "And I told you no."

CHAPTER SEVENTEEN

FORD

Joey's squeak had my gaze shooting to the rearview mirror.

"What?"

"I lost my tooth!" She smiled, revealing the hole where her eye tooth had been.

"Nice." I chuckled as she held it up, slimy with a little bit of blood. "We've been waiting for that one to fall out," I told Millie.

The permanent tooth was already poking through and hopefully this would give it space to come in straight. Though Joey was going to need braces. There was no avoiding that with the gap between her front teeth.

I thought it was adorable. I doubted she'd agree when she was fifteen.

"Think the tooth fairy will give you a quarter?" Millie asked.

"He's the tooth fairy." Joey leaned forward to poke my arm. "And he gives me five dollars for every tooth."

Millie whistled. "Prices have gone up since I was a kid."

"Daddy says I'm expensive."

I chuckled. "You are expensive."

Joey's and Millie's laughter filled the truck's cab. The radio was on, low in the background, but I reached forward to shut it off. I'd listen to them laugh for the rest of my life over any music, even my favorite classic rock.

Millie glanced over, a flush rising in her cheeks.

Fuck, I could kiss her again. And I'd made the decision that every time she told me to stop, I'd kiss her twice instead.

"Can I call Mom to tell her about my tooth?" Joey's question doused my mood like a fire extinguisher.

If she called Sienna, chances were Millie's name would come up. And after Sienna's reaction the night Joey had told her about the cookie and cake baking Saturday . . .

I wasn't jazzed about fighting with my ex-wife.

"We're just about to the trailhead," I said.

Joey pouted. "But I didn't get to talk to her last night."

Sienna had been too busy to call her daughter.

"Please?" Joey begged.

Goddamn it. I'd promised myself, no matter how much resentment I had toward Sienna, I'd do my best to hide it from Joey. I wasn't always successful, but I tried. I could count on my hand the number of times Joey had asked to call Sienna since we'd moved to Montana. So I took the phone from the console and hit Sienna's name.

It rang three times. Maybe I'd get lucky and she wouldn't answer.

"Hey."

Not lucky.

"What's up?" Sienna's voice was groggy, like I'd woken her up.

"Joey wants to talk to you." I handed the phone to the back seat, then glanced at Millie.

Her lower lip was worried between her teeth and her shoulders were curled inward, like she was trying to disappear into the seat. Her gaze was locked straight ahead at the road, so focused it was like she was driving, not me.

"Hi, Mom," Joey said, followed by a long pause. She nodded at whatever Sienna had said to her. "I lost my tooth."

The excitement in her voice was gone. It had been like that for a while now. Joey would be smiling and happy, but the minute I gave her the phone, it was like someone had turned the volume down on my daughter.

"Did you plan your trip?" Joey asked.

Hold up. Trip? What trip? Was Sienna planning to come here? They'd talked a few nights ago, and I'd let Joey have my phone in the other room. But if there was a trip, it was news to me.

"Oh."

Yeah, there was no trip.

Fucking Sienna.

Joey muttered a yes, then a no. "We're going hiking to the T. Me and Daddy and Millie."

Boom. Yep, this was going to suck.

"Here, Daddy." Joey stretched the phone forward. "She wants to talk to you."

Of course she did. I pressed it to my ear. "Yeah?"

"Are you fucking kidding me?" Sienna seethed. Guess she was awake now. "I told you how I feel about her, Ford."

"And I don't care," I clipped, then yanked the phone from my ear and ended the call.

It rang immediately, so I declined it, then turned the volume to silent before glancing in the mirror.

Joey's chin touched her chest.

"Sorry, princess," I said.

She lifted a shoulder. "She has to work so she can't come here to go school shopping with me."

They'd talked about school shopping? News to me. I made a mental note to take her tomorrow night after work. She had cute clothes already but if she wanted something special for her first day, we'd go buy it.

Fucking Sienna.

Someday, her antics would stop pissing me off. Today was not that day. My knuckles were white as I strangled the steering wheel, my molars grinding together.

The rest of the ride to the trailhead was silent and tense. I parked in the crowded lot, scrubbing a hand over my face. When I looked at Millie, her gaze was waiting.

"Sorry," she mouthed.

"Not your fault."

She gave me a sad smile, then climbed out, opening the back door for Joey. Maybe she wasn't sure what to say. Or maybe there was nothing to say, because Millie just held out her hand, helping my daughter to the ground, then put her arm around Joey's shoulders. "Have you been up to the T before?"

Joey shook her head.

"Whenever I get to the top, I close my eyes and make a wish."

"Have they ever come true?" my daughter asked.

"Sometimes they do," Millie said. "Sometimes they don't."

Joey cast her eyes up the trail. "I'm going to make a wish at the top."

"Me too." Millie held out her hand for a fist bump.

"Want to hear a funny story? The very first time I came up here to hike, I bent over to tie my shoe and ripped a hole in the butt of my shorts."

Joey snorted. "Seriously?"

"Yeah, and it gets worse. I was with this boy I had a crush on and he saw my underwear. It was *so* embarrassing."

Joey giggled as Millie feigned a cringe.

"Who was the boy you had a crush on?" Joey asked.

Me.

"Oh, just a guy from the past," Millie said, waving it off.

Maybe someday, when she was older, I'd be able to tell Joey the whole story. That the guy Millie had been hiking with that day was me.

It had been the spring of my senior year. I'd been dating Sienna for months, and Millie had become a regular at our hangouts. She was the first girl I'd met who understood football. It was awesome.

A few of us guys had wanted to hike the T, and I'd asked Sienna to come along. She'd been hungover from a party the night before—I'd told her not to drink so much, especially during the track and field season when it was prohibited—but she hadn't listened.

So while Sienna had spent the day in bed, Toren had invited Millie to come with us.

Mills had been wearing a pair of shorts, not the second-skin biker style like she was in today, but running shorts with that slick fabric that didn't really stretch. Maybe they'd been old but as she'd bent to tie her shoe . . . *rip*.

We'd all laughed, even Millie. She'd been a hell of a sport about it, taking one of my old sweatshirts to tie around her waist.

I hadn't had a damn clue she'd had a crush on me. Not then.

Maybe things would have gone differently if I'd known. If I'd paid more attention to those pretty hazel eyes, her shy smile or the flush of her cheeks.

There was no point in dwelling on what might have been, not with Joey. So I took the backpack I'd brought out of the truck and got ready for our hike. The bag was full of water bottles and granola bars. I added Millie's pink bottle, then strapped it to my shoulders.

"Want to lead the way?" I asked Joey.

"Um, sure." She shrugged. "Where do we go?"

I pointed to the trail. "Up."

She let me slather her with sunscreen before we embarked, then we fell in line, taking the first few corners single file.

The incline was gradual, but I let Joey set the pace, glancing back every once in a while to see Millie close behind.

"Do you ever come up here?" I asked her as the trail widened, falling back to walk by her side.

"Sometimes. I'll hike up, then jog down."

Joey marched on about twenty feet ahead, oblivious to our conversation.

But I lowered my voice anyway. "Sorry about the phone call earlier."

"I take it Sienna isn't thrilled I'm spending time with you and Joey?"

"No, she's not." It was a truth Millie deserved.

Sienna's jealousy was as colossal as the mountain we were climbing. After we'd gotten married and moved to Seattle, she'd asked me if anything had ever happened with

Millie. I'd stupidly admitted to the kiss in the name of full disclosure to my new wife.

Sienna hadn't spoken to me for a week.

"I can't say I'm surprised." Millie sighed. "I don't want to cause any problems."

"You're not. She's going to have to get over it," I said. "She doesn't get to dictate my life anymore. Or Joey's."

Ahead of us, my daughter's blond ponytail swished across her shoulders.

"Where is she, Ford?" Millie asked. "Why isn't she here with Joey?"

I inhaled a long breath, slowing my pace just a bit to let Joey gain a bit more space. "She's in Seattle. About five years ago, she decided she wanted to start a lifestyle blog. It started small, mostly photos of our house and her daily outfits, but grew quickly. She'd post on social media every day and play up her role as an NFL player's wife. It got her a lot of followers."

Sienna used to come to my games and would spend the entire time on her phone. She couldn't have cared less about football. All she'd wanted was to take pictures and videos at the stadium to then splash over Instagram and TikTok.

"We didn't have a good marriage," I admitted. That was the one thing Sienna and I would always agree on. "About eighteen months ago, after my injury, I told her I wanted a divorce. She was rarely home, always planning these trips with friends and whoever else. Joey was never her priority and it pissed me off. So I was done. Her biggest concern with a separation wasn't our daughter. She was worried what it would do to her *brand*."

Sienna threw that term around as often as I threw a football.

Millie cringed. "Wow."

"Exactly."

Sienna had made friends with some of the other players' wives and girlfriends. A few were models. One an actress. The football world had become her identity, yet she didn't know anything about the sport.

"So I take it the divorce wasn't an amicable one?" Millie asked.

"Not at first. Sienna wanted to try and work it out. But then I found out she'd been sleeping with one of my teammates."

Millie gasped. "Who?"

"Jordan Powell."

"Oh." Her nose scrunched up. "He's a showboat."

"Yes, he is."

Jordan was all about flash. So was Sienna. They were actually perfect together.

"The divorce went fairly smoothly after that point. I knew there was only a slim chance I'd ever play again and was in discussions to take on the coaching position. I wasn't the star anymore and dating an assistant coach wasn't nearly as attractive to Sienna as scoring a player."

"Maybe for her," Millie muttered so quietly I barely made it out. "She didn't want custody of Joey?"

"Oh, she did. She wanted fifty-fifty. I just refused," I told her. "We were in the very beginning stages of the divorce, a little over a year ago, and a TV producer approached Sienna about a reality show. Or maybe she approached them. I never did get a straight answer. But there are five women doing it. Each is either married to, engaged to or dating a Seahawks player."

"A reality show? You're kidding."

"Nope." I shook my head. "It hasn't aired yet but apparently they're wrapping up the first season. I don't know. I don't ask many questions. I just knew that I didn't want Joey anywhere near it. I refused to let her be in that sort of situation where everything is on display for the world to see. No kid needs that kind of public scrutiny. So I told Sienna that the only way I'd agree to shared custody was if she refused the show."

Millie's mouth parted. "She chose the show?"

I looked ahead at my beautiful daughter. "We're in Montana, aren't we?"

Sienna had given up Joey for a chance at fame.

"Oh my God." Millie put her hands on her cheeks. "I mean, I hate her. She was a total bitch to me in college. But wow. I'm so sorry, Ford."

"I'm sorry for Joey." Not a day had gone by that I'd mourned my marriage. "It's ugly. Not many people know what happened. I don't talk about it."

Millie nudged her arm against mine. "Then I'm a vault."

Vault. Without question, Millie wouldn't tell a soul. It was why she'd always been an incredible friend. The best, actually.

Joey looked over her shoulder, cocking her head when she saw how far we'd fallen back. "Are you guys coming?"

Millie smiled, taking off at a jog to catch up. I hung back a bit, letting them talk as they hiked.

It didn't take long before we reached the top. They'd added a bench at the base of the T since the last time I'd been here, so I took a seat, staring out over the green valley surrounded by mountain peaks.

"Do you think we can see our house from here?" Joey

cupped her hands around her eyes, squinting into the distance.

Millie stood at her side, pointing toward our neighborhood.

The two of them together were picture perfect. Better than any staged photo Sienna could conjure for social media.

This was real. This was life.

I dug my phone from my pocket, snapping a quick picture of Millie and Joey together as they stared into the distance.

It was the best photo I'd taken in years, so I set it as my wallpaper.

Then I tucked my phone away and enjoyed the view.

And when a breeze wafted the scent of pine and earth through the air, I closed my eyes and tipped my face to the sun. I made my silent wish at the base of the T.

I wished that Millie might have a crush on me again.

CHAPTER EIGHTEEN

MILLIE

"I have a confession," I said, answering Autumn's call.

"You've been hanging out with Ford."

"Yes." I slouched in my office chair. "How did you know?"

"Because for the past five years, I've talked to you at least four times a week. Since he showed up in Mission, you've been quiet."

"Sorry." I sighed.

"Don't be. I get it. This is a tough situation."

"I'm just . . . confused."

"And you're trying to figure it all out on your own. How's that going for you?"

It was equally wonderful and annoying to have a friend who knew me so well. "Not great," I muttered.

Autumn hummed and I didn't need to see her face to know she wore a smug smile. "Spill."

I filled my lungs, holding the breath until it hurt. I exhaled.

I spilled.

I told her everything, from bumping into him at the grocery store, to the cookies, to Kurt's warning, to our hike, to the three times Ford had kissed me. I told her every tiny detail, hoping maybe she'd be able to help me make sense of my feelings.

"What should I do?" I asked.

"I mean, I think there's really only one option."

My heart sank. "End it now. Before it gets even more complicated."

"No, dummy. Bang him."

I laughed. Of course that was Autumn's advice. "That's not helpful. I could lose my job over this."

"Then it will have to be a secret affair. Those are the most fun anyway."

"Autumn," I deadpanned. "I'm serious. What should I do?"

"I'm serious too, Millie." The teasing in her tone was gone. "You pined after Ford for years while he dated that bitch Sienna. You settled for being his friend. And when he finally cut her loose, you went for it."

"And look how well that turned out for me," I muttered. Total humiliation.

"That's my point," she said. "You went for it and got burned. You've been guarded ever since."

I scoffed. "I'm not guarded."

"Oh, you're not guarded? How many men have I dated in the past five years?"

Oh shit. Was I supposed to be keeping track? "Um . . . a lot?"

"A lot. I put myself out there. And yeah, I've found a lot of losers, but I don't regret them."

I drew an invisible circle on my desk. "What about the douchey lawyer?"

"Fine, maybe the douchey lawyer. Whatever. We're not talking about me."

"You're the one who brought it up. I was talking about me and then you started talking about—"

"Millie," she snapped. "I have a client coming in ten minutes, so shut up and listen."

I giggled, having missed my friend these past few weeks. "Okay."

"Adrian is the one and only man I've seen you let in. But even then, it was like you cracked a window and expected him to crawl through it because the doors were still locked."

"Ouch." I winced. "Maybe I don't want to talk to you anymore."

"The truth hurts, sweetie." Autumn's voice softened. "For the record, I'm glad you didn't move in with Adrian and marry the man. There was always something missing between you."

I closed my eyes, wishing she wasn't so . . . right.

There had been something missing with Adrian. I wished I had realized that sooner. That I hadn't hurt him. But Adrian was a topic for another day.

"How does having sex with Ford solve my problem?" I asked.

"You'll always wonder what might have been. This is your chance to find out. So keep it a secret. Don't put your career at risk. But let the guy give you an orgasm and then maybe you can really let go of the past. Besides, it will also be like a big *fuck you* to Sienna."

"This is true."

Autumn hated Sienna arguably more than me. She hated that Sienna had betrayed my friendship.

It was a sour note for me too, though not as bitter as it had been to watch Ford and Sienna together.

Their relationship had started strong, and seeing them kissing and cuddling around campus had been excruciating. My crush never did go away. But by the end of their first year together, they'd had plenty of ups and downs. By our junior year, it had mostly been downs.

It had been Ford's last semester, the semester we'd been trapped together in philosophy, and he'd spent less and less time alone with her at parties.

Instead, he'd spent more time with the rest of us, watching a game. Whenever he'd see me walking across campus, he'd rush to catch up and say hello. Most times, he'd carry my backpack too. He'd tease me mercilessly about my addiction to tennis shoes, and whenever he got a new tattoo, he'd send me the first picture.

I'd confided in him about my dad's death. He'd told me about high school in Vegas and never feeling like a part of the school. How people would befriend him because of his talent on the football field and how others would resent him for the same. We'd shared our dreams. Mine, to work with a university sports program. His, to get drafted and go pro.

Through it all, Sienna had stayed exactly the same. The mean girl. And oh, how she hated that her boyfriend was my friend.

But no matter how much she had gossiped about me, no matter how rudely she had behaved, I'd refused to give Ford up. And not once had I told him how awful she could be.

When Ford eventually broke up with Sienna, it certainly hadn't ruined my day. But the next afternoon at practice, she'd gotten in my face and spewed her venom. She'd asked if Ford had fucked me yet, then called me a whore. She'd accused me of cheating and said I'd get what was coming to me.

Bitch.

As much as I loathed Sienna, I didn't like the idea of using sex with Ford to get revenge. It just wasn't . . . me.

"I think I just need to tell him we're done," I told Autumn. "At this point, I don't even think friendship is a good idea."

"Also an option," she said. "It's the option without orgasms, but that's your prerogative."

I smiled. "I've missed you."

"Missed you too. Drinks tonight?"

"Yes. Text me later. Have a good day at work."

She smooched into the phone. "You too."

I ended the call and set my phone aside, spinning in a slow circle in front of my desk. When I started to get dizzy, I stood, walking to the window that overlooked the parking lot and practice field.

A line of football players streamed from the fieldhouse, all walking toward the grass. I spotted Toren, Parks and the other coaches, but not Ford.

We hadn't seen each other since he and Joey had dropped me off after the hike on Sunday. And though school hadn't started, campus was beginning to flourish with activity. Football was about to begin. This coming weekend, there would be a scrimmage at the stadium. Then the following weekend, the first home game.

If there was ever a time to cut Ford out, it was now. For the next three months, he'd be consumed with work. Maybe I wouldn't have to do a thing. Maybe if I just kept my distance, his schedule would become the wall between us. By the time the season was over, he might very well have forgotten about me.

Ick. My stomach churned.

I'd already been forgotten by Ford once. Not a great experience or one I cared to repeat.

A ding from my phone pulled me away from the glass. I was due to meet the facilities manager in five minutes to talk about the basketball season. Both the men's and women's teams practiced in a smaller gym but they had their games in the fieldhouse. The weekends they were away, we'd tear the court down and make room for other events, like the college rodeo and a local home exhibition. We'd had a few stumbles last year with setup, and I wanted to make sure we didn't repeat those past mistakes.

Since Kurt was so set on keeping men's basketball and football under his umbrella, he should technically be at this meeting. But he'd delegated logistics to me, so I collected my laptop, walked out of the office and headed downstairs.

The moment I opened the door to the first floor, I was met with angry voices.

"Are you calling me a whore?" There was a tremble in the woman's voice.

What the hell?

"No! Fuck. Would you just listen to me?" The man's voice sounded vaguely familiar.

I changed course, veering down the hallway toward the noise. Feet away, Rush Ramsey was dragging both hands through his hair while a petite girl with a strawberry-blond ponytail stood in front of him, her arms wrapped around her waist as tears streaked down her cheeks.

"You think I planned this, don't you?" she asked, her entire body shaking.

"That's not what I'm saying, Faye!" His arms stretched wide at his sides.

"Then what?"

Oh, boy. It was too early in the year for this level of student drama.

I cleared my throat.

Both students jerked, their eyes widening as they turned my way, just as Ford rounded the corner behind them.

"What the hell is going on?" His presence, large and commanding, chased away the anger from the previous moment. "Do you realize that everyone in this part of the building can hear you?"

Rush's arms dropped, his head hanging. "Sorry, Coach."

"How about we take this conversation into a conference room?" I met Ford's gaze, waiting until he gave me a nod, then I led the way into a nearby room, closing the door once everyone was inside.

"Okay, what is going on?" Ford asked them, standing at my side against a wall.

Faye sniffled, wiping at her cheeks.

"Just a misunderstanding," Rush mumbled.

Wrong thing to say. Faye's eyes blazed as she raised her chin. "In a single breath, you asked me for a paternity test and how many guys from the team I've slept with."

Yikes.

Wait. She was pregnant? My gaze whipped to Ford's profile but he looked entirely unshocked, like he already knew.

"Rush." Ford shook his head. "Listen, let's all sit down. Talk this through."

Faye didn't budge from her spot in the corner, but Rush obeyed instantly, pulling out a chair from the table and slumping in the seat.

Ford took the spot beside Rush while I stayed on my feet, inching closer to Faye.

She glanced at me, her pretty eyes swimming with unshed tears.

I offered a kind smile and waved to a chair. "Come on."

She finally moved, sitting stiffly on the seat's edge while I sat beside her.

"I'm Millie," I said. "I work upstairs."

"Faye," she whispered.

"And I'm Coach Ellis." Ford leaned forward, his hands folded together. "Nice to meet you."

She swallowed hard, nodding. But she kept her eyes on the table, her chin ducked.

"I hope you don't mind, but Rush told me what's happening," Ford said.

He was so calm. So collected.

I guess he should be.

He'd lived through this before.

"How about we start at the beginning?" I asked.

Rush glanced to Faye, waiting until she gave him a nod, then he told me about how they'd met and hooked up. And how they'd be parents in the not-so-distant future.

"I didn't mean to insinuate anything in the hallway." Rush dragged a hand through his hair. "I'm just . . . I don't know what I'm doing or saying. I only asked about other guys so that I wouldn't be surprised. I don't like surprises."

"And the paternity test?" Ford asked.

"It's fine," Faye said. Her hands were fisted on her lap. Her eyes held unshed tears. "I'll get one."

"You don't have to." Rush shook his head. There was an apology written on his face. But Faye didn't see it because she wouldn't look at him.

"No." Faye's voice was sharp. Pained. "I'll get the test. Then there won't be any doubt."

We all heard the conviction in her tone. There wasn't any question in my mind that this baby was Rush's.

"Bit of advice," Ford said once it was clear Faye had nothing else to say. "Find a way to talk to each other. In person. Texts. Calls. Emails. Whatever. You're going to get a lot of external input, but at the end of the day, all that matters is what you both decide together."

Faye's chin began to quiver.

I reached over and put my hand on hers. "You'll be okay."

She sniffled, a single tear falling down her cheek. "I'll be okay." She spoke so quietly I barely heard the words.

Rush nodded. "Thanks, Coach."

Ford blew out a long breath. "You're late for practice, Rush."

"Yes, sir." He stood, leaving the conference room.

Faye waited until he was gone, then without a word, stood and left too.

The tension in the room should have vanished with them. But it was there, charged in the air and bunched in Ford's shoulders.

His blue eyes shifted from the doorway to meet mine.

"Was it like that?" I asked. "With you and Sienna?" Strained meetings. Accusations. Tears and pain.

"More or less."

Was it hard for him to watch this? To be on the outside

this time? "Did you ever find a way to communicate with each other?"

"Not really." He shook his head, his eyes softening. "I was always better at talking to you than I was Sienna. Part of the problem."

Then why did you choose her instead of me?

That question had been plaguing me for years.

And still, I didn't have the courage to ask. The answer, no matter what it was, would only hurt.

So I stood from my chair and left the room.

I was late for my meeting.

CHAPTER NINETEEN

FORD

I was tired of watching Millie walk away from me.

But considering that the pregnancy thing with Rush had sent me reeling, it had probably resurfaced memories for Millie too.

Rather than talk it through with me—or look at me—she'd marched out of the conference room and disappeared. I always seemed to be chasing her around this building. Not today—I was late for practice.

So I swung by my office to get a hat, then headed out to the field and got to work.

By the time practice was over and the players were all filtering into the locker room for a shower, I had sweat beading at my temples and could use a rinse myself.

"It's going to be a hot son of a bitch on Saturday for the scrimmage," Toren said as we walked inside the fieldhouse, following the other coaches to a conference room for our regular post-practice meeting.

"Yep. I'll ask Patti to ensure we've got plenty of water."

Patti was my new assistant. She was sixty-one years old,

something she'd announced during our interview, along with her Zodiac sign—a fellow Taurus. She'd started two weeks ago, and so far she'd proven to be a dream, taking care of the administrative tasks that would have otherwise buried me.

I was the last man to enter the conference room, so I closed the door behind me and took my regular seat at the head of the table, pulling off my hat to run a hand through my damp hair.

My phone was in the back pocket of my shorts. I shifted, digging it out to make sure there wasn't a text or missed call from Joey or Stephanie. The screen was blank, so I set it down on the table.

When I looked up, Parks was staring at my screen. On the wallpaper set behind the time and date. On the photo I'd taken of Millie and Joey on our hike.

That wasn't a moment I wanted to share with anyone, so I grabbed my phone and returned it to my shorts pocket. Then I leaned my elbows on the table, glancing around the room. "Good practice today."

That statement was met with nods all around.

Day by day, we were becoming a team. A solid team. There were still a few kinks to iron out, but we had a couple more practices and then the scrimmage. I was just hoping we'd win our first game.

The rivalry with the Grizzlies would be the pinnacle of our regular-season play. But damn, I loved having a first-game victory in my grasp. It set the pace for the season.

"Who wants to go first?" I asked.

Toren raised his hand. "I will."

One by one, my coaches each went over their strengths and weaknesses. We talked about their players, who'd had noticeable improvement, who was on tap to be a starter and who'd be backup. Then we hammered through the playbook, making a few tweaks as needed and picking the plays we'd be focusing on for tomorrow's practice.

By the time our meeting adjourned, I was ready for that shower.

It was four thirty, about time to head home to relieve Stephanie. But I had a couple emails to send, so I hustled to my office and busted them out, doing only what was urgent so I'd wrap up by five. The rest would happen tonight, after Joey was asleep.

Except just as I was about to leave, my office phone rang. Kurt's name popped up on the screen.

"Hey, Kurt." I stood from my desk, pushing in my chair and grabbing my truck keys from the top drawer.

"Hi, Ford. Do you have a minute to swing up to my office?" There was tension in his voice. Kurt's normal kiss-ass tone was missing.

"Sure. Be right up." I put the headset in its cradle, then walked out, hitting the lights on my way.

I waved to the coaches still in their offices, then jogged up the stairs two at a time. Kurt was in his corner office with his hands steepled in front of his chin.

"Come on in." He waved me forward. "Close the door if you would."

Damn it. I wasn't going to like this conversation, was I? With the door shut, I took a seat across from his desk, trying not to scowl. "What's up?"

"Well, Ford . . . I, uh, just got a complaint."

I raised my eyebrows. "A complaint." This had better not be about Millie. *Fuck.* "About?"

Kurt blew out a long breath. "About you bringing your daughter to work."

I blinked. "Excuse me?"

"I understand you're dealing with a lot." He held up his hands. "For the record, I don't have a problem if she has to come occasionally. We'll do whatever we can to accommodate you. But you're also under a microscope. These are sensitive times. And we just need to know that you're focused."

Focused. So the evenings when Joey had to tag along to second practice and the one day when I'd had her here for lunch and a campus tour equated to me being unfocused? This was fucking absurd.

"Who complained?" I asked, my jaw clenching.

"That's, um . . . confidential." Kurt gave me a pacifying smile as he folded his hands in his lap.

Confidential my ass. Had there really been a phone call? Or was this *Kurt's* complaint?

The only person who'd ever looked twice at Joey was Kurt. That, and Millie, but there was no way she'd complain.

No, this *complaint* had Kurt's name written all over it.

"Noted," I clipped.

Joey was starting school next week and would soon have her own schedule. Stephanie would help by picking Joey up every afternoon and staying overnight during away games. The only time Kurt would see Joey was if she came to a game, and luckily, there'd be twenty thousand other people there for him to fret over.

"Anything else?" I asked.

"No. Sorry about this."

Except he sure didn't seem sorry.

If someone had legitimately complained, Kurt could have squashed it immediately. He could have told the person who'd griped that I was doing my job and Joey's occasional visits were nothing to get riled about. Instead, Kurt had called me into his office to slap my hand.

"It's fine," I lied.

It wasn't fucking fine. Joey was my priority and if this program couldn't be a bit more family friendly, then we'd find somewhere else to go after the year was done.

"You're doing a fantastic job," he said. "I was just telling someone earlier today that it's like you've been here for years, not weeks. I can't wait for Saturday."

And now ass-kissing Kurt was back.

"Me too." I forced a smile, then made my way to the door, ripping it open too hard. I stormed down the hallway, my hands fisted at my sides, and just as I was about to head for the stairs, a swish of brown hair caught my eye.

Millie came out of an office, talking to another assistant AD. She laughed at something, her smile bright and beautiful. Then the other woman—*Tiffani? Tina?*—returned to the office.

When she glanced up, Millie spotted me and that smile dimmed. Then she spun on a heel and retreated to her own office.

Yeah, I was fucking tired of watching Millie walk away.

I should have let her go. But my shoes pounded on the floor as I followed.

She was fast but her legs just weren't as long as mine and it only took a moment to catch up.

"Millie."

She kept walking.

"Are you going to stop and talk to me?" I asked.

"Nope." She shot me a frown over her shoulder and quickened her steps.

She bypassed her office, probably because she had to

know I'd just follow her in there. She was practically jogging every other step as she rushed forward, heading straight for the women's restroom.

Did she really think that was going to stop me?

She shoved through the door.

I followed.

"Ford," she hissed.

"No more walking away from me, Millie." I let the door swing closed, then flipped the lock.

Her eyes widened as she turned, bending low to check each of the stalls for shoes. But the bathroom was empty. "What are you doing? If someone finds you in here, it will just lead to a bunch of questions."

"So?"

"So." She threw her hands in the air. "I'll get fired. I can't get fired."

"What are you talking about? You're not going to get fired, Millie." Not a soul I'd met here didn't hold her in the highest regard. Everyone loved Millie. If there was anyone on the chopping block, it was me. Especially after that conversation with Kurt.

"We have a no-fraternization policy."

"We do?"

"Yes. And Kurt has been strictly enforcing it lately."

All right, that complicated things. This was what I got for not combing through the human resources paperwork. I hadn't realized there was a policy, let alone one that was so strictly enforced.

She pinched the bridge of her nose. "You're the head football coach."

"So?"

"So I'm just an assistant AD." Her shoulders slumped.

"Who do you think Kurt will choose?"

I wanted to argue. I really did. But she truly believed she'd get fired and I wasn't entirely sure she was wrong.

"Mills—"

"I'm not giving up my career for you."

I wouldn't have asked her to give it up, never, but the way she delivered that statement was like a slap to the face. "I'm not asking you to give up anything."

She looked up, her hazel eyes so full of defeat it made my chest pinch. "Then what do you want, Ford?"

"You. A chance to see what's happening here. Thought I'd made that pretty clear."

"Oh." Millie drew her lower lip between her teeth.

Oh. That was it? The bathroom went quiet as I stared at her. As she stared at the tiled floor. Her silence was shredding me to ribbons.

Was her hesitation entirely about the job? Or was there more holding her back? Guess there was only one way to find out.

"We'll keep it a secret." I crossed the space between us, taking her face in my hands. "I want you enough to hide a relationship. I'll fucking hate it. But I'll do it."

She gulped. "What if we're better off as friends?"

Friends? Hell no.

I brushed my lips across her mouth, running them back and forth, just a barely there touch. It was all she'd get this time. If she actually wanted me, it was time to show it.

"Ford." Her breath hitched. She rose up on her toes, searching for more.

Yes. That was it. That was the sign. She wanted this too.

Rather than kiss her, I pulled away, locking my gaze with

her because I needed to know she'd hear what I said next. "We're not friends. Not this time around. Clear?"

She nodded.

We'd hide. We'd sneak around like goddamn teenagers. If that was what it took to explore this thing, fine. Progress.

"Good." I let her go because I really didn't feel like getting caught in the ladies' room, and turned for the door. Except before I could flip the lock free, Millie's whisper stopped me cold.

"I can't let you hurt me."

My hands balled into fists. So much for progress. "And you're so sure I will? For fuck's sake, Millie."

"I won't pretend I'm not scared, Ford."

Not what I'd expected to hear. And I wasn't sure what she expected me to say.

So I stormed out of the bathroom, not certain if I was angry at Millie.

Or angry at myself.

CHAPTER TWENTY

FORD

A thousand tiny hurricanes raged inside my veins. They rained nerves and anticipation and excitement and dread. It was an effort to keep my hands from shaking as I strode out of the fieldhouse, following the team marching to the stadium.

Fans were lined up along the path, clapping and cheering for the Wildcats. It couldn't have been a nicer day for our first home game. A cloudless blue sky. A gentle breeze to combat the sun's heat.

Damn. Sunscreen. I'd left the house this morning knowing I'd forgotten something. It was sunscreen.

Hopefully with this hat and my sunglasses, my face wouldn't burn. But my forearms and calves were probably going to get roasted.

"Ready for this?" Toren asked as we walked side by side.

"Nope."

We could use another week of practice, but that was always the case. No matter the role, player or coach, I'd never once felt prepared for a first game. But I hadn't been this anxious before a game in years.

Keyed up was an understatement. Every time I drew in a long breath, I expected to exhale these crippling nerves. This wasn't my first game. I'd done this countless times before. So why couldn't I relax?

The scrimmage last weekend had gone well, but today we'd be running our plays against another team and another coach who wanted to win too. Guess we'd find out who wanted to win more.

And who had the talent to bring in a victory.

God, I hoped it was us. For the thousands and thousands of fans who'd be in the stadium, for my staff and my players, I hoped like hell we'd win.

And maybe for Millie too.

It had been eight days since I'd stormed out of the ladies' bathroom. Eight days since I'd seen her face. This time, it hadn't been her avoiding me, but the other way around. I'd made sure to stay far away from her office, focusing my time and energy on my corner of the world.

Joey had started school, and so far, fourth grade had been a hit. She'd made a few friends already and liked her teacher. But it was still early on. Every night when I went home, I held my breath as I walked through the door, wondering if I'd find her in tears.

She hadn't wanted to come to today's game, choosing to stay home with Stephanie instead. Next week, Joey started volleyball, and somehow, I'd need to figure out how to balance my schedule and hers so that I made it to a few games—also on Saturdays, because why would anyone make it easy on me?

Maybe if her game was early enough, I could go watch

for a bit before coming here. Stephanie would need to help and take a video or maybe live stream it and—

Later, Ford. That would all need to wait until later.

The list of shit I needed to figure out was growing and it was all pushed to later.

Millie included.

Was she here working today? Would she be watching the game?

As we walked toward the stadium, I glanced up to the sky boxes. The clear glass windows reflected the sky, hiding anyone inside.

"Go Big Blue!" a man carrying a beer cheered as we passed.

"Don't *fuckitup*, Coach," the guy's drunken friend slurred before they both started laughing.

Toren chuckled. "Now that sounds like football."

Normally, I'd laugh too. Not today.

Don't fuck it up, Coach.

The polo shirt I'd chosen to wear today felt too tight across my chest. My legs felt wobbly, like I'd just run five miles, not walked a few hundred yards. What the hell was wrong with me?

I shook my head, hoping to clear some of the haze, and when I looked up, my gaze instantly landed on a silky, brown ponytail.

The entrance to the stadium was guarded by a fence. Millie stood beyond the nearest gate, in the end zone, talking to a man with a TV camera at his feet. She was wearing a pair of gray slacks and a white polo, the outfit accentuating her lean figure and the slight curve of her breasts. Whatever he said made her laugh.

Who was that guy? He looked her up and down, his

perusal blatant and nauseating. What the fuck? Was he flirting with her? Clearly he was on the television crew. Didn't he have work to do? The game was starting in an hour.

I clenched my jaw as he touched her arm—too affectionate, too familiar. Then he bent and hoisted the camera onto a shoulder before walking away.

Millie turned, watching as the players streamed through the gates, heading for our locker room at the stadium.

Most of our time was spent at the fieldhouse, on the practice field, in the weight room or locker room. But for games—before kickoff, during halftime and after a win or a loss—we'd congregate here.

Toren stepped in front of me so we could file through the gate. When he spotted Millie, he waved.

She waved back, her eyes sparkling. Millie had always looked beautiful on game days, especially with that smile.

He might be my friend, but I hated that she gave that smile to Toren so effortlessly.

After he turned to follow the team inside, Millie's eyes swung my direction.

My footsteps slowed as I waited for her smile to dim. For her to dismiss me with a swish of that ponytail and disappear into the crowd. Or maybe she'd glare, still pissed at me from our last conversation.

Except she just stood there, her smile as breathtaking as ever. It was like she knew I needed it.

Calm swept through my body, chasing away the jitters. My next breath was easy. Light.

"Good luck," she mouthed.

I winked and walked inside.

It was game time.

———

THIRTY-FIVE TO SEVEN.

We were one minute and sixteen seconds away from our first victory.

The noise in the stadium was ear-piercing. The Wildcat defense was on the field, and though there was no chance we'd lose this game, the fans were on their feet, screaming, like if we didn't stop the other team three and out, the sun would fall from the sky.

I crossed my arms over my chest, watching from my post on the sideline. The calm I'd found before the game, the calm from Millie, had settled deep in my bones. But it was fading in time with the game clock. A rush of excitement—and relief—took hold.

We'd won this game.

Thank God.

The referee placed the ball on the line of scrimmage, raising his hand as he jogged backward while the other ref brought a whistle to his lips. One blow and the teams took their positions, the center crouched over the ball.

The opposing quarterback took the snap and stepped back, his gaze searching for an open receiver in the backfield. He found his target and launched the ball.

Yeah, we were going to win this game, but my heart stopped anyway as the football soared, my pulse stopping as I waited for the receiver to catch it.

He did.

Damn it. The air rushed from my lungs as he took off,

sprinting away from the fifty yard line, his legs pumping as he tried to break free from the safeties running to chase him down.

"Come on," I said. "Get there. Stop him."

Forty yard line. Thirty yard line. Twenty.

The receiver had the ball tucked under an arm. He was fast.

Just not fast enough.

Our star safety leapt, arms wide, and wrapped the receiver up, both players crashing into the turf.

"Yes." I fist pumped, finally breathing as the stadium erupted in a fresh wave of shouts.

The teams both jogged to the new line of scrimmage.

On the opposite side of the field, the other coach was waving his arm in a wide circle, trying to get his team to move faster. But part of the reason we'd dominated on the field today was because our team was in better shape. Both their offense and defense were gassed.

Less than one minute.

They'd earned a first down, but if we stopped them on this run, game over. Hell, it was already game over, but I didn't like ending a game with the other team scoring the final points.

"Let's go." I clapped, my heart racing.

Just as I was about to walk down the sideline to get a closer look at these next couple plays, a chant started in the stands.

Go Big Blue. Go Big Blue. Go Big Blue.

Each word was accentuated with a clap.

I let the rhythm of that cheer sink into my blood, feeding off the excitement as I walked the sideline. I glanced up, another check of the clock, just as the image on the jumbotron changed.

Millie's face filled the screen. She had no idea she was on camera. Her focus was entirely on the field, her face a mask of concentration. She was in the end zone, like she had been earlier, standing in a reserved section for special guests and wealthy donors. Her forearms were resting on a metal rail. A lanyard with an all-access was looped around her neck.

Why was she on the screen? Was that her friend the cameraman's doing? Maybe he was as obsessed with her face as I was.

It took an effort to force my eyes away, to focus on the field just as the center snapped the ball.

Their quarterback took a handful of steps and that was all he got before the line broke and he was pummeled into the ground. A sack and loss of five yards.

"Yes." I glanced up to the screen again.

To Millie, who was screaming with the people around her. Her arms were raised in the air as she jumped up and down.

My God, she was stunning. And gone too soon. The camera panned to another area of ecstatic fans.

The other team's offense fell apart after the sack. They managed two yards and attempted to go for it on fourth down, but we held them until the clock ran to zero.

The stadium erupted.

"Yes." A smile stretched across my face as my heart climbed out of my throat.

Toren reached me first, smacking me on the shoulder. "Congratulations, Coach!" He had to shout in my ear and still, I could barely hear him over the noise.

"First win." I laughed.

"Not the last." He grinned as we were mobbed by the team.

I smacked helmets. I clapped kids on the shoulders. I weaved through the crush, making my way to the center of the field to shake the other coach's hand.

A reporter from the local radio station found me next, followed by a news reporter who wanted a sound bite to finish the live broadcast.

I went through the motions, giving the lines I'd rehearsed over the past week, commending our team and my staff on their hard work. I praised the other team for a great game and when asked if I was glad to be in Montana, I answered honestly with a wholehearted *yes*.

Then finally, I was able to jog down the field, to join the team in the locker room and give them a congratulations of their own before releasing them to the fieldhouse to get showered and changed.

I was the last one to come out of the locker room, the stadium having mostly emptied out while I'd been talking to the team.

I was about to head to the fieldhouse myself when a familiar laugh caught my ear.

Millie was still in the end zone, shaking hands with a few boosters decked out in royal blue and silver.

Part of me wanted to talk to her. To seal this victory with a kiss. Except the moment the people she'd been talking to left, others took their place. She was working. She was busy.

And our relationship—if we even had a relationship— was a secret.

So I turned and followed my team to the fieldhouse, retreating to my office, where I sat in my chair and called to check on Joey.

"Hey, Daddy," she answered Stephanie's phone.

"Hi, princess. How's your day going?"

"Good. You guys won, huh?"

"Yep. Did you watch?"

"Yeah, a little."

Better than nothing. "Next time, maybe you'll come too."

Kurt could go fuck himself if he ever told me not to bring Joey to a game.

"Sure. Can I go with Millie?"

"Uh, maybe." I sighed. "Remember, tonight, I have to go to an event. It starts in about an hour. Then I'll be home."

"When are you getting home? Before or after my bedtime?"

"Probably before."

"But what if it's after? Can I stay up late and wait?"

I chuckled. "Yeah. You can stay up late."

"Sweet." Joey would be rooting for me to get home after nine.

I closed my eyes, wishing I didn't have this damn event so I could just go home and spend time with my kid. "See you later. Be good for Stephanie."

"I will."

The minute she ended the call, I sagged in my chair, the adrenaline from the game still coursing through my blood. My knees bounced. My fingers tapped on the armrests. I was about to leave, to wander the halls or head downtown early to the bar where this event was being held, when a knock came at my office door.

Millie appeared in the doorway. "Good game, Coach."

"Thanks. I wasn't sure I'd see you today. Figured you'd be in the suites, schmoozing donors."

"Normally, yes. But it was over eighty degrees and Kurt

doesn't like getting hot. Or cold, for that matter. He takes the suites on the days when the weather isn't perfect. We had some guests in the end zone, so I entertained them today."

"Ah." I was guessing she preferred it that way too.

She glanced around the space, looking anywhere but at me.

How could she do that? When she was in the room, I struggled to look anywhere but at her.

I hadn't bothered with the lights when I'd come in, but even with the blinds drawn over the windows at my back, the space was still bright. Enough that I could study the sleek line of Millie's nose. The soft, pink pout of her lips.

How I'd ever ended up with Sienna over Millie was still a damn mystery. Maybe because Sienna had been so bold. So aggressive in her pursuit. She was beautiful. She'd been an athlete too, so we'd had that in common. And she'd fucked me the night we'd met. Chalk it up to a stupid guy too busy thinking with his dick.

"Saw you on camera today," I said, standing from my chair to round the desk, then sitting on its edge.

She blushed. "I know the camera guy. He puts me on the jumbotron from time to time."

Another ex? I bit back the question. For now. "What are you doing here?"

For the first time, she'd sought me out. Why?

Millie worried her bottom lip between her teeth. "About what happened in the bathroom the other day. I'm sorry."

"Don't be." I'd replayed that conversation countless times. She'd only been honest. I couldn't fault her for that. "I don't want to hurt you, Mills. I don't know where this is going, but I'd like the chance to find out. If you're up for it."

A crease formed between her eyebrows. She stayed

firmly fixed in the doorway. Not outside. Not inside. Just on the line. Then on a breath, that crease disappeared. Her hazel eyes softened. She took one step into the office, turning to close the door behind her and flip the lock.

My pulse raced as she closed the distance between us. And just like she'd done ten years ago, *she* kissed *me*.

CHAPTER TWENTY-ONE

MILLIE

What am I doing?

My lips pressed against Ford's and a moan escaped my throat as he licked my bottom lip. No man should have this amount of power over me, the ability to blank my mind and turn my insides to mush with a single stroke of his tongue.

He stood from the edge of his desk and his arms banded around me, hauling me flush against his broad chest.

Why did he have to taste so good? I'd done such a good job this past week, steeling my defenses and putting some distance between us. Except today, watching him on the sidelines, seeing his face on the massive screens around the stadium, hearing the other women in the end zone talking about how hot he was.

This kiss was envy's fault.

That bitch had led me to his office and made me lock the door.

Autumn's advice echoed in the back of my mind. *You'll*

always wonder what might have been. This is your chance to find out.

This was my chance. I was going to take it.

"Fuck, Millie." Ford tore away, panting against my mouth. Then he leaned back to meet my gaze.

His blue irises were darker than normal, the heat between us making the shade a rich cobalt. Those women in the end zone hadn't gotten his eyes today. He'd had them shielded behind mirrored sunglasses. These blues . . . they were just for me.

So was the hardness pressing against my hip.

Our eyes stayed locked, searching.

"What do you want, Mills?" he asked, his low voice sending a shiver down my spine.

You. He was what I'd always wanted. Except admitting that would be too much. So I lifted on my toes, my lips brushing against the corner of his mouth.

How many times had I wished to be the woman to kiss Ford Ellis after a game?

This was my chance.

His arms loosened. He shifted, like he was going to round the desk and put it between us.

If he stopped this now, we'd have to start this dance all over. I'd have to work up the courage to kiss him again. I wouldn't. In my heart, I knew I wouldn't have the guts to lay it all out there again, especially if he shut me down today.

So I reached between us, in a move so bold I startled myself, and palmed his erection through his gray shorts, dragging my hand up his length.

Ford's pained groan filled the room, mingling with our ragged breaths.

"Millicent," he warned on a growl. His body went taut,

195

like every muscle had tightened, turning him into a statue. "Don't fucking tempt me."

A shiver zoomed down my spine. My entire body felt like it was on edge, primed and electric. Like any touch and *zap*, the spark would ignite. The ache between my legs began to throb, matching my pulse's thundering beat. It begged for more than just a kiss.

I inched closer and lifted the hat from his head with my other hand, tossing it to the side. Then my arm wrapped around his neck so I could pull myself higher and lick the seam of his lips.

My skin felt too hot. These clothes were too tight. I'd stood outside all morning and afternoon, never once breaking a sweat, even in the heat. But God, it was sweltering in this office.

"Ford." I peppered that sharp, stubbled jaw with kisses. Then I closed my eyes. And waited.

My courage was fading fast, like someone had tipped over a bottle and the water inside was slowly leaking to the floor. This wasn't me. I wasn't a brazen woman. I didn't initiate sex. Ever.

Not in a bedroom. Certainly not in an office at work.

Did Ford have any clue how far out of my comfort zone I was walking here?

A flush crept into my cheeks. The reality of the situation slapped me in the face, and I was about to turn, to run out of this room and chastise Autumn for putting the idea of sex with Ford in my mind, but before I could move, Ford's hands skimmed up my hips, trailing across the smooth fabric of my pants until his hands palmed my ass.

God, he had big hands. And that hardness between us was like a steel rod.

I gulped.

"Look at me," he ordered.

Breathe. I sucked in a short inhale, then tilted up my chin.

If his blue eyes had been heated before, an inferno burned in his irises, the pools as dark as midnight.

"We're in my office."

The world around us was blurry. We could be anywhere in the world and all I'd see was him.

"Fuck, I want you, Millie."

I craved him. I ached for him. I needed him to put out this fire. For once, I needed him to choose me. Not the proper path. Not the other girl. Me. Just me.

Maybe my insecurities had come so close to the surface he could see them in my eyes. Because one moment, he stared at me like he didn't have a clue what I was thinking. Then something flashed across his gaze, like he could read my thoughts.

Ford slammed his mouth down on mine, swallowing a gasp. Then his arms wrapped around me again, hauling me off my feet as he stood to his full height.

My legs wrapped around his narrow hips as he hoisted me up higher, enough that my core pressed against his erection. I rolled my hips, seeking any friction I could get against my clit.

A rumble came from deep in his chest, the vibration pebbling my nipples beneath my bra. I clawed at his shoulders, unable to get close enough. "More. I need more."

Ford gripped me tighter, his hold nearly crushing, like he felt exactly the same. Then with a quick spin, he turned us, laying me down on the top of his desk, never once breaking our kiss.

My fingers started grappling for fistfuls of his shirt, pulling and tugging, trying to get it over his head while I kicked off my shoes.

He yanked my polo out of the waistband of my pants, then reached between us, frantically working free the button. "Millie." His lips left mine to trail across my neck. His tongue darted out to lick my pulse.

I arched into him, my hands abandoning his shirt to thread in his hair, savoring the feel of his mouth sucking on my skin.

He nipped at my earlobe, sending a new wave of heat to my center.

"Ford." My breath hitched. "I want you. God, I want you."

With that sexy, addicting growl filling the room, he stood, reaching behind his neck to yank off his shirt. It went sailing to the floor as he reached for the waistband of my pants, ripping them off my hips. My black panties came with them.

With a quick tug on my arm, he hauled me up to a seat. Then my own shirt was gone, joining his in a heap, and with a single flick of the clasp, my bra came off next.

The moment the air hit my naked skin, Ford's mouth was there, latching on to a nipple and sucking it into his hot mouth.

"Oh, yes." My eyes fluttered closed as my fingers dove into his hair again, holding him close as he trailed to the other nipple. My legs lifted, my toes shoving at his shorts but they were still fastened.

He shifted, his mouth never leaving my breast, as the thud of his shoes landed on the floor. Then with a shove, his shorts were gone and his cock was between us, the tip pressing against my slit.

"Are you wet for me, baby?"

"Soaked." I arched into him, desperate to feel him inside, but Ford leaned away, his palms flat on the desk beside my head as he stared down at me. The intensity of that stare made my mouth go dry.

His gaze raked over my skin, like he was memorizing it inch by inch, from my throat to my breasts to my belly. "Look at what you do to me, Millie."

My eyes widened at the sight of his cock. Long and thick. Hard and weeping. *For me.*

Ford took my chin in a hand, forcing my eyes to meet his. Then he held me there as he pressed his cock into my slick center, his jaw clenching as he thrust forward.

I hissed at the stretch, the fullness. Damn, he was big.

"Fuck," he bit out, his teeth clenched.

"Move." My fingertips dug into the solid muscle of his arms.

He pulled out only to rock us together again, this time going so deep it stole my breath. "You feel so fucking good, Mills."

My inner walls fluttered. My toes curled. His scent, like wind and sunshine and spice, filled my nose. The heat from his body was like kindling to my own, a sheen coating my skin.

Ford powered into me, each thrust a slap that joined my whimpers and his groans.

Was this really happening? I looked at us, to where he disappeared inside my body. It was erotic. It was surreal. It was breathtaking and overwhelming and the build kept going, higher and higher until all I could do was feel.

My orgasm was seconds away from exploding when Ford suddenly stopped, his cock pressed deep and the root hard against my clit. "No, don't stop."

Ford's hand came to my face, brushing away a lock of hair I hadn't noticed had fallen out of my ponytail. "Millie, I—"

I waited but he didn't continue. "What?"

He shook his head, then crushed his mouth to mine, our tongues tangling. With a single, effortless sweep, he pulled me from the desk and walked us, connected, to the nearest wall. My back collided with the cold surface as Ford pressed himself against me, sending his cock deeper and surrounding me entirely.

My legs hooked around his back, my arms holding tight to his shoulders. Not that I needed to hold on. He held me like I weighed nothing. He was a work of art, from the muscled arms to the washboard abs. His hands palmed my ass, spreading my cheeks apart as he pulled out, then pistoned forward.

Stroke after stroke, his cock hit that spot inside that made me tremble. The intensity climbed. The pleasure climaxed.

"Ford, I—" My orgasm broke, silencing my warning as I detonated. Pulse after pulse, I came apart, my body shaking as I clenched around him, my head falling back against the wall as stars broke across my vision.

"Fuck, Millie." In the haze, I heard Ford's curse. Then I felt his own body shake and tense as he poured into me.

I was ruined. Cataclysmically ruined.

Never in my life had I come apart like this and when I finally came down, my chest heaving against Ford's, I cracked my eyes open to find his waiting.

He looked sexy and disheveled. An arrogant smirk

tugged at his mouth before he bent to pull my bottom lip between his teeth. His chest glistened with sweat but he didn't let me down. He kept me pinned against the wall, his come dripping down my thigh.

"We didn't use a condom," I whispered.

He dropped his gaze to where we were still connected. "Fuck. Sorry."

"I'm, um . . . I'm on birth control. And I haven't been with anyone in a while."

Ford dropped his forehead to mine, blowing out a long sigh. "Neither have I."

The air rushed from my lungs.

My heart was still thundering, but I unlocked my legs until he set me on my feet. My knees wobbled as I slipped past him to collect my clothes.

The room smelled like Ford and sex. My cheeks flamed. What if he had a meeting later? What if someone had overheard?

Oh, shit. I needed to get out of here. I needed to breathe and think and oh my God, I'd just had sex with Ford. In his office. On his desk. Against a wall.

I just had sex with Ford.

Everything was different. Everything had changed.

What now?

I didn't have the slightest clue. Not even an inkling.

I was about to pull on my panties and get dressed, to race out of here and find a quiet corner to rock in for a few hours, when an arm banded around my chest.

Ford's naked chest pressed against my back as he held me to him, his lips a whisper against my shoulder blade. "No, you don't."

"Huh?"

"You're not running out of here." His hand dipped lower, trailing down my belly. He curled his fingers around my sex, pushing the come that continued to leak down my thigh back inside my body.

My heart tumbled. Oh, damn that was sexy. Why was that hot?

"Get dressed. We've got to get downtown for the event. I'll drive."

I tensed. "Ford, I—"

"We'll walk in separately. But we're riding together, Mills."

There was no arguing with that tone, so I sighed. "'Kay."

"She finally listens." He chuckled, dropping a kiss to my neck, then let me go to get dressed.

Ford did the same, stepping into his black boxer briefs, the cotton molding to his thighs and ass. The sight of him in just underwear was so glorious, I didn't realize I'd stopped moving until he reached out and pinched my leg. "Millie. Clothes. We're going to be late."

"Right." I jerked, quickly pulling on my bra and shirt. When I stepped into my pants, I caught a whiff of my skin.

I smelled like sex and Ford. And I was about to walk into a bar teeming with my coworkers and my boss. *Shit.*

My hands were shaking so bad it was a struggle to button my pants. Could Ford hear my panicked heart? It was too quiet in here. Why wasn't he saying anything?

"Excited to celebrate the win?" *Small talk, Millie? Really?* My voice was as shaky as my fingers.

Ford straightened, his torso still bare. In a single step, he closed the gap between us, taking my chin in his hand. Then he grinned, planting a kiss on my mouth. "I thought that's what we just did."

CHAPTER TWENTY-TWO

FORD

The post-game event was held at a bar in downtown Mission. It had been one of the more popular hangouts during my college days, and according to Toren, that hadn't changed. Though the owners had done an extensive remodel a few years ago, and when I'd walked through the door, I'd barely recognized the place.

The center of the room was the bar itself, a rectangle where patrons could order from any side. Dark wood posts bracketed the mirrored liquor shelves. Tall-backed leather booths hugged the red brick walls. Instead of windows overlooking Main Street, a large garage door made entirely of black-paned windows had been raised, letting the late evening air chase away the heat from so many bodies crammed together.

Toren nudged my elbow with his.

I tore my gaze from Millie. "Huh? What did you say?"

"I don't know why you're standing here when you clearly want to be over there." He chuckled, shaking his head as he pointed to the other side of the bar.

To Millie's side.

"What's happening there?" he asked.

"Nothing," I lied.

Other than the fact that I'd had my cock inside Millie less than an hour ago.

On the drive over, she'd barely spoken ten words. We'd ridden in silence downtown, parking a couple blocks away from the bar. Then she'd hopped out of the truck so fast I hadn't had the chance to say a word.

She'd jogged ahead, her ponytail swishing across her shoulder blades, then hurried inside. When I'd walked into the bar, she'd already had a glass of wine in her hand and been in a deep conversation with another one of the ADs.

She hadn't looked at me once. In the hour we'd been here, not a glance. Aloof Millie was in attendance tonight.

"You're staring." Toren shifted, turning his back to the bar so he could look me in the face.

In the rush out of my office, I'd forgotten my hat, so I dragged my hands through my hair for the hundredth time in the past thirty minutes.

I could still feel Millie pulsing around my dick. I could still taste her sweet mouth and hear her breathy moans.

Was she closing me out because this was a work function? Or was she spooked because we'd fucked?

This event had been a horrible idea. I should have hauled her to my house and locked her in my bedroom. Worshiped her body until there wasn't a goddamn doubt in her mind about how I intended this to go.

I'd suspected it after our first kiss, but now that I'd had her, there was no going back.

Maybe this was happening fast. But Millie would catch up.

I glanced at my phone, checking the time. "What time does this go until?"

"The email said we had to stay until eight," Toren answered.

Fuck my life. That was another hour.

I searched for Kurt, and as always, he wasn't far.

He stood about twenty feet away, talking to Parks and an older couple that I recognized from the stadium event this summer. But Kurt was about as distracted as I was. His gaze kept sweeping the room, landing on one staff member, then the next, like he was taking attendance.

When he looked over at me, he nodded, like he was giving me his sign of approval for the day.

I fought an eye roll and gave him my own nod. Then, because she was a magnet, my gaze settled on Millie once more.

"Ford, if you keep looking at her, everyone in this bar is going to know something's going on." Despite being surrounded by loud conversation and a background of booming music, Toren spoke low enough that only I could hear him.

I sighed, rubbing a hand over my jaw. She'd twisted me inside out. My bones felt hollow. My muscles twitchy. And yet she looked so . . . normal. Unaffected. How could she be so aloof?

That was the best damn sex of my life. And we'd only done it on a desk and against a wall. What would it be like if we had an actual bed? Room to play?

I wanted to find out. Tonight.

Toren raised a hand, flagging down the bartender. "Two shots of tequila, please. Best you've got. He's buying."

"Do I get one of these shots?" I quirked an eyebrow, digging into a back pocket for my wallet.

Toren smirked, waiting until two shots of cold, clear liquid appeared on the bar.

I handed my credit card to the bartender, then lifted a glass.

Toren clinked his with mine. "Congratulations, Coach."

"Same to you." The tequila burned on its path down my throat, warming my belly. Hopefully it would take the edge off.

I should be thinking about next weekend's game. I should be talking to my coaches and making nice with the donors. But that unsettled feeling only seemed to get worse as the night progressed, and every time I found Millie in the crush, the knot in my gut twisted.

Was she ever going to look at me?

No. The answer was no. As the minutes ticked by, as I stood in my place with Toren at my side, as people approached me, offering smiles and handshakes and gratitude for the team's win, Millie stayed firmly on her side of the bar.

Whenever I glanced over, unable to help myself, she was engrossed in everything other than me.

It had to be because this was a work function, right? Once I got her alone, we'd be fine. Her Kia was on campus. I just needed to endure this event and once it was over, I'd drive her to my place and we'd talk. We'd pick up where we'd left off in the office.

As often as I looked to Millie, I checked the clock. And when the numbers on my phone's screen finally turned to eight, I breathed. "I'm taking off. Thanks for everything today."

"Welcome." Toren smacked me on the shoulder. "Monday."

I nodded. "Monday."

With a wave to Kurt, I weaved through the bar, rounding one side to get to Millie's. She'd been in basically the same spot all night. Like me, people had come to her. But when I reached her space, it was empty.

I scanned the room, finding her just as she escaped through the front door.

And into a waiting car.

"What the fuck?" I muttered, my hands fisting.

An Uber? Seriously?

No. Just . . . no.

The cool evening air did nothing to temper my boiling blood as I strode outside, my legs eating up the sidewalk as I made my way to the Silverado. I climbed in, slamming the door, and raced across town.

Millie was standing beside her car, keys in hand, when I turned into the fieldhouse parking lot. The moment my headlights flashed, she paused beside her door, watching as I skidded to a stop. Her frame slumped when I parked and climbed out.

My chest heaved as I stared at her, pissed and confused and not sure exactly what I wanted to say. So I stood there, hands fisted on my hips, jaw clenched.

"Ford—"

"Don't fucking run away from me, Millie." Guess I did know what I wanted to say.

"That's not what I was doing," she said, her gaze on the asphalt beneath our feet.

I wanted her to look at me. So I took her chin, lifting it until she had no choice but to meet my eyes. The fear in her expression was like a dagger to the heart. My hand dropped like her skin was on fire. "Mills."

"We had sex."

"Yes."

"I liked it."

Thank fuck. "So did I."

"I'm not good at this, this . . ." She see-sawed her hand between us. "This."

"This?" What was this?

"Yes. This. I don't know what to say." This time, both hands flew in the air. "When I came into your office, I just wanted to say congratulations. I didn't expect to kiss you or for us to . . . you know. And then we went to the event, and I knew that if I looked at you, the entire bar would know that we . . . well, you know."

I inched closer, taking her face in my hands. "Millicent—"

"I'm freaking out."

"I gathered that."

She let her forehead fall against my chest. "I need to go home."

"Okay."

"Just . . ." She leaned back, giving me a shy smile. "Will you kiss me good night?"

She didn't even need to ask. I bent, sealing my lips over hers.

One sweep of my tongue against her mouth and she melted, a sweet moan coming from her throat and shooting straight to my cock.

She opened for me, letting me have a taste. Then Millie rose up on her toes, searching for more.

Our tongues dueled. Our lips were frantic, our teeth clattering as I banded my arms around her, pressing my arousal against her hip. Then I dropped my mouth to her neck, sucking and licking. "Feel how much I want you, Mills."

"Yes."

Above us, a parking lot light flickered, like a warning that we were standing out in the open for anyone driving by to see. I tore my mouth away, ready to put some distance between us.

But Millie reached behind me for the back door of the truck. As soon as it opened, she planted her hand on my chest and shoved.

Fuck yeah. I hopped inside, and the moment my ass hit the seat, Millie jumped in too, closing us in. Then she straddled my waist, her mouth coming down on mine.

I reached for her hair tie, tugging it from her hair and tossing it to the floor. Then I let her kiss me as her hair draped around us. Citrus and sweet. I growled when she started grinding against my dick.

"Get these off." I ripped at the button on her pants.

Stripping her bare was clumsy and fast. She shifted to the seat beside me, tugging and pulling at her clothes while I did the same, furiously shoving my shorts and boxers free until they were bunched at my ankles. The moment her panties were gone, I took her by the hips and swung her to my lap, her head nearly colliding with the cab's roof.

Then her mouth was on mine again and she sank down on my shaft, sheathing herself fully.

"Fuck, baby." I squeezed my eyes closed, letting my head fall back against the headrest. The fact that I'd lasted as long as I had in the office had been astounding. This, feeling her inner walls flutter around me, was delicious torture.

My stamina was shot, thanks to years of a sexless marriage. With any luck, Millie would help me build it up.

She lifted on her knees, only to sink back down and slam us together again. "Oh, God, Ford."

I held her at the hips, letting her set the pace. Over and over she brought us together, our breaths heavy. The windows fogged. Millie didn't tire. She kept working us together, using the strength in those gorgeous, toned, mile-long legs.

Next time, I wanted those legs spread wide on my mattress or hooked over my shoulders. *Next time.*

She rode me hard, taking us both to the brink as her perfect breasts bounced between us. Millie leaned in for a kiss but before she could find my mouth, her forehead came to mine, her jaw dropping as a cry escaped right before she shattered.

"Yes." I nipped at her lower lip, feeling her pussy clench. God, this woman. This tight wet heat. Heaven.

My own legs trembled. The pressure at the base of my spine reached its peak and I let go of my control, pouring inside her as I came on a roar. The release racked my muscles and sent me shooting to the stars, only to float back down minutes later.

My arms fell limp at my sides as the haze cleared.

Millie collapsed against my chest, our bodies sticky with sweat. "Wow."

"Damn." I threaded my fingers into her hair, holding her to me as she buried her face in my neck.

Her giggle was music to my ears.

I held her closer, wrapping her tight as I kissed her temple. My muscles began to relax, my cock still in her body beginning to soften. But before I could pull her off my lap, a pinch came in my calf, tightening like a rubber band about to snap.

"Oh, hell." I grunted, swinging her off me as I massaged the muscle.

"What's wrong?" Millie asked, shoving the hair out of her face.

"Cramp." This was what happened when you had your shorts bunched at your ankles. I shifted my hips, pulling up my boxers and shorts, then stretched the leg across the center console to the front seat, breathing through the cramp until it loosened.

Millie's mouth twisted as she tried to hide a smile.

"You think this is funny?" I smirked. "Next time we're doing this in a bed. Understood? I'm too big for sex in the back of my truck."

A flush crept into her cheeks. "Next time?"

I twisted to face her, running a hand over her naked chest, down her heart to the space between her breasts. "Make me a deal. Every time we win, this is how we celebrate."

"With fogged-up windows like we're horny teenagers?"

"No, with orgasms, baby." I chuckled, flicking one of her nipples. "We'll celebrate with orgasms."

Her entire body shivered. "Then you'd better keep winning."

CHAPTER TWENTY-THREE

FORD

The drop-off line at Joey's school stretched for a block. Vehicles inched forward. The mother ahead of me had her arm out the open driver's side window and was tapping the side of her minivan, like it would make the process move faster. But this line had become one of the best parts of my day.

Joey was a captive audience in the back seat. From home to school, I had her all to myself for thirty minutes each morning.

"What should we have for dinner tonight?" I asked.

"Corn dogs? Chicken nuggets? Mac 'n' cheese?"

I really needed to learn how to cook healthier meals. "Corn dogs."

There was a bagged salad kit in the fridge. We'd have that too and call it balance.

"Did you remember your gym shoes?" I asked.

"Yep." She smacked her backpack.

"And your homework?" We'd spent our Sunday afternoon doing three worksheets that her teacher had sent home on Friday.

"Got it."

"Stephanie will pick you up this afternoon. Then I'll be home around five."

"Can we do something fun tonight?" she asked.

"Sure." I smiled at her through the rearview mirror. "Like what?"

She lifted a shoulder, inspecting her fingernails. "Maybe we could ask Millie to come over again and make more cookies."

My heart swelled.

It sounded like the perfect idea, but I wasn't sure where Millie's head was at after Saturday. I'd fought the urge to call her a hundred times yesterday. Instead, I'd settled for a single text.

Hi.

She'd replied with the same.

That was a good sign, right? At least she'd responded.

I'd pushed hard on Saturday. My only regret was that we'd been too reckless on campus. That we could have been caught and our jobs could have suffered.

But that woman was irresistible.

My instinct was to haul her into my life. To complicate the hell out of everything and run into this at a full sprint.

Millie was so *good*. I wanted that goodness wrapped around Joey like a bear hug. Except what I wanted might not be what Joey needed.

She undoubtedly liked Millie. But Joey knew her as my old friend from college. How would Joey feel about me having a girlfriend?

I wouldn't have given it a second thought except it had been hard on Joey when Sienna had started dating Jordan. Even harder when they'd moved in together and gotten engaged.

Joey hadn't told me exactly how she felt but I think there were a lot of mixed emotions. Sadness as the permanence of the divorce sank in. Rejection as Sienna settled into a new home where Joey didn't even have a designated bedroom.

Joey had endured enough change in the last few months. New town. New school. New friends.

Maybe adding a girlfriend was too much.

"How about we try to make cookies together? You and me?" I asked. "I kind of want to try it to see if we can do it."

"Okay." Her voice gave nothing away.

Was she disappointed I wasn't inviting Millie? Was the reason she'd asked for Millie to come over because she wanted cookies?

Was it this hard for all dads to read their daughters?

The minivan ahead of us reached the curb and the sliding door flew open, two kids piling out and waving before they headed for the playground.

My time with Joey was up this morning. When the van was gone, I took its place and twisted to give my daughter a smile. "Love you, princess."

"Love you too, Daddy." She unbuckled, grabbed her backpack and stretched forward to kiss my cheek. Then she was gone, rushing to join a group of girls on the sidewalk.

"Have a good day," I murmured, then left the school and drove to work.

The parking lot was already crowded by the time I pulled in and headed for the fieldhouse. I grinned when I passed Millie's Kia, parked just one row away from where it had been Saturday night.

The memory of her in the back seat of my truck made my cock twitch behind my zipper.

We'd been explosive together. I craved her with every cell in my body.

Maybe I wasn't ready to make a big announcement to Joey, but that didn't mean I was letting Millie go.

Not again. We had shit to work out. We'd be keeping this a secret at work. For a time, we'd be keeping this a secret at home. But that was temporary. We'd figure this out. Somehow.

The familiar scent of cement and bleach greeted me when I walked inside. As I headed for my office, my to-go cup of coffee in hand, I breathed in the start of a new week.

About half of my staff had beat me into the office. A couple of the other coaches had kids too so they were probably also making the drop-off loop. We'd have a busy week, rehashing the game, watching film and tweaking plays. This morning, there was a large department meeting with each of the head coaches to start discussing budgets for the next school year since planning took place twelve months in advance.

I flipped on the lights in my office, another grin forming on my mouth when I moved behind the desk.

Not a day would go by that I wouldn't think about Millie spread on its surface. That I wouldn't picture her perfect body, naked and trembling, beneath my touch. That I wouldn't see my come leaking down her thighs.

She'd asked me to keep my distance at work, but fuck it. I picked up my desk phone and dialed her extension.

It rang twice before she answered. "Hello."

"Hi." Yeah, definitely should have called her yesterday. I'd missed that voice. "You okay?"

"I'm, um . . . yes."

"Still freaking out?"

"A little," she admitted.

"We'll figure it out. Promise."

She blew out a long breath. "Okay."

A knock came at my door.

Kurt walked in, wearing a tight smile as he closed the door behind him, clearly not caring that I was on the damn phone. What the hell? Was he like this with everyone?

"I'll let you go," I told Millie.

"Bye."

With the phone back in its cradle, I leaned back in my chair. "Morning."

"Ford." He took a seat across from my desk.

"What's up?"

"I, uh . . ." He pinched the bridge of his nose. "I just got a strange call. It was about Saturday."

Oh. Fuck. No.

I hadn't noticed anyone else in the parking lot. Or maybe someone had overheard us in here? *Shit. Shit. Shit.*

She hadn't said anything on the phone. She hadn't sounded upset. Was Kurt going to go to her office next? Millie was going to flip out.

"What about Saturday?" Maybe I could deny it. Maybe if Millie denied it too, we'd be fine. And next time, a hell of a lot more careful.

"Something about excessive drinking at the event."

It took a moment for his words to register. "Hold up. Say that again?"

"You were seen drinking with Coach Greely. Apparently, in excess."

"Is this a joke?" What the fuck was going on?

Kurt shook his head. "I'm afraid not."

I held up a finger as my nostrils flared. "I had one shot with Toren. One. And other than water, that was the only thing I had to drink at the event. An event held at. A. Bar." If they had expected it to be a dry function, then maybe they should have chosen a different location.

Kurt held up his hands. "I'm just relaying information."

"And I assume you won't tell me who lodged this complaint either?" Was this like the previous grievance about Joey? Was this really Kurt's issue?

"It's confidential."

Fucking confidential. If this was real, the coward bitching about my perfectly acceptable behavior was going to get an ass-chewing if I ever figured out who it was.

My nostrils flared. "What did you say? To this confidential complaint?"

"Look, Ford, this is a unique year."

Meaning Kurt hadn't defended me. Hell, he'd been standing feet away all night. He knew goddamn well that I hadn't been *excessively* drinking.

"You're the head coach," he said.

"Your point?" Venom dripped from my voice.

Kurt dropped his gaze, swallowing hard. "We're just trying to fly under the radar this year."

And apparently having a shot of tequila with Toren wasn't *under the radar*.

"Fine," I clipped. We told the players absolutely no public drinking. At this morning's staff meeting, I'd tell the coaches the same. "Anything else?"

"Sorry, Ford. I really am. But I wanted you to know." Kurt shook his head, standing from his chair. Bad news delivered, he headed for the door. "Oh, and uh, great win this weekend. Great way to start the season. Weather is supposed to be perfect this weekend. I'm looking forward to being on the sidelines with you guys."

I had nothing nice to say at the moment so I kept my mouth shut, waiting until he was gone.

What the hell? How could anyone who'd been in that bar say I'd been excessively drinking? The complaint about Joey coming to work this summer had pissed me right the fuck off, but this? This felt a lot like I had a target on my back.

I shot out of my chair, shoving it away so hard that it rolled and slammed into the wall. Ignoring it, I stormed out of my office and jogged to the second floor.

When I reached Millie's office, she was in her chair, fingers flying over the keyboard. She spotted me and froze, her eyes widening as they glanced past me.

"Can we visit about the weight room schedule?" I spoke loud enough that anyone listening would hear.

"Oh, um, sure."

I closed the door behind me, then paced from it to the corner of her desk, too fucking pissed to sit. "Kurt has reprimanded me twice in the past two weeks. He claims that someone has complained to him."

She jerked back. "What?"

"The first was right when school started. Someone was pissed about that day I had Joey with me."

"Who?"

I shrugged, still pacing. "Kurt won't tell me. It's *confidential*."

She rolled her eyes. "It was probably him. He's weird about kids. What was the second complaint?"

"That I was drinking excessively at the bar on Saturday night."

"What?" Her voice was so loud she flinched. "No, you weren't. I was watching you all night long. You had one shot with Toren."

"Exactly. I—" My feet stopped moving. "You were watching me? Because every time I looked at you, you pretended like I didn't exist."

She lifted a shoulder. "I was trying not to make it obvious. Speaking of, you need to work on that or everyone in Mission is going to know we're, um . . . you know."

Yeah. I knew. "You sound like Toren." I chuckled, some of my anger deflating. I rounded the corner of her desk, bent low and took her mouth for a chaste kiss. "I'll try to stop staring."

Her cheeks flushed, her eyes flicking to the door. "People can't find out, Ford."

"I know, baby. We'll keep it a secret." At least the complaint hadn't been about Millie. As much as it burned to know that someone was watching my every move, at least she was safe.

"Thank you," she whispered.

I kissed her again, licking her soft pout, then went back to pacing before I did something reckless, like break in *her* desk this time. "Who would do this? Let's assume Kurt really did get two complaints. Who would want me in trouble?"

"I have no idea. I mean, the event was at a bar."

"Exactly."

"There's no rule that coaches can't drink. I mean, it's always been implied to keep it under control, but I see nothing wrong with what you did."

I rubbed a hand over my jaw. "This feels a lot like someone is gunning for my job."

"Who?"

"Not a damn clue." My gut twisted. Could it have been one of the other coaches? Another department employee? "Could this be Kurt? Maybe he has a problem with my daughter and me drinking. But why wouldn't he just tell me that?"

"If you figure him out, please pass it along," she muttered. "He's . . . Kurt."

Footsteps and dulled conversation came from the hallway outside her door as people passed.

"I'll get out of here." I gave her a smile, then opened the door, again talking loud enough for people to hear. "Thanks for the help, Millie."

"Anytime. Great game on Saturday."

"See ya around." With a wave, I headed down the hall. As I passed cubicle walls on the way to the stairs, Kurt stood at the mouth of the break room.

His eyes were locked on me, and I had no doubt that he'd seen exactly where I'd just been.

Millie had been hell bent on hiding this from the start. She was borderline panicked about keeping this hidden.

At first, I'd thought she was just being paranoid. That she'd taken that no-fraternization policy too literally.

But now, with two bullshit complaints and a boss who hovered like a hornet at a picnic, well . . .

Maybe she was onto something.

CHAPTER TWENTY-FOUR

MILLIE

Beyond the Stadium Club's floor-to-ceiling windows, the Wildcats were crushing the opposing team, fifty-six to three. I actually felt bad for the other coaches and players. Well, sort of.

I really liked it when we won.

It would have been the perfect Saturday, other than the fact that I'd been trapped inside. Oh, what I'd give to be outside with the other fans, enjoying the sunshine and riding the high of impending victory. Instead, I'd only caught brief glimpses of the game in between conversations with boosters and alums.

"Millie." Fingertips grazed my elbow. Familiar fingertips. Though not the fingertips I'd been dreaming about all week.

"Hey, Adrian." I pivoted away from his touch, taking a step back because he'd come too close for two people who were supposed to be friends and colleagues. "How's it going?"

He sighed, not missing the distance I'd just put between

us. "Fine. Is there a reason you haven't been returning my texts?"

"I've been busy." A half-truth. This was not the time or place for the full truth.

We needed to have a long conversation. I needed to remind him that we were over, that the daily texts needed to stop.

At first, I'd responded when he'd asked me about my day or how I was doing. The few times he'd asked me out, I'd just said I was busy. Except lately, there'd been an urgency to his texts. An insistence. Every day, he asked me out to lunch or dinner. Yesterday, he'd stopped by my office again to take me out for a drink after work.

I'd declined. I'd declined over and over, yet here he was, persistent as always.

Was that why we'd dated for so long? Because he'd worn me down? Because I'd been a coward and it had been too exhausting to constantly say no?

"Busy? Too busy to return a quick text?" Adrian shook his head. "What the hell is going on with you lately?"

"I've just had a lot on my mind."

"Like what? What happened that you can't confide in me anymore?"

Our breakup. That was what had happened.

"I'm trying here, Millie. I thought we were in a good place. Working toward something. What changed?"

Oh, Adrian. Nothing had changed. And everything had changed. All it would take was me saying no. That I was interested in someone else. A quick, brutal rejection and this conversation would be over. But I'd never been good at brutal.

"Listen, how about we meet up later? Talk when there aren't so many people around."

He sighed. "Yeah. Okay."

"Find me after the game."

"All right." He touched my arm again, a sweet caress that had once made me feel special. But today, it took effort not to jerk my arm away.

The only man I wanted touching me was currently standing on the football field.

"See you later." I waited until Adrian walked away, then turned toward the window and let out a big breath that fogged the glass. "Ugh."

My eyes drifted to Ford.

My heart skipped.

Something had happened on the previous play that had caused an uproar. I'd missed it, talking to Adrian.

Ford's arms flew out at the sides before he shook his head, clearly pissed.

Boos filled the stadium.

"Offsides? Are you kidding me?" A man behind me scoffed. "These refs."

Ford appeared on the jumbotron, the camera cataloging his reaction. But other than the immediate response, he went right back to steady, stoic Ford.

We hadn't spoken this week. Not since he'd come to my office on Monday.

I shouldn't have missed him. But I missed him.

Was it because of those complaints that he'd kept his distance?

Who would do that? Nothing Ford had done was outside what other coaches had done. Our dance team coach brought her daughters to practice all the time. No one had ever been bothered. And the fact that someone had accused him of excessive drinking was ludicrous. In all my time with Ford at college parties, I'd only ever seen him drunk once.

Everyone, especially Kurt, was extremely cautious at the moment. But there was an undercurrent of malice with these complaints that had plagued me all week. Like someone was intentionally out to get Ford fired.

At least the team was winning. No one had expected the Wildcats to do so well off the bat this season.

As much as it sucked to admit, college coaches were rarely fired if they had a winning record. Unless . . . there was a scandal.

Like the football coach fucking an assistant athletic director in his office.

My cheeks flamed thinking about last Saturday.

No matter what happened today, I would not repeat that mistake. After the game, I was going straight home. I didn't trust myself not to venture to Ford's office again, so I'd even put my car key in my pocket instead of leaving it on my desk like usual, just so there was no reason for me to set foot in the fieldhouse.

The Wildcat defense held the other team on a desperate fourth-down attempt. As the offense jogged onto the field, led by Rush Ramsey, Ford walked over to Toren, the two talking about something with their heads bent together. Then Toren nodded and walked away, leaving Ford alone again.

My mouth watered.

In college, I'd thought the sexiest sight in the world was Ford dressed in his royal blue and silver uniform. Those pants, molded to his ass? Perfection. Except I hadn't known what I'd been missing.

Ford as the head coach, confident and in control, was practically erotic. Waves of authority rolled off his broad frame, rolling all the way from his side of the stadium to mine, permeating the glass and sending a shiver down my spine.

Okay, so maybe I'd venture into the fieldhouse after all. It would be rude not to at least say congratulations, right?

Watch the game, Millie. Not the coach.

I shook my head, locking my gaze with Rush just as he threw the ball toward an open receiver.

"Touchdown," I called before the receiver even reached the end zone.

Rush had been flawless today—at least during the plays I'd been able to watch. Was Faye watching today? Or was she avoiding everything football? Were they keeping her pregnancy a secret?

I hoped, for her sake, that her secret wasn't eating her alive.

Mine was starting to gnaw at me.

What were we going to do? If Ford and I wanted to have an actual relationship, we couldn't hide forever. Was this even going to last? If it did, how was I going to keep my job? How was he going to keep coaching?

Kurt wouldn't make an exception. My gaze drifted to my boss, also standing on the sidelines. He'd been hovering closer to Ford at the beginning of the game, but Ford must have said something because Kurt had latched on to Parks instead after halftime.

What happened if he decided coaching at TSU wasn't all it was cracked up to be and he left again? What if he decided Joey was better off somewhere else? Did Joey even want her dad to have a girlfriend? Would Sienna poison her toward me?

Oh, God, Sienna. I'd thought the day she'd moved away I'd never see that woman again. If I stayed with Ford, I'd have to face her again.

I grimaced.

Why was I stressing about this already? We'd only had sex twice. That was hardly a relationship.

But what if . . .

What if this time around, my dream came true?

I sighed, my eyes glued to Ford again.

He was perfect on that sideline. He was made to lead a team. As the crowd celebrated yet another touchdown, Ford smiled and clapped. My heart tumbled.

Once upon a time, I'd dreamed of kissing him after a win. It had been a fantasy in college. A dream I'd always known wouldn't come true but I'd dreamed it anyway.

It seemed almost sentimental now.

I still wanted to kiss him after a win. That was what had driven me to his office last weekend. And fool that I was, in my heart of hearts, I knew I'd go again tonight.

"You're drooling, Millie."

I jerked away from the window, my head whipping toward President Cruz as she took the place at my side.

"Um . . ." I gulped. "What?"

"Millie." I'd never seen President Cruz roll her eyes, but she was good at it.

"He's just a friend."

"And I'm six feet tall."

Okay, this was bad. Really, really bad. But I knew that if I opened my mouth, a string of word vomit would come out, and in my excuses to explain how I was not totally infatuated with Ford Ellis, I'd tell her exactly how I was, in fact, totally infatuated with Ford Ellis.

So I turned my back on the glass, facing the crowd in the club and the people celebrating another win. "The season is off to a great start." My voice was too cheery, almost panicked thanks to my racing heart.

President Cruz arched an eyebrow, but thankfully, she let me off the hook. "It's fantastic. And from what I can tell, Ford is quickly winning everyone over."

My chest swelled with pride that she liked him. His adoration would be the death of my career if we kept seeing each other. No one, including President Cruz, would pick me over Ford. But I was proud of him all the same.

"Are you heading down to the field after the game?" I asked.

"Oh, I think I'll just sneak out. Leave the celebrations to the younger generations." Her eyes crinkled at the sides when she smiled. "Have a good time, Millie."

Was there a hint of innuendo in her voice? Or was that just my paranoia running rampant? She couldn't know about Ford's office, right?

No. No freaking way.

"You too, President Cruz." Still too cheery. I waited until she walked away before I let out a groan. "I'm doomed."

Goodbye, career.

Hello, unemployment.

But I hadn't been fired yet. So I squared my shoulders and mingled with the crowd, sharing high fives and fist bumps as the Stadium Club slowly emptied. As the last of the fans hopped on the elevator, I joined them, making my way to the field.

The reserved end zone section where I'd been last weekend was still full of people celebrating.

I spotted Kurt first, smiling and shaking hands like he'd had some key role in the team's win today. If I did lose my job, I wasn't going to miss my boss.

"Two for two." An alum I'd known for years walked over. "Heck of a way to start the season."

"It sure is."

For the next thirty minutes, after the team had ducked into the locker room, I made small talk, smiling and nodding because that was my job. And I loved my job. But I'd also been up since five to go on my run, then make it to the field-house to watch the women's volleyball game.

My energy was draining and most of the people were leaving, so I waited until there was a break in the conversation. Just as I was about to make my escape—to ditch Adrian, force myself to go home and avoid Ford—I heard my name.

"Millie." Adrian came stalking toward me, his body tense and his jaw clenched like he was pissed. Maybe he knew I'd been about to leave without meeting him.

"Hey, can we resched—"

Adrian moved so fast I didn't have a chance to stop him.

I froze as he pressed his lips to mine. My eyes widened when he licked my bottom lip. It took a second for me to snap out of it. To plant a hand over his chest and shove. Hard.

"Adrian," I hissed, wiping my mouth dry.

"Millie." He scoffed. "Two years ago, you wouldn't have cared if I kissed you after a game."

"Two years ago, we were together." Sparing him from that brutal rejection felt too generous at the moment. He'd crossed the line. "We're not together anymore. And we're not getting back together either."

Hurt flashed in his eyes before they hardened. Then he strode past me, leaving as quickly as he'd arrived.

"What the hell was that?" I pushed a hair off my forehead, glancing around, grateful that no one had been close enough to overhear. Most of the end zone was empty now, except for a few people milling toward the exit.

Except before I could slip past them and duck out, my gaze caught on blue.

Brilliant blue. Angry blue.

Ford.

"Oh boy."

CHAPTER TWENTY-FIVE

FORD

The plates and glasses inside the dishwasher rattled as I slammed the bottom rack closed. I didn't even care if something had broken. I'd deal with it tomorrow.

"Can I watch TV?" Joey asked.

"Yeah." After spending all day at the game and coming home just in time for dinner, I'd normally insist we do something together, like play outside or do odd jobs around the house. But I was shit company at the moment.

And Joey was in a bad mood too.

Maybe because I'd been gone all day. Maybe because her mother hadn't called yet. Maybe because my attitude was contagious.

Whatever the reason, the atmosphere in this house was, well . . . awful.

"Before you start watching TV, spend a couple minutes picking up your room," I told her.

"Why? Stephanie will do it for me on Monday."

"No," I drawled. "That's not what Stephanie is here to do. You're responsible for keeping your room clean."

"You let her clean up your messes."

Well, shit. I'd hired a housekeeper to do the heavy cleaning, but Stephanie had been great about tidying up around here. But I didn't want Joey slacking on her chores and expecting Stephanie to do it. "Just . . . clean your room. Now."

"Whatever." Her eye roll looked so much like Sienna's that I wanted to rip my hair out.

"Watch your attitude, Josalynn."

"Me?" She gaped, pointing to her chest. "You're the one who's been acting like an ass all night."

I blinked. "Did you just call me an ass?"

"Yeah, and now I'm going to get in trouble even though it's true." Her voice wobbled along with her chin.

As much as I wanted to deny it, to reprimand her about her language, she was right. I'd been an ass tonight.

"I don't want to fight with you." I sighed. "I'm asking you to spend five minutes picking up your room. Can you do that or not?"

"Yes," she muttered.

"Thank you."

She spun on a heel and stormed away, her arms crossed over her chest and her blond hair swinging across her shoulders.

When she rounded the corner and slammed her bedroom door, I blew out a long breath. Did all parents feel like they couldn't do a damn thing right? Or was that just me?

I'd hoped that these arguments would stop once school started, but it was the same as it had been in August. Either we were happy and smiling. Or at each other's throats.

Was it still because of the move to Montana? Was it me?

Was it Sienna? Or did all girls get an attitude when they reached a certain age? I'd hoped to avoid this until she was in her teens. Nine seemed too young to be so sassy and . . . angry.

Joey was just angry.

And tonight, so was I.

Every time I closed my eyes, I saw Adrian kiss Millie at the stadium. I saw red.

"Motherfucker." I stomped to the cabinet above the fridge, taking out a bottle of whiskey. After pouring myself a tumbler, I stalked to the living room, too pissed off to sit, so I stood by the window, watching the horizon as the evening light faded.

The only thing keeping me from chugging this drink was the fact that we'd won today's game. Had we lost, Joey would have been justified in calling me much worse than an *ass*.

Immediately after the game, I'd met with the team, congratulated the guys on a great win. Then I'd cut them loose to walk to the fieldhouse to shower and change. I'd held back, mostly because I'd hoped to find Millie.

And oh, I'd found her.

She'd been in the end zone again, just like last weekend. The moment my eyes had locked on her, it had been impossible to tear them away.

Maybe one day, I'd look at her and my heart wouldn't skip. Maybe one day, I'd stop thinking about how many years I'd missed. Maybe one day, I wouldn't have to hold myself back from going to her.

I'd felt eyes on me. While I'd been staring at Millie, Adrian had been staring at me.

His nostrils had flared before he'd stalked toward her.

For a moment, I'd thought he was going to yell at her. I'd taken a step, ready to haul ass over there and tell him to fuck off.

Except then he'd kissed her, and I'd nearly screamed.

For a split second, I'd thought she wanted him to kiss her. They had a history. They had freedom. There'd be no hiding. No pretending.

But she'd shoved him away, and I'd been able to breathe again. Clearly, it hadn't been her idea. So why was I this mad?

Instead of talking to her about it, I'd marched to the field-house and locked myself in my office. Part of me had hoped Millie would show. That she'd knock on my door.

Except when I'd finally ripped the door open to come home, the hallways had been empty. There'd been no sign of her car in the emptying parking lot.

She was mine. For fuck's sake, she was mine. And if we weren't being forced to keep it a secret, I would have pummeled Adrian for daring to think he could touch what belonged to me.

My hand squeezed the tumbler so hard I feared the glass would break, so I tossed back the whiskey and retreated to the kitchen for a refill. Except before I could take out the bottle, Joey's door opened.

"My room's clean," she barked, then went to the bathroom and slammed yet another door.

"This has been a lovely evening," I deadpanned and reached for the bottle.

Its glug, the splash of the whiskey in my glass, was music to my ears.

"Here I am, excessively drinking again." I scoffed, then

took my glass to the living room, this time sitting on the edge of the couch as the shower turned on.

I sat in silence, in the darkening room, not bothering with the lights.

Joey walked out of the bathroom.

"Josalynn," I called before she could shut herself in her room. "Come here, please."

Her hair was combed and wet. She was dressed in yellow pajama pants and a tee printed with tiny daisies. *Happy pajamas*. Oh, how I wished her face would be happy too.

That shower must have washed off some of the attitude because the defiant lift of her chin was missing. Her shoulders sagged as she shuffled into the living room. "Yeah?"

My heart pinched. "I love you."

"I love you too," she said, except instead of looking at me, she told her toes.

"Got a hug for me?"

She walked over, her arms limp as she placed them over my shoulders.

I wrapped her up tight, breathing in the scent of her watermelon soap. Another father probably would have known what to say. How to make his kid smile. How to fix this.

All I could do was hug her.

"Can I go watch TV now?" she asked, pulling away.

I sighed. "Sure."

She practically jogged out of the room.

I lifted my tumbler, inspecting the rolling waves of caramel liquor, then tipped it to my lips, grateful for the burn as I swallowed.

There was no chugging this time. I sat on the edge of the

couch, still too frustrated and tense to relax, and sipped my drink until darkness had fallen beyond the windows. Then I checked my phone as I took my empty glass to the sink.

Eight thirty. And not a peep from Sienna.

The Seahawks had a home game tomorrow. The first game of the regular season. There was likely a fundraiser or event tonight. Sienna was probably at a party, surrounded by people who didn't give a flying fuck about her. Meanwhile, the one person who did care was in her bedroom, watching TV.

I gave it another hour, hoping she'd at least send a text. She didn't.

The only saving grace was that when I walked into Joey's room, she'd already fallen asleep. I wouldn't have to tell her tonight that her mom hadn't called.

The remote dangled from her fingertips, so I picked it up, shutting off her show before kissing her forehead and tucking her in. A surge of new anger hit as I closed her door and padded down the hallway.

Fucking Sienna. Fucking Adrian.

Not a chance I'd sleep. I was too mad. But I moved through the house anyway, killing the lights, then aimed my feet for my bedroom because what else did I have to do?

So I'd force myself to get in bed. To toss and turn until I finally crashed. And in the morning, hopefully Joey and I could start fresh.

I was just about to close my door when my phone vibrated in my pocket.

"About goddamn time," I muttered, taking it out and expecting Sienna's name.

Except it was a text.

From Millie.

Are you asleep?

My footsteps halted as I typed a quick reply. *No.*

Can I come in?

Hold up. She was here?

I spun around so fast I nearly gave myself whiplash as I hustled to open the front door.

Millie was in the same clothes from the game. Navy slacks. Gray Wildcat polo. Her hair was down today, curled in silky waves.

The image of Adrian kissing her flashed again and my hands balled into fists.

She noticed. "You're still mad."

"Yes, I'm mad."

"I told him it was over."

I arched an eyebrow. Either Adrian was hard of hearing or she needed to work on the delivery.

She frowned. "It's not like I asked him to kiss me."

I leaned down, my eyes locked with hers. "The only man who kisses your mouth is me. Clear?"

Millie looked like she was going to argue—apparently everyone was arguing with me tonight—but then she must have changed her mind because she simply nodded.

"Fuck." I raked a hand through my hair. "Woman. What the hell are you doing to me?"

She lifted a shoulder. "I don't know."

"That was a rhetorical question."

"Oh." She pulled her bottom lip between her teeth, and all I could think was that the last man to kiss her hadn't been me.

Fuck that asshole. I reached forward, snagging the cotton collar of her shirt, and hauled her close.

Millie gasped and teetered, but before she lost her balance, I wrapped her in my arms and sealed my mouth over hers.

I'd erase Adrian's kiss. I'd erase everyone's until the only man she remembered kissing was me.

My tongue slipped between her teeth for a taste of her sweet. Millie. *My* Millie. And tonight, she was in my bed.

With a quick lift, I picked her up off her feet, backing up until we cleared the door. Then I shoved it closed with a foot before spinning us around, stalking through the dark house toward my bedroom.

Millie ripped her mouth away, her eyes shooting over my shoulder as I walked. "Wait," she whispered. "What about Joey?"

"Asleep." I kept walking, my hold on her tight.

Tomorrow, I'd worry about what to do with Joey. But no more keeping my distance. No more staying away from Millie. No more letting another motherfucking man kiss her in *my* football stadium.

No more.

"Kiss me," I ordered.

She was still looking over my shoulder.

So I stopped walking and waited. "Kiss me, Millie."

"But—"

"Do not argue with me. And don't even think about leaving. You're here for the whole night."

"Sheesh." She rolled her eyes. "You're grumpy."

"Another man kissed you today. Fuck yes, I'm grumpy."

Her gaze softened. "I'm sorry."

"Then kiss me."

"Okay," she whispered, gently pressing her lips to the corner of my mouth.

It was a sweet kiss. "I don't want sweet, Mills. We're going to fuck. Hard. Then I'll give you sweet. But right now? Fucking. Kiss. Me."

It took her a heartbeat, then she crushed her mouth to mine, her hands diving into my hair and tugging hard on the roots.

My tongue plunged into her mouth, tangling with hers and sliding deep. My cock swelled, desperate to sink into her body.

We reached the bedroom and I shut us inside, flipping the lock. Then I strode for the bed, tearing my mouth from Millie's to toss her on the bed.

She bounced, instantly sitting up to strip off her clothes.

I reached behind my head, yanking off my shirt. My shorts came next, along with my boxers.

Millie was still working her pants off by the time I was naked, so I fisted my shaft, stroking a few times until she was naked. When she finally looked up, she saw what I was doing. If the lights were on, no doubt I'd see her cheeks flush.

"Spread," I ordered, still stroking. "I want to see you."

One leg at a time, she bared her pussy, letting her knees fall open. Pink. Perfect. And fucking drenched.

"I need you, baby." I swallowed hard, dropping my cock before I spilled too soon. Then I planted a knee in the bed, moving between her thighs.

She relaxed on her back, taking the weight of my chest as my hips fell into the cradle of hers. Then I reached between us, dragging a finger through her slit and earning a hiss. "Ford. Fuck me."

I lined up and thrust home.

Holy fucking hell.

Millie squeezed, her moan filling the room. Her legs opened wider, her body already trembling.

Hard and fast. This time, we'd take the edge off. So I pulled out, then slammed inside again, doing exactly as promised. I fucked her. Hard. I pistoned my hips, my eyes falling closed as her inner walls fluttered around my length.

"Oh God, Ford." Her nails dug into my shoulders, the sting adding to the pleasure.

"Again. Say my name again."

Her breath hitched. "Ford."

Damn right. I'd kiss her, worship her, and when a name escaped her lips, it would only be mine.

I moved faster, thrust after thrust, driving her to the brink. Her moans mingled with my groans and the sound of our bodies coming together. She felt too good. Not a chance I'd last much longer.

"Come, Millie," I ordered, going deep and rocking my cock against her clit. That was all it took.

Her back arched off the mattress and she writhed beneath me, her hands fisting in the sheets as she pulsed around me.

That tight clench triggered my own release and I poured into her, my mind, my body, entirely consumed by Millie. A woman so perfect she must have been made for me.

Our bodies were sticky with sweat. Our breaths labored.

I shifted off Millie, rolling to my back and hauling her onto my chest, where my heart thundered.

"Still grumpy?" she teased.

I chuckled. "Depends. Are you still arguing with me?"

"I barely argued."

"So that means yes."

She giggled, relaxing to kiss the dusting of hair over my pecs. "Good game today, Coach."

"Is that why you came over? To tell me good game?"

"No." She propped up on an elbow. "You promised me orgasms for each win."

I leaned up, nipping at an earlobe as my hand slid to palm her ass. "I guess I did."

CHAPTER TWENTY-SIX

MILLIE

"Hold up." Ford reached for me before I could slip away, his hand capturing mine.

"Ford," I whispered. "I have to go."

"One more." He hauled me close, his mouth dropping to mine.

I didn't put up a fight. I never did. Instead, I let him kiss me again and again, the heat from his lips chasing away the cold morning air.

I rose up on my tiptoes, sinking into his arms as his tongue stroked mine.

We'd had one month of these goodbyes. A month of late nights when I'd drive to his house and slip into his bed. A month of worshiping his body and letting him do the same to mine. A month of four a.m. alarms so I could get out of the house before Joey woke up.

One month of secrets.

The flash of headlights drove us apart. A neighbor, up early, rolled past, and I let my hair fall to curtain my face.

A familiar frown marred Ford's handsome face. "I'm

tired of hiding this, Mills. We can't do this forever, baby." He tucked a lock of hair behind my ear as our breaths billowed around us.

"I know." I gave him a sad smile. "I don't know what to do."

He moved closer, his bare toes next to mine. "Neither do I."

I'd spent an hour yesterday, in between Friday afternoon meetings, reviewing the department's HR policies. I'd read the no-fraternization document no less than twenty times—it was surprisingly short, considering it was the bane of my existence. In a nutshell, relationships between employees within the athletics department were strictly prohibited.

"Let's just get through this season," I said. Another month, maybe two if the team did well in the playoffs.

Ford blew out a deep breath, his forehead dropping to mine. "Okay. But I want to tell Joey after the game today. We can hide this at work, but I'm tired of sneaking around my own house."

I tensed and pulled away. "Maybe we should wait."

"Why?"

Because what if you leave again?

"Um . . . because." Now I sounded like my mother. As a kid, whenever she wanted me to do something but was in too much of a rush to explain her reasoning, or just didn't have a good reason, she'd answer my *why*s with a *because*.

Given the way Ford's expression hardened, he hated hearing *because* as much as I hated saying it.

"What if she hates me?" I threw out a hand. "What if she doesn't want you to have a girlfriend?"

"Joey doesn't hate you. It's not like you're a stranger. And I don't know how she's going to react to a girlfriend in my life, but I've thought about it a lot this month, Millie. I'm willing to give her the chance to figure it out."

"Sienna will go ballistic." My lip curled on her name. We hadn't broached the Sienna topic yet, but my stomach twisted just thinking about her.

"Who the fuck cares about Sienna?"

"Joey," I shot back.

He sighed, dragging a hand through his messy hair. It was sexy in the morning, tousled and sticking up at odd angles, mostly because of my fingers from last night. "Millie, I will hide this at work. But not here."

"Just for a little longer," I countered. "Until the season is over."

"No. It's just Joey. Who's she going to tell?"

"Please?"

"Millicent." His eyes narrowed. "Talk to me. Why don't you want me to tell Joey?"

"Because . . ." I swallowed hard, squeezing my eyes. "Because what if this falls apart like it did last time?"

I didn't have to see it to know he winced.

He was silent for three heartbeats. I counted.

"Look at me." He hooked a finger under my chin, waiting until I was drowning in those blue eyes. "I'm not leaving."

"You might," I whispered.

He shuffled closer, taking my face in his hands. "Then this time, I'll take you with me."

The air rushed from my lungs. "Really?"

Ford chuckled. "What do you think is happening here?"

"Um . . ." Other than spending nights in his bed, I hadn't let myself hope for more. "Maybe you'd better tell me, just to make sure."

His eyes crinkled at the sides. "Thought I did last night. And the night before that. And the night before that."

I closed my eyes, falling forward as my arms snaked around his narrow waist. "I promise to be more observant tonight."

"Good." His arms wrapped around me tight, his cheek falling to my hair. "We can hold off on telling Joey. For a little while longer."

"Thank you." It wasn't what he wanted to hear. Tension crept into his frame. But it was what I needed.

Until I knew what to do, secrecy was my shield.

"I'd better go," I said, shifting away. Then I picked up my purse from beside our feet and dug my keys from my coat pocket. "See you later?"

"Yeah. Appreciate you taking Joey."

"No problem." I smiled. "We'll have fun."

Today, I was making good on my promise to take her to a game.

Kurt had begrudgingly agreed to give me this weekend off, not because he was a good boss, but because I'd reminded him that in ten years, I hadn't missed a single home game. That, and I'd made sure there were two other assistant directors to help cover for me in the Stadium Club.

I hadn't told anyone that I was still coming to the game and bringing Joey. We'd just be two more faces in a sea of twenty thousand fans.

My first year at TSU, when I'd only been an associate AD, I hadn't needed to attend every game. But I'd wanted to show up for the Wildcats, so I'd bought two season tickets, one for me and one in case I wanted to bring a friend—I'd always gone alone. They'd been okay seats, about midway up in the stands.

But the following year, our ticket manager had stopped by my desk asking if I wanted to change my seats. There'd been a rare opening on the fifty yard line, second row up. And since he knew how much I loved Wildcat football, he'd offered them to me first.

Those two seats cost me a fortune every year. Most would think it was a waste of money, since I rarely used them. But I refused to give them up.

I gave away tickets to other people in the department to use when I couldn't. Those seats were never empty.

Only today, it would be my butt on the bench alongside Joey's.

Ford stood on the threshold of his door as I rushed to my Kia. We'd gotten an early cold snap, and I was shivering by the time I made it behind the wheel. Even having let the car warm up and the windows defrost, my teeth chattered on the drive home.

Not even a cup of coffee and a hot shower chased away the chill in my bones. Maybe it had nothing to do with the weather. Maybe it had everything to do with a four a.m. conversation on Ford's front stoop.

He seemed so . . . sure. About us. About the future.

"So what the hell is my problem?" I muttered to myself as I swept through the house, tidying up before I had to meet Ford.

Why couldn't I let go of the past? Why couldn't I stop fearing the worst?

Part of me wanted to call Autumn. I had no doubt she'd tell me exactly what she thought about this situation. She'd tell me to pull my head out of the sand and just be . . . happy.

Why did that seem so terrifying? I was sick of sneaking around. Telling Joey would need to happen eventually.

Except once the world—and his daughter—saw us together, well . . . then everyone would know if he broke my heart.

Just like last time.

This was different from college. I told myself that ten times every day. But the words weren't sinking in.

And on top of everything, I was nervous to spend a solo day with Joey. She liked me, right? She'd have fun?

My stomach was in a knot as I left the house to drive to the stadium. The parking lot was already full of tailgaters. The scent of charcoal barbeques and portable fire pits infused the fresh air with a smoky aroma. People dressed in winter coats and Wildcat hats carried Koozie-clad beer cans.

Like the masses, I'd dressed in extra layers today. Despite the brilliant October sun, the forecast called for a high just above freezing. The mountain peaks in the distance had a fresh dusting of snow capping their indigo peaks.

The energy inside the fieldhouse was buzzing, the noise from the men's locker room drifting through the closed door.

Ford was in his office, decked out in Wildcat gear as he sat on the edge of his desk, scrolling through his phone. It was impossible to look at that desk and not think of him inside me. So I concentrated on the other person in the room.

Joey was slouched in his chair, swiveling it back and forth, with a Nintendo Switch in her hands. She'd probably been playing while Ford had been busy with the team this morning.

"Hi." I knocked, drawing their attention.

Joey sat up straight, a bright smile lighting up her face as the Nintendo was set aside. "Hey, Millie."

Ford glanced to her, then to me. For the briefest of seconds, I thought I saw pain in his expression. Like this secret was hurting him. But whatever I saw was gone in a snap as he grinned. "Hey, Mills."

"Ready for the game?" I asked them both.

"Yep." Joey popped out of the chair, crossing the room. "Let's go."

"Hold up." Ford held up a finger, reaching for the beanie beside his keyboard. "You need to wear this."

"Oh, yeah." She snatched it from the air as he tossed it over.

"And you have your money."

She nodded. "Yep."

"Gloves?"

"Yes." She patted her coat pocket. "Can we go now?"

"Not even going to wish me good luck?" He smacked a hand to his chest. "Ouch."

Joey flew across the space between them, launching herself into his arms to kiss his cheek. "Good luck."

"Thanks, princess." He kissed her hair. "Be good, okay?"

"I will."

He let her go, then stood, walking over. Ford shoved his hands in his pants pockets, like if he didn't, he'd pull me into his arms too.

"After the game is over, do you want me to bring her here or to the field?"

"Either one," he said. "Thank you."

"Welcome." It took effort not to bury my nose in his shirt, to draw in his cologne and wish him luck with a kiss. "Good luck."

Joey darted into the hallway, leaving us alone for a brief moment.

"You good?" he asked.

"More or less."

Ford reached out, his thumb caressing my cheek. "Tonight?"

I nodded. "Tonight."

Joey was bouncing on her feet when I joined her in the hallway, and even though we had nearly an hour before we needed to be in the stadium, we set off in that direction.

"So . . ." Was it stupid to ask about school? Maybe she hated it here, and I'd just be bringing up a sore subject. Why hadn't I had Ford prep me for this? We'd spent our nights giving each other orgasms, not updates.

"So . . . what?" she asked, those blue eyes staring up at me.

"Um, nothing." I waved it off. "How is, uh . . ."

What was the nanny's name? Was that a safe topic? Or did Joey resent the fact that she had to have a nanny because her mother was noticeably absent?

"How is what?" Joey asked, this time giving me a sideways glance. "Are you okay?"

I loosened a breath. "I'm nervous."

"For the game? Dad never admits it but he gets nervous too. He, like, can't stop moving around the house and stuff."

"I know how he feels," I muttered. "And no, I'm not nervous for the game. I mean, I want them to win, but that's not what's making me nervous."

"Then what is?"

"You."

Joey's eyebrows came together. "Me? Why?"

"I want you to have fun today. With me. I guess . . ." This was pathetic. I was pathetic. "I want you to like me," I blurted.

Her cheeks flushed as she gave me a shy smile. "I like you. A lot."

"Really?" This girl had no idea how much I needed to hear that. "I like you a lot too."

A man rushed in front of us waving a pom-pom and wearing a football helmet. When he spotted us, he stopped, dropped to a squat and roared, "Go Big Blue!"

Joey and I stared at him.

"Woo!" the man screamed, then jogged away to attack some other people with his Wildcat spirit.

Joey and I stared at one another for a long moment, then burst out laughing.

It was okay. We were okay.

"They have the best hot chocolate and cookies at the stadium," I told her.

"Better than your cookies? No way."

"Aww. Thanks." I smiled down at her, reaching to take her hand. "Come on. Let's get loaded up on sugar and find our seats."

By halftime, Joey and I had shared two cookies, two hot cocoas and more laughs than I could count. The Wildcats were ahead by ten, and even though it wasn't a blowout, the crowd acted like victory was already in the bag. The faith in this team, in Ford, was glorious.

"Hot dog or pizza?" I asked Joey as we headed to the concession stand for the third time.

"Pizza," she said.

"That's what I want too." I led her to the line, my cheeks pinching from smiling so much. I was just about to move up and order when I heard my name.

"Millie." Kurt came walking my way.

Oh, shit. My smile dropped. My shoulders stiffened. "Hey, Kurt."

"Thought you weren't going to be here today."

Technically, I hadn't told him I wasn't going to be here. I'd just told him I wasn't going to work. "No, I'm here. Just not working."

He frowned, his eyes darting to Joey. Then he did a double take, like he'd forgotten who she was and was just realizing it now. "Is that . . . Joey, right?"

She nodded, looking between the two of us.

"Yes, this is Ford's daughter. I'm hanging with her at today's game."

Kurt, like me, didn't have a poker face. Either he was mad that I hadn't shared every detail of my weekend agenda, or he was irritated that I'd brought Ford's daughter. Probably both.

A muscle in his jaw ticked. "We could have had one of the students sit with her."

Joey could hear him. He realized that, right? That kids had ears?

"I wanted to bring her today." I put my arm around Joey's shoulders, not wanting her to feel like she was an inconvenience. "This was my idea."

His mouth flattened in a thin line just as someone called his name.

"I'll let you get back to it," I said, spinning Joey for the concession stand. When she gave him a sideways glance, I just smiled and shuffled her forward. Then I turned my back to my boss, feeling his glare on my head.

I ordered our pizzas and drinks, then risked a glance over my shoulder. Kurt was gone. The air rushed from my lungs.

Had I done anything wrong? No. Would I still get a lecture on Monday morning? Undoubtedly.

My stomach was in free fall, but I plastered on a smile, not wanting it to put a damper on Joey's day. We returned to our seats, we ate our pizza, and I pretended like everything was perfect. When the Wildcats won, I clapped and cheered, ignoring the dread swimming in my veins.

I wasn't doing anything wrong. Well, as far as Kurt knew. But he'd warned me away from Ford already. To find me with Ford's daughter . . .

Oh, I was in trouble.

"Can we go on the field?" Joey asked the moment the game was over.

"Sure," I said, taking her hand to lead her through the crush.

We reached the gated entrance, and I flashed my access pass to security, then slipped onto the field, where the teams were still shaking hands.

Joey followed me as we weaved past players toward the man in the center of the field. "Daddy!" she hollered when she spotted Ford, then took off running.

The smile on his face was blinding. He bent, arms wide when she rushed over. Then he swept her into a hug.

He asked her something, his mouth by her ear so she could hear over the noise. She pointed my direction and he followed her finger.

The smile he sent me was equally devastating. Carefree. Victorious. Handsome. My heart skipped.

"Good game," I said. "You're on a winning streak."

"Thanks, baby." Ford leaned in, like he was about to kiss me.

And for a split second, I was going to let him. Kissing him was as natural as breathing. I'd been doing it for a month.

Then the noise registered. So did Joey, clinging to his side.

And I pulled away. One step. Then two.

Baby. He'd called me baby in front of his daughter.

I glanced around. Both Toren and Parks were close. Had they overheard? Had any of the players?

I took another step away, glancing at Ford.

His jaw clenched. Either because he realized his mistake, or because he knew what I was about to do.

After a quick wave to Joey, I turned around.

And jogged away.

CHAPTER TWENTY-SEVEN

FORD

"Did you have a good time at the game with Millie?" I asked Joey as we drove home.

"Yeah, it was really fun." She met my eyes through the rearview mirror. "Daddy?"

"Joey?"

Her forehead furrowed. "Why did you call her baby? And why did she run away?"

So she had noticed. *Damn.*

I'd hoped that during the commotion after the game, maybe Joey hadn't heard my slipup. Or that in the excitement afterward, meeting with the team before walking back to the fieldhouse, she would have spaced it.

Of course she hadn't. This was my daughter, the girl who remembered every promise made—and broken.

Sienna would suffer the consequences of Joey's memory one of these days. But that was her problem to handle. At the moment, I had my own.

My problem's name was Millicent Cunningham.

Damn it, I'd messed up. I'd been so caught up in the win, in seeing Millie and Joey together on the field, that I'd forgotten we'd been standing in a sea of people. That there were cameras and fans. That too many eyes had been aimed my way.

Millie's smile had blocked out the world. So I'd called her baby. And I'd leaned in to kiss her.

I was so sick of hiding this, especially from my daughter. It felt like a betrayal to let Millie into our home each night and keep that a secret from Joey.

Though, I guess that was over now. Joey sat quietly, waiting for my answer.

"I like Millie." Like was an understatement. "A lot."

"Is she your girlfriend?"

"Would that be okay with you?"

She nodded. "Yeah."

No hesitation.

I loved my kid.

Her answer wasn't a surprise, but I released the breath I'd been holding. "There's just one thing, princess. Millie and I work together. So her being my girlfriend? It's a secret. You can't tell anyone."

"Not even Stephanie?"

I shook my head. "Not even Stephanie."

Asking Joey to keep a secret grated on my nerves, but it wasn't like we had another choice. Millie's job depended on it. So did mine.

There hadn't been any complaints in the past month. I'd made sure that anyone watching could only say I was working my ass off as head coach. But I wasn't out of the woods. By the end of the season, if Kurt didn't think I was a good fit for the TSU program, there'd be no contract renewal. My head would be on the chopping block.

Just as long as it was mine, not Millie's, I'd deal with whatever outcome.

So I'd ask my daughter to keep this a secret, for a little while, and hope like hell nothing slipped.

Millie wasn't going to like it. After this morning's conversation, there was a chance she thought I'd done this on purpose. A chance I'd be sleeping alone tonight. How pissed was she right now?

I turned down our block, ready to be home, ready to have some privacy to call Millie, when I spotted a black Audi parked in my driveway.

"Who's that?" Joey asked, sitting straighter and shifting to look past the seat in front of her.

"I don't know." I hit the button for the garage, trying to peer into the car's windows, but they were tinted. But then I looked at the license plates. "You've got to be fucking kidding," I muttered, easing into the driveway.

Today? She showed up today?

The Audi's door opened. And Sienna stepped out.

"Mom?!" Joey scrambled to unbuckle her seat belt.

"Just wait until I'm parked," I said, pulling into the garage.

The moment the truck's wheels stopped, Joey shoved her door open and flew down the driveway, straight into Sienna's open arms.

My day had started on such a good note. Waking up with Millie's naked body pressed against mine. Then a win for the team. My good day was unraveling. Fast.

"Would it kill her to call first?" I grumbled, shoving out

of the truck and walking out of the garage, tucking my hands into my pockets to keep them warm.

Joey clung to her mother as Sienna stroked her hair.

When she saw me coming down the driveway, Sienna offered a small smile. "Hi, Ford."

"Sienna."

She'd taken out her hair extensions since our last Face-Time. Gone were the long, straight blond strands that had fallen to her waist. Now her bob, curled in loose waves, brushed the tops of her shoulder blades. Other than that, she looked the same. A lot like Joey.

"How are you?" she asked me.

"Good." I lifted a shoulder. "Coming in?" For Joey's sake, I needed her answer to be yes. For mine, a no would suffice.

"Yes."

"Excellent."

Her eyes narrowed at the lie, but she covered it with a smile for Joey as she ran her fingers through our daughter's hair.

"How long are you here?" Joey asked her.

"Let's talk about it inside." Sienna nodded to the house.

Joey snatched Sienna's hand, holding it tight. She was probably afraid Sienna would disappear soon. A valid fear. "Want to see my room?"

"Sure." Sienna let Joey tug her in while I stood in my cold driveway, letting my breath turn into white clouds.

I dug my phone from my pocket and pulled up Millie's name, typing out a text I would have sent hours ago if not for the chaos after the game.

Sorry

I stared at the screen for a few long moments, hoping I'd get a quick reply. Nothing.

Yep, she was mad.

So I retreated to the warm house, finding Sienna with Joey in her bedroom. "How about pizza for dinner?" I asked.

Joey's blue eyes, brimming with hope, shot to Sienna's in a silent plea for her to stay.

"Would you order me a salad, please?" Sienna asked.

"Yep." Without another word, I strode for the living room, sitting on the couch to check my phone again. There still wasn't a text from Millie, so I dialed her number, the call going straight to voicemail.

"Hey, it's me. Call me when you can. I'm sorry. About earlier. I wasn't thinking and just . . ." I pinched the bridge of my nose. "Call me, okay?"

After ending the message, I ordered dinner from a local pizza place. Then I kicked off my tennis shoes, willing my phone to ring with Millie's name on the screen.

Instead, Sienna emerged from the hallway, joining me in the living room. Joey trailed not far behind, like she didn't want to let her mother out of her sight.

"Sorry I didn't call first," Sienna said, taking the chair closest to the fireplace while Joey perched on its stone ledge. "I wasn't sure how the drive would go today."

"It's fine," I lied.

That earned me another narrowing of Sienna's eyes. We'd learned to lie to each other during our marriage. We'd learned to spot them too.

"It was a last-minute decision to visit," she said.

"Did you get a hotel? I can make a few calls while we wait for dinner if you haven't yet." No way she was staying here.

Sienna didn't miss my lack of an invitation. But she must have expected it because she sat straighter. "I actually found a vacation rental."

Vacation rentals usually meant long-term visits. I swallowed a groan. "How long are you in Montana?"

Joey stared at her mother, unblinking, that hope so vivid and bright in her blue eyes.

If Sienna crushed it, we'd have the fight to end all fights. I was done letting her hurt our daughter.

"Two or three weeks," Sienna said, giving Joey a small smile. "I missed you too much."

"I missed you too." Joey stood from the fireplace and went to sit on Sienna's lap.

"And Jordan?" I asked. "Will he be visiting?"

Sienna shook her head. "He's got a busy month."

Meaning the Seahawks had a string of away games and he'd be on the road. Now the timing of this visit made sense. Or maybe there was trouble between them. I didn't give a damn enough to ask.

"And your show?" I asked.

"On a filming break."

As long as a camera crew hadn't followed her here, I also didn't give a shit.

"Well"—I smacked my palms on my knees and stood—"think I'll take a quick shower while we wait for dinner. Warm up from the game."

Sienna and Joey had their heads bent together, whispering and giggling, as I walked out of the room.

By the time I emerged from the shower, dressed in a pair of sweats, the delivery driver had texted they were on their way. And still, nothing from Millie.

I growled, gripping my phone tight, wishing I could

squeeze out a reply like juice from an orange. But it stayed silent all the way through dinner.

While Sienna peppered Joey with questions about school and friends and volleyball, I ate pizza to keep my mouth occupied so I wouldn't say something I'd regret. Like the fact that Sienna should have been asking those questions for weeks.

She should already know Joey had volleyball practice on Tuesdays and Thursdays. She should already know Joey's two favorite friends were Maddy with a *y* and Maddie with an *ie*. Sienna should already know Joey loved her teacher and, as of two weeks ago, had decided green was better than pink—Maddy with a *y* was to thank for that change. At least we hadn't painted her room yet.

But Sienna didn't know any of that because her phone calls had become more and more sporadic. Her absence had been as noticeable as the change in weather.

Until now, apparently.

I wasn't holding my breath that this trip of hers would last two or three weeks. Maybe she'd surprise me. Maybe, for once, our daughter would take priority over Sienna's thirst for fame.

Once dinner was over, I did the dishes while Joey took her shower. Then she stole Sienna away to her room until well past nine, when I went in to say good night.

Joey didn't beg Sienna to stay with us, maybe because she knew it would be a hard no. Or maybe my girl was a little bit hurt still that her mother was just now visiting after we'd lived in Montana for months.

"See you tomorrow," Sienna said.

"Bye, Mom." Joey yawned. "Night, Daddy."

"Night, princess." I blew her another kiss, then closed her door.

Sienna stood in the hallway, a look on her face I'd seen before. A look I didn't like. "Can we talk for a few minutes?"

Yep, this wasn't going to be good.

"What's up?" I asked, walking past her. I didn't stop in the living room, but moved straight for the entryway, ready to show her out as soon as this little chat was over.

Millie still hadn't texted, and if it took me calling her all night so we could talk, well . . . so be it.

"I've been thinking about our custody arrangement," Sienna said, crossing her arms over her chest.

"What about it?"

"I'd like to spend more time with Joey."

"No one is stopping you."

She rolled her eyes. "You live in Montana."

"Really," I deadpanned.

"Ford," she snapped. "I'm telling you I want more time with my daughter."

"Then move."

"I can't move." She huffed. "You know that."

"Why do you want more time now? Why not when we lived in Seattle? Why not when we were going through the divorce? Why wait until we're settled somewhere new to decide you want to be more active in Joey's life?"

"I've missed her."

I narrowed my gaze. It wasn't entirely a lie. Sienna seemed genuine. But there was more to this request. More to this trip.

"We can't do this forever," she said.

"Then. Move."

Her nostrils flared. "You're asking me to give up my entire life."

"For your daughter. Yes. Yes, I am."

"My work is in Seattle."

"Really? Because I was under the impression you could post on social media from just about anywhere on Planet Earth."

"I have my show."

"That show was your choice. You knew exactly what you'd be giving up when you took it on, so don't use it as an excuse."

Sienna tossed up her hands. "I knew this conversation would be pointless. We either do things your way or not at all."

"That's the beauty of having full custody of our daughter." I leaned in closer, pointing a finger at my chest. "*I'm* in charge."

She jutted up her chin. "I've been talking to a lawyer."

"Do not threaten me, Sienna."

Her bravado disintegrated like a snowflake in hell at the harsh edge to my voice. "I just wanted to know my options."

"You have no options." I'd fight. I'd fight her ruthlessly.

After her behavior before and after the divorce, it was unlikely a judge would give her partial custody of Joey. But it wasn't beyond the realm of possibility. The idea of a custody battle made my stomach churn, but I kept my temper on its leash.

"By all means, talk to a lawyer. It's your money to piss away. This lawyer of yours can contact my attorney if he or she has questions."

"Or we could figure this out together."

"No."

"Ford." Her jaw clenched as she sneered my name.

"Sienna."

She could glare at me all she wanted. I wouldn't change my mind. "You're so stubborn."

"When it comes to what's best for Joey, damn straight, I'm stubborn." I reached for the door, wrenching it open. "Good night."

She took a step, like she was about to leave, but she paused, turning back. "I left my phone in Joey's room."

"Stay here." I held up a hand, stopping her before she could go for it. "I'll get it."

I didn't trust her to be around Joey at the moment. The last thing I needed was for her to march into our daughter's room, wake Joey up and do something stupid. Like blame me for her shitty parenting. Or ask a nine-year-old girl if she wanted to fly back and forth across two states to split time with her parents.

Mostly, I feared that Joey might say yes.

Then I'd have to tell her no too.

I strode through the house and slipped into Joey's room. Sienna's phone was on the nightstand so I snatched it up and left as quietly as I'd entered, retreating to the entryway.

Sienna had closed the front door.

So I opened it for her again.

"It's good to see you, Ford," she said, her voice dripping with honey.

Was this some new tactic? Maybe that sultry purr worked on Jordan but it sure as fuck wouldn't work on me.

But before I could tell her to get the fuck out, Sienna slid a hand up my chest, placing her palm over my heart. Then kissed the underside of my jaw.

I reared away. "What the—"

"Night, babe."

Babe? Was she high?

Sienna plucked her phone from my hand, then walked outside.

I tracked her steps, not sure what that goodbye was about.

Until I looked past Sienna's car.

And saw Millie standing in the cold.

CHAPTER TWENTY-EIGHT

MILLIE

I hated her.

I hated her with every fiber of my being.

Sienna wore the same snide smirk I remembered from college as she walked to her car. *Bitch.*

But ten years later, and I still didn't have the guts to say it aloud. Instead, I stood on the sidewalk in front of Ford's house, stuck, as she walked to her Audi and climbed inside. It wasn't until she'd reversed to the street that I faced Ford.

Sienna had kissed him. I zeroed in on his jaw, fury burning through my veins that she'd put her lips on his skin.

Was that how Ford had felt when Adrian had kissed me? No wonder he'd been so pissed that night.

"Millie." Ford's voice carried across his frozen lawn.

I unglued my feet and crossed the walkway, stopping on the stoop. Had it just been this morning that we'd talked in this exact spot? It felt like a lifetime ago.

Ford stared at me for a long moment, jerking his chin toward the house. "Are you coming in?"

If I stepped past the threshold, he'd kiss me. And if he

kissed me, I'd lose the nerve to do what I'd come here to do. To hit pause.

It was time to pause.

After the game, I'd gone home to my empty house. I'd immediately changed into some running gear and raced outside. It had taken every step of the ten miles I'd run, my body sweating, my breath freezing, to sort through my feelings. To find a sense of calm. Of direction.

Through stretching, through my shower, through the drive to Ford's, I'd kept that peace.

All it had taken was a single look at Sienna and now I wanted to scream.

I hated her.

Oh, how I hated her.

I hated that I'd once considered her my greatest friend. I hated that she'd turned out to be so awful. I hated that she'd had Ford for so long. I hated that she'd been his wife. I hated that he'd chosen her over me.

I hated that she'd won.

Would it always be this way? Would I always feel like second place?

"I'm sorry about earlier, Mills." Ford sighed. "Just come inside so we can talk about this."

It took every ounce of my resolve not to budge. "I got your text. And voicemail."

"But you're still mad."

"No." I shook my head. No, I wasn't mad. I hadn't even been mad at the stadium. "I'm just . . ." Defeated. So entirely defeated.

We couldn't keep hiding from the world. This was never going to work between us, not without a sacrifice. Ford Ellis was the Treasure State University head football coach. I was an assistant athletics director.

Until one of those facts changed, we'd always be a secret.

"Just what?" Ford took a step closer but he stopped short. Maybe he sensed that I needed those three feet between us. Or maybe I'd reinforced my walls so thoroughly that they kept him back.

"Did you tell Joey?" I asked.

He nodded.

"Even though I asked you not to," I whispered.

His frame deflated. "I slipped up at the game. Joey noticed. She asked. I won't lie to her."

"I won't ask you to. Not anymore." I gave him a sad smile.

It didn't surprise me at all that Joey had picked up on Ford's endearment. She was too smart, too observant. Who else had noticed us today?

There had been cameras around. Had that interaction been caught on video? One clip was all it would take for Kurt to fire me. Then what?

"We can't keep doing this," I said, bracing myself when Ford's expression turned to granite.

"What are you saying, Millie?"

"I'm saying . . ." My heart climbed into my throat. "I'm saying that we need to press pause."

"*Pause.*" Ford spoke that word with such disgust it made me cringe. "No. What the fuck does pause even mean?"

"Ford, we jumped into this, running full-steam ahead. It means we slow down. It means we take a breather."

He grumbled something under his breath, his hands raking through his hair. "You've got to be fucking kidding me."

"I'm not asking for forever. Just until the football season is over."

His hands balled into fists. "That's a month or more. No. It's too long. I'm not *pausing* this for over a month."

I loved him for that. I loved him for a lot more.

I'd been in love with him for over a decade. Those feelings hadn't vanished, they'd just gone into hibernation.

They'd stirred awake the day he'd returned to Mission.

"I don't know what else to do, Ford."

"I do." He crashed through my invisible wall, his hands going to my face, his fingertips threading into my hair. "I do, Millie. I do. We figure this out together."

My heart. It cracked as my chin began to quiver. "After my dad died, I got lost. Dad was the person who believed in me most. He was *my* pilot. Mom was always so tight with Macie. They clung together after Dad, and I drifted along until graduation."

Ford was one of the few people at TSU who knew about Dad. But even this wasn't something I'd shared.

"When I came here, I started to find myself. To find my footing. Sienna was a big part of that. She was my friend. She was my roommate. I loved her once. The way she treated me, dismissed me, was like running at full speed and being tripped."

"If this is about what Sienna did tonight—"

"It's not." I shook my head. "It's not about her at all. I realized soon enough I didn't need or want her as a friend. Especially after I met you. But then you left and . . ." And I'd been in the dirt once more.

Ford sighed, dropping his forehead to mine. "Millie."

"I've built this whole life for myself. I look in the mirror and I know my dad would be so proud." My eyes flooded.

"But a big part of that is my job. I will give it up, Ford. I will give it up for you. But give me a month to say goodbye to the job I love. Give me a month to figure out who I am without the career I've built."

He let me go but held my gaze. "I know who you are. You're brilliant. You're beautiful. You're smart and sassy. You love football arguably more than I do. You never shy away from a bet. You're capable of anything and everything. You are my Millie. That's who you are. And I don't want to go a month without you."

"Ford—"

"Why do you have to let your job go? You're not the only one in this. I'll quit. I'll resign as coach."

I reached up, placing my hand over his heart. "No."

"Why not?"

"Joey. If she's settling here, you can't uproot her again. And because I don't know what would be sadder. Me, not working as a Wildcat. Or me, not being able to cheer for you on the sidelines."

Ford growled, frustration vibrating in his bones, until he hauled me into his chest, holding me so tight it nearly hurt. "This is ridiculous."

"Not to me." I breathed in the smell of his soap and natural spice, soaking in that scent to tide me over for the next month. "How long is Sienna here?"

"She said two or three weeks."

"Then this is perfect. We'll pause while she's here. Until the end of the season."

Another angry growl rumbled from his chest.

"I don't trust her," I said. "If she learns that we're hiding our relationship, I don't trust her not to share it."

"Fuck." He blew out a long breath. "Neither do I."

"So maybe this is good timing. Give Joey a chance to spend time with her mom. Finish the season. Then we'll figure out the rest."

I knew I'd struck the right chord when Ford's body sagged, just slightly, but enough to know I was making my point.

"What happens after the season?" he asked.

"I'll go to Kurt. Tell him we're together." Then promptly get fired.

Maybe I'd get lucky. Maybe this would work out. Maybe I just needed to hold on to hope.

"This is a horrible fucking idea," Ford muttered, letting me go to drag both hands over his face.

"It's not like we won't see each other."

His hands dropped. Behind them was a frown. "Millie."

"It's not forever." I took a step away. "See you at work, Coach."

It was painful to return to my car. My heart squeezed with every step.

If we got caught, the outcome would be the same. I'd lose my job. Except if I had to go, it would be on my terms. So I kept walking, one foot in front of the other.

Ford stood watching as I climbed inside the Kia.

But he let me go.

And we took our pause.

CHAPTER TWENTY-NINE

FORD

I slammed the recruiting notebook closed, dropping my elbows to the desk and burying my face in my palms. My jaw was scruffy, the hairs scratching against my skin. I hadn't bothered shaving today. Or yesterday.

Last night, unable to sleep, I'd stayed up watching film until three. Finally, I'd crashed on the couch only to sleep through my six o'clock alarm. Luckily, my body had jolted awake at six thirty, so I'd managed to get ready in time. Joey had been pissed that I'd woken her up late, so after demanding an alarm clock for her own room, she'd hustled to get dressed.

By some miracle, I'd dropped her off in time for school, then hurried to get to work myself.

A yawn stretched my mouth, and I shook my head, hoping it would wake me up. It didn't.

Dead. I was absolutely dead on my feet.

And it was Millie's fault. She was the reason I hadn't slept well in the past month. No, this *pause* was the reason.

I'd gotten used to her in my bed, and now that it was empty, I couldn't seem to shut off my mind.

Fuck, but I missed her. More and more each day. I was a wreck without her. If not for the team, the coaches and players counting on me, I would have marched my ass up to Kurt's office and handed in my resignation.

But I'd honored her request. I'd stayed away. I'd given her time. And I'd focused on doing my job.

This morning, after the disastrous start at home, I'd spent a grueling hour on a conference call to review upcoming changes to a few NCAA regulations. Then I'd spent the rest of my hours before lunch weeding through the recruiting notebook and reading about potential players. If I did end up leaving the Wildcats, I wanted to position them for a solid season next year. We had a pretty large group of seniors who'd be graduating. But the sophomores and juniors were solid. This year's freshmen had potential. I'd like to be able to say the same next fall.

Work had become my salvation. My distraction.

Would Millie really quit her job? Could she walk away? Could I let her?

My biggest fear at the moment was that, after this month, she'd decide I wasn't worth the hassle. I meant what I'd told her. If quitting as coach meant keeping Millie, I'd turn in my resignation today.

Why hadn't I already?

I hated this pause. I knew exactly how to end it.

I just . . . couldn't. Not yet.

I'd told myself I'd give it a year. I owed it to the coaches. To the players. I owed it to myself. Millie wasn't the only one who needed time to say goodbye to a career.

Who was I without football?

The answer to that question scared the shit out of me.

My phone rang. For a brief moment, I hoped it was Millie. I always hoped it was Millie. But when I snatched it up, it was Sienna's name on the screen.

"Hello," I answered.

"Hi. I was hoping to take Joey to dinner after volleyball practice tonight."

"Okay."

"Could she spend the night with me?"

"It's a school night." Meaning no.

She huffed on the other end of the line. "Fine."

"Anything else?"

Without answering my question, she ended the call.

"Guess not," I muttered.

Sienna hadn't brought up shared custody or her lawyer again. In a month, not a peep. Which should have been a relief but had only put me on guard, especially since she'd extended her stay in Montana not once, but twice. Instead of a two- or three-week visit, she'd stayed a month and was now planning on returning to Seattle next week.

When I'd asked why, Sienna had insisted she was simply making up time lost with Joey. I'd wanted to believe her. For Joey's sake, I'd wanted that sentiment from her mother.

But Sienna and I had known each other for too long. So I'd made a few calls to some friends in Seattle. The gossip I had was secondhand at best, coming from a former teammate's wife. Still, my gut said it was true.

The rumor floating around the Seahawks universe was that Jordan hadn't exactly been faithful to Sienna. No surprise. He hadn't had any issue sleeping with her when she'd been my wife.

So she'd come to Montana because her life in Washington was in shambles.

Maybe Sienna didn't want to face that sort of humiliation on her reality show. Hell, maybe it had all been staged for the reality show.

None of it really mattered.

For Joey, her mother was here, showering her with attention. Sure, Joey was second priority. But she hadn't figured that out yet. I hoped for my girl's precious heart, she never did.

As long as Sienna didn't try to pull some stunt to convince Joey that traveling back and forth between Mission and Seattle was a good idea, I'd tolerate Sienna's presence.

But after the stunt Sienna had pulled with Millie a month ago, kissing me, I'd made exactly zero effort to do anything asked by my ex-wife.

It was nearly lunch time but the peanut butter and jelly sandwich I'd stowed in the staff lounge's refrigerator held no appeal. So I collected the backpack I'd brought along this morning and headed for the locker room.

A punishing, daily workout had become part of my routine over the past month. Something to break a sweat. Something to clear my head. Though I would have much preferred daily sex with Millie over an hour spent lifting and doing cardio.

"What the fuck does taking a pause even mean?" I asked myself as I changed into a pair of shorts and a T-shirt.

"What was that, Coach?"

I whirled around as Rush Ramsey walked my way, dressed similarly to hit the weight room. "Oh, nothing. How's it going?"

"Good. I had a break between classes. Thought I'd come lift."

"I'm headed that way myself," I said, walking toward the weight room. "Everything going okay?"

Rush shrugged. "I guess."

"Need to talk anything through?"

"I, uh . . . I think today, I'll just lift."

So Rush had come to the gym to shut off his mind too. "You know where I am if you change your mind."

"Thanks, Coach."

I nodded, pulling my earbuds from my shorts pocket. Then I cranked up some music and spent the next sixty minutes pushing my body to the extreme.

By the time I quit, sweat dripped down my face and my muscles were on fire. Maybe tonight, I'd actually be able to sleep.

I snagged a towel from the rack, drying my forehead, then walked to the drinking fountain. But before I could guzzle some water, the door to the weight room opened.

And the woman of my dreams, of my current nightmare, stepped inside.

Millie pulled up short when she spotted me. "Oh, uh . . . hi."

She wore a pair of black slacks and a floral-print blouse. The reds and oranges of the shirt were different for her. Brighter. Bolder. I was used to seeing her in neutral shades, but the warmer colors brought out the caramel and gold flecks in her eyes.

Beautiful, my Millie. Absolutely fucking beautiful.

I wanted to kiss her. I balled my hands into fists instead. Goddamn it, I hated this.

"Hi." It came out angrier than I'd intended. Or not. I was

pissed that I missed her and pissed that she'd made a lot of good points last month and pissed that I hadn't been able to change her mind and, well . . . I was just pissed.

She'd asked for time, but when that time was up, would she come to me? Would I have to chase her down?

I would. If that was what it took, I'd chase her down.

I'd quit my job as coach. I'd give up football. I'd turn my life upside down.

That was how much I wanted Millie.

Metal weights clanged across the room. Millie glanced past me to where Rush was positioning a bar on his traps, about to do a set of squats.

"You, um . . ." She cleared her throat, then forced a too wide smile that didn't reach those pretty hazel eyes. God, I'd missed nights staring into those eyes. "Away game this weekend?"

"Yep." That came out snappy too.

She pulled that bottom lip between her teeth, worrying it for a moment. Then she stood taller, squaring her shoulders. "Good luck, Ford."

I huffed. I didn't need luck. I needed her. What the hell did I have to do to prove that?

Without another word, Millie turned, about to escape through the door.

"Mills," I said.

"Yeah?" She stopped, turning back.

I sighed, taking a step closer so only she could hear. "I miss you."

Her eyes flooded. "I miss you too."

It was something.

Just not enough.

Millie opened the door and walked away.

CHAPTER THIRTY

MILLIE

My fingers flew across my phone's screen as I typed out a furious reply to Kurt's latest email about next year's budget. "Why does he always want to cut from *my* programs?"

Every day this week I'd had to fight for my teams. Monday, volleyball. Tuesday, tennis. Wednesday, cross country. Thursday, indoor track and field. And today, golf. If I didn't advocate for the smaller programs, who would?

But arguing with Kurt had become an outlet to my misery. The past month without Ford had been the worst in a long, long time.

"I only have myself to blame," I muttered, storming down a hallway at the fieldhouse, my heels clicking hard on the floor. I rounded a corner and slammed into a wall that hadn't been there yesterday.

A six-foot-something wall made of solid muscle.

He didn't budge as we collided.

I bounced off his large frame.

"Eep!" My ankle twisted as I lost my balance.

But Rush stretched to grab my arm before I could fall on my butt. "Shit. Sorry."

I righted my feet, waving it off. "No, my fault. I wasn't watching where I was going."

Rush was dressed in a pair of royal blue warm-ups, the Wildcat logo stitched into both the jacket and pants. Over one shoulder, he carried a duffel bag.

"Taking off for the bus?" I asked.

Two buses, to be exact, that would drive the team to the airport where they'd fly to Idaho for their away game tomorrow.

"Yeah. But I'm early."

"I used to always be the first person on the bus because then I got to pick whatever seat I wanted." I shifted out of the way so he could head outside. "Good luck this weekend."

"Thank you." Rush dipped his chin but before he could leave, Faye rounded the corner.

She was hurrying and her cheeks were flushed, like she'd been running. "Oh. Um, hi . . ."

"Millie," I said.

"I remember." She nodded, then glanced at Rush, pulling out a phone from her pocket. "Here. You forgot this on the counter."

"Shit." He shifted his bag, patting the front pocket. "Thanks for bringing it."

"Yeah." Faye handed it over.

Rush took his phone, then reached for her, like he was going to touch her shoulder or arm. But before he could, she shied away. Her eyes dropped to the floor. His spirits seemed to join them beside their feet.

"Better get on the bus," he muttered, then walked away.

I waited until he was gone, then gave Faye a sad smile. "How's it going?"

She shrugged, looking over her shoulder to make sure no one else was around. But the hallway was empty except for us. "Kind of . . . bad."

"Sorry."

"We moved in together. I was living with my ex-boyfriend, but when he found out about us, the baby, he kicked me out."

"Oof. Jerkface."

"Pretty much."

"How is living with Rush?"

She shrugged again. "Awkward? We argue a lot."

These poor kids. "You both have a lot to navigate. I'd say arguing is expected. Give it time."

"Yeah." The hopelessness in her gaze twisted my heart.

"He told me not to get a paternity test. That he didn't need one." She stood a little taller. "I wouldn't lie about something like this."

"I believe you."

Faye's frame deflated. "It's just temporary. Us living together."

"Does it have to be? Rush seems like a nice guy. I don't know him very well, but I get the impression he's trying to do the right thing."

"He is." She wrapped her arms around her waist. "I don't think . . . It will be better if we keep some boundaries between us. Easier, I think."

"Okay."

She took a step back, giving me a sad smile. "I've got class."

"Bye, Faye."

"Bye." She hurried away, her chin ducked and that strawberry-blond hair a curtain around her face.

That girl was terrified, wasn't she? If she'd had walls around her heart the last time I'd seen her, she'd since reinforced them with locks and chains. All to protect herself from Rush when he seemed like all he wanted to do was break through. To help. To care.

She was too scared to let him in. So instead, she'd push. She'd keep him at arm's length.

Just like I was doing with Ford.

Oh my God. Faye and I weren't all that different, were we?

Ford wanted commitment, and I'd found a way to shut him out by taking this *pause*.

A pause. Where had I come up with that idiotic brainchild? Ford was more important than my career.

Deep down, I knew that my job had just been an excuse. The problem wasn't unemployment. It was fear. I'd let my fears and insecurities take control.

I was so scared Ford wouldn't choose me. That he'd leave. But he'd already chosen me. He wasn't leaving me behind. Not this time.

What was I doing?

"What am I doing?"

I missed Ford. I missed him so much I ached. Why had I thought this break would be a good idea? Secrecy was better than this.

I spun around so quickly I almost careened into the actual wall, but I shoved off and jogged down the hallway toward Ford's office.

The door to the locker room opened and a line of players emerged, all dressed in the same warm-ups as Rush. They stopped and stared at me as I raced by, but I dismissed them and hurried past the line of offices.

I skidded to a stop outside of Ford's dark, empty office. Where was he? His chair was pushed into his desk and only a hint of his cologne clung to the air.

Was he already on the bus?

I whirled and, for the second time today, ran into a body. This time, it was Toren.

"Everything okay?" he asked. "You came flying by my door like the building was on fire."

"Where's Ford? I need to talk to him."

A knowing smirk spread across his mouth. "About time. He's been a grumpy bastard all month, and I figured it wasn't just because Sienna was in town. Have you seen her yet? How did that reunion go? Ford hasn't told me a damn thing, and every time I ask, he changes the subject."

"Toren," I snapped. "Can we play twenty questions a different day? I want to talk to Ford before you guys leave."

"Fine," he muttered. "He already left for the bus. I was just about to head that way. Let me get my bag and I'll walk—"

Before he could finish his sentence, I breezed past him and raced down the hallway again, weaving past the players all making their way to the parking lot.

When we reached the exit, I fell in line with them, stuck as they all shuffled outside. As soon as I was clear, I shifted out of line, searching for Ford.

Both buses were parked and waiting. Their storage compartments were open and the players dropped off their bags before climbing the stairs and disappearing inside.

I stood on my toes, trying to spot Ford. Where was he? I checked behind me at the door, making sure I hadn't passed him somehow. I was just about to run for a bus to look inside when a familiar stride caught my eye.

Ford rounded the front of the first bus. His hair was trapped beneath a gray Wildcat hat. He had on the same pants as the players, navy with a stripe down the side and the stitched logo. But instead of the matching jacket, he wore a gray pullover that molded to his broad chest.

He said something to the guys waiting to climb on the bus. They all nodded, then jogged up the steps, moving faster than they had been.

Then he took up the spot behind them, about to climb those stairs too.

"Ford," I called.

He stopped, twisting to stare at me over his shoulder.

My heart hammered as his eyes locked on mine.

In my rush to find him, I hadn't thought at all about what to say. There were twenty feet between us. I guess that gave me twenty feet to figure it out.

I steeled my spine, about to walk over, when the door behind me clattered open.

"Guess we had the same idea, Millie." Kurt stopped at my side. "Came to see the team off?"

"Oh, um. Yeah." *Damn.* So much for talking to Ford. I guess this wasn't really the place for a serious conversation anyway.

When I looked back at the bus, Ford's blue eyes were waiting. A million words hung between us.

They'd all have to wait.

Kurt left my side and walked to Ford, hand extended. Whatever he said, Ford simply nodded as Kurt smacked him on the shoulder.

I doubted anyone but me noticed the clench in Ford's

jaw. The coolness in his gaze as Kurt went to the other bus, jogging up the stairs.

Ford's gaze found mine again.

A breeze swept through the air, carrying the scent of pine trees and the promise of snow.

Football weather. And Ford had a plane to catch.

So I lifted a hand in the air.

He lifted his too, giving me a small nod. Then he faced forward and climbed the stairs for the bus.

CHAPTER THIRTY-ONE

MILLIE

"Throw it!" I screamed at the TV, my hands diving into my hair to tug at the strands. If I had any hair left by the end of this game, it would be a miracle.

Rush searched for an open receiver, but they were all covered. He lifted the ball, about to launch it, but a defensive end broke free from the line, barreling toward Rush for a sack.

"Run!"

Rush tucked the ball and took off, trying to break free, but one moment he was on his feet, the next slamming into the turf. He'd lost two yards.

"Damn it."

Fourth down with twelve to go.

The score was twenty-one to three. For the first time all season, we were getting our asses kicked.

The offense jogged off the field and special teams came on to punt. Ford was probably going to catch flack for not taking a fourth-down attempt. But at this point, I think he was just trying to stop the bleeding.

"It's been a rough day for the Wildcats," the announcer said. "They've been so dominating thus far this season, but Idaho has just ruled the game today."

"Shut up." I swiped the remote from the coffee table and punched the mute button. Then I paced the living room, barely able to watch the last minute of the game.

It was too painful.

Oh, how I hated to lose.

I risked a look at the screen. The clock was at zero. The Idaho Vandals were celebrating a victory.

"Ugh." I was about to shut the TV off when the picture changed to Ford shaking hands with the Vandals coach.

Ford looked gorgeous in his royal blue jacket. And furious. I wasn't the only one who hated to lose.

I hit the power button and slumped to a seat on the couch.

It felt like a lifetime since I'd watched the buses leave the fieldhouse parking lot yesterday. If time had gone slowly this past month, the past twenty-four hours had been glacial. The next six or eight or however many it took for Ford to get home would be equally as vicious.

My phone rang on the cushion beside me so I picked it up.

"Hi, Mom," I answered.

"Hi, there. How are you?"

If she paid any attention to Wildcat sports, she'd know the answer to that question. "Good," I lied. "You?"

"I'm good. I'm actually at your sister's house. We were just talking about dates for her baby shower."

"Oh, okay." This was Macie's third baby. I hadn't expected Mom to plan another shower, but I'd happily go, just like I had for the previous two. "When are you thinking?"

"January nineteenth. That's a Sunday. I wasn't sure if you had a game or a function you needed to attend."

January was a busy time for basketball, wrestling and skiing. Other sports were wrapping up. Others kicking off. But since I'd likely be unemployed sooner rather than later, I guess that didn't matter. Maybe I could find a job where I had weekends off.

"Sure," I said. "Count me in."

"Great," Mom cheered. "All right, I'd better let you go. We've got some planning to do. It's either going to be safari or circus themed."

Even if they picked safari, this shower would be a circus, just like the previous two. "Both excellent options."

"I want circus. We could do so much with balloons." Mom wasn't speaking to me, but Macie.

"Bye, Mom," I said, ending the call. Then I fell onto my back, staring up at the ceiling.

If I was pregnant someday, would Mom be as excited about planning my baby shower as she was Macie's? *No.*

I was strangely okay with that idea today.

Mom and Macie had a bond. Even if Dad hadn't been killed in that car crash, they would have been this close. Maybe it had never been about Mom choosing Macie over me. That was just what life had gifted them. A daughter—a mother—as a best friend.

Ford would choose me. I'd be his number one. I'd doubted that for ten years, but life had gifted us a second chance.

"Which I immediately screwed up." I groaned, burying my face in my hands.

I twisted to look at the clock on the wall and sighed. It would be hours before Ford got home. I wouldn't be able to sit still, so I pushed up to my feet. A deep clean was in order.

It was after ten by the time my house was spotless.

I snagged my toothbrush from my bathroom and an extra pair of panties from my closet, then climbed in my car to make the drive to Ford's neighborhood.

Most of the lights in his house were off except those in the living room. The driveway was empty, so Joey's nanny must have already left because Ford was home.

I parked on the street, my pulse a dull roar in my ears. Then I collected my purse to hurry across the walkway and knock on the front door. My insides knotted, my breath lodged in my throat, as I waited.

The deadbolt flipped.

But it wasn't Ford who stood in the threshold.

It was Sienna.

She was still in Mission? *Ugh*.

"What are you doing here?" She arched an eyebrow, crossing her arms over her chest.

Once upon a time, that glare of hers had been intimidating. Hurtful.

Now I just found it pathetic. Weak.

So I flashed her a saccharine smile. "Is Ford home yet?"

"No."

I was about to return to my car and wait for him there but stopped myself. Why should she get to stay inside? Before she could block me, I shoved past her through the open door.

She scoffed. "Excuse me. What do you think you're doing? You just can't come in here."

"Oh, get over yourself, Sienna." I rolled my eyes and

unzipped my coat, hanging it on a hook in the entryway. "I'm in Ford's life. I'm not going anywhere. So somehow, you and I will have to figure out how to coexist." Which had been a lot easier when she'd lived in Seattle. When was she leaving?

Sienna huffed, looking to the nearest wall.

What? No comeback? I swallowed the retort because I didn't want to stir up trouble. Besides, for the first time in my life, I knew that if it came down to a fight with Sienna, I'd win.

I'd win Ford, no contest.

I already had.

I'd won him ten years ago.

After toeing off my shoes, I left her in the entryway, moving through the house to the living room. Strange that I'd been here so many times and had never actually sat on the couch.

I took a seat, brushing a hand over the buttery leather. Then I relaxed, breathing in the scent of Ford's home. The smell I'd missed this month.

Sienna, arms still crossed, took a chair beside the couch. "You always wanted him."

"Yep." That wasn't the dig she'd intended it to be. I pulled my phone from my pocket, unlocking the screen with a swipe. "I'm staying here tonight, if you want to take off."

Sienna opened her mouth, but before she could speak, a door opened.

I twisted, rising from the couch as footsteps came our way.

Ford strode through the kitchen, dropping a duffel bag on the island. He must have pulled into the garage when I'd been in the entryway with Sienna, so we hadn't heard him.

His face was unreadable, his jaw granite as he strode to the living room.

He looked pissed, like he had in the weight room on Thursday.

Okay, maybe I should have called first. But if an argument, even one in front of Sienna, was what it took to put us back together, so be it.

I squared my shoulders and kept my gaze locked on his as he rounded the end of the couch.

"Hi, I—"

Ford stretched out a hand, engulfing mine, and with a single tug, he hauled me into his chest. "Hey, baby."

The air rushed from my lungs. I sagged into his hold, my arms sliding around his narrow waist as he wrapped me up tight. Then I buried my nose in his shirt, breathing him in deep. Until every molecule of oxygen in my lungs was coated in Ford.

"Sorry about the game."

He held me closer. "It's all good now."

CHAPTER THIRTY-TWO

FORD

"**F**uck, but I missed you," I murmured against Millie's hair.

She clung to my waist, her face pressed so deep into my shirt I could barely make out the words when she whispered, "Me too."

Sienna's throat cleared.

But I didn't let Millie go. Never again. This fucking pause was over, effective immediately.

"How was Joey?" I asked Sienna, not bothering to look at her as I spoke.

"Fine."

"Great. Have a good night."

Millie's shoulders began to shake with a silent laugh.

"Nice, Ford." Sienna stood, likely shooting me a glare, but she left the room, heading toward the garage, where she'd parked her car. Her suitcase had been waiting by the door too.

She'd asked to stay last night with Joey while I'd been away at the game this weekend. The only reason I'd agreed was because she was leaving for Seattle in the morning, so this sleepover had been a farewell.

Sienna's reality show would resume filming next week, and whatever had been happening with Jordan must have worked itself out because I'd overheard her on the phone this past week talking to him about coming home soon.

There hadn't been another word about changing Joey's custody arrangement. Either Sienna had realized that Joey had a good thing going in Montana, or it had been an idle threat to piss me off. Knowing my ex-wife, I was fairly confident it was the latter.

Sienna would return to the city and be consumed with her moment of fame. And whenever the roller coaster that was her life hit a low point, she'd remember she had a daughter. Whatever. She wasn't the woman I wanted to think about tonight.

I focused on the woman in my arms, loosening my hold to thread my fingers in her hair.

"Hi," she whispered. The gold flecks in her hazel eyes glowed like midnight stars. "We're unpaused."

"About fucking time."

"Not my best idea ever."

"Nope." I chuckled. "My bed, Mills. You're in my bed from here on out. If we need to sneak around for a while, fine. We'll get through this season. But I'm not doing this apart anymore. We're together. Clear?"

The corner of her mouth turned up. "Clear."

I'd made a decision today on the flight home. As soon as this season was over, I'd resign. It wasn't like I needed the money, not with the millions I'd saved from my time with the NFL. It was the game that would be tough to give up. But I'd be a stay-at-home dad, give Joey my fullest attention. Maybe see if the high school needed some volunteer help with their team.

As long as I had my Millie, I didn't need football.

"I love you."

Millie's eyes went wide before they flooded. Then she burst into tears, collapsing against my chest.

"Not exactly the reaction I'd hoped for," I teased, wrapping her up again.

She shook her head, pulling away to swipe at her eyes. "I just didn't expect you to say that."

"Ah." I caught a tear with my thumb at the corner of her eye. "Ready for it now if I say it again?"

She nodded.

"I love you."

Her expression softened. She closed her eyes, soaking in those three words. Then she made my whole goddamn life. "I love you too."

"Look at me," I ordered, waiting until I had those pretty eyes. "Say it again."

She smiled. "I love you."

Ten years. Three words, ten years in the making. They were sweet. So fucking sweet.

I crushed my lips to hers, sliding my tongue inside as she opened for me. I did a lazy swirl, her frame melting against me as I sank into the kiss.

She'd be the last. The last woman I'd kiss until the end of my days. It was Millie. It always had been Millie.

My arms looped around her as she clung to my shoulders, rising up on her toes when I picked her up and carried her away, our mouths fused. When we reached the dark bedroom, I shut the door and flipped the lock. Then we were a mess of frantic hands and sloppy kisses as we stripped each other out of our clothes, leaving a short trail on the floor to the bed.

"My beautiful Millie." My hands roamed her smooth skin, feeling every inch. Then I took her hand, bringing it to my steel cock. "Look at what you do to me."

Her cheeks flushed as she wrapped her fist around me, stroking hard.

I closed my eyes, savoring the feel of her hand while the other reached to cup my sack. "Fuck," I hissed.

Millie shifted, about to drop to her knees, but I stopped her, picking her up so fast she yelped. With a spin, I lifted her to the bed, setting her on her knees. Then I climbed up behind her, letting my cock settle between her cheeks.

Millie moaned, her back falling against my chest as she wiggled her ass.

"You want to suck me off?"

She nodded, reaching a hand back to cup the nape of my neck, pulling my lips to her shoulder.

"Later," I murmured against her skin. "I'm going to fuck you first."

"Ford," she whimpered as I rocked my erection against her ass. One of these days, I'd take her there too. I'd own every inch of this woman's body.

My hands shifted across her ribs, cupping her breasts and tugging hard on her nipples, rolling them between my thumbs and fingers. Then I let her go, planting one hand in her spine to push her forward.

Without any hesitation, I lined up at her slick entrance and thrust home, filling her completely.

"Oh God." She gasped, her inner walls fluttering around my length. "I love you."

I eased out slowly, then with a fast shift of my hips,

buried myself to the root, falling forward against her trembling body. "I love you, Millie. I fucking love you, baby."

"More," she panted. "I need—"

"I know what you need." With an arm banded around her chest, I shoved back up to my knees, bringing her with me. My ass rested against my calves, Millie still impaled and sitting on my cock.

God, I was deep. Deep into this woman and I was never letting her go. Never again.

I rocked out, then in again, gentle and slow this time. Then I did it again, over and over. Millie fell into the rhythm, our bodies moving in perfect sync.

My mouth latched on to the side of her throat, sucking and licking, wanting to leave a mark for the world to see. My hands cupped her breasts again, rolling and flicking and tugging. "You feel so good, Mills."

"Yes." She put her hands over mine, threading our fingers together as I thrust faster and faster.

With one of our laced hands, I brought our fingers to her clit. Then just like I had been with her nipples, I played with her, working her up higher until every muscle in her body was shaking.

The pressure built in the base of my spine, the urge to fill this woman with my come so overpowering I groaned, my release barreling into me like a freight train.

"Ford." Millie shattered, clenching around me so tightly I lost any hope of holding back.

I came on a roar, burying my face in her hair as I poured inside her. White spots erased my vision. The scent of Millie and sex blanked my mind. All that kept me tethered to the world was the woman in my arms.

We collapsed in a sweaty heap of tangled limbs and

ragged breaths. When my heart stopped pounding in my chest, I forced myself up and to the bathroom to get a warm cloth to clean Millie up. Then I tucked her beneath the sheets, kissing her forehead. "Be back."

She hummed, sinking into a pillow.

"Don't fall asleep without me."

Her eyes popped open.

Not a chance she'd be awake when I came back. My woman crashed. Hard.

I snagged my boxers from the floor, tugging them on before slipping out of the bedroom. I hit the lights in the living room and padded to the garage, closing the overhead door. The opener I'd let Sienna borrow was on the workbench.

Then with the house closed up for the night, I headed for Joey's room, cracking the door to peek in on her. The light she liked to sleep with was on, casting rotating pink and white stars around the walls and ceiling.

I eased the door closed, about to return to Millie, but stopped when a pair of arms snaked around my waist. "She okay?"

"Yeah. But tomorrow is going to be rough." While I was more than ready for Sienna to leave Montana, Joey had loved having her mom close.

"You're a good dad, Ford."

"Am I?"

Millie kissed my spine, a hand sliding up to cover my heart. "Don't ask silly questions."

"I feel like I make a lot of the wrong decisions," I whispered.

"She's happy. But if you think she isn't, you could always ask her."

How had that thought never occurred to me? "Truth? I'm scared of her answer."

"I'm not." Her arms banded tighter.

I blew out a long breath. "Figured you'd be asleep."

"Not yet." Her hand moved away from my chest, trailing down my stomach, her fingers sliding into the peaks and valleys of my abs.

My cock stirred, ready for a second round. So I turned, sweeping Millie off her feet. And carried her to my bed again, exhausting our bodies until we both crashed.

When my alarm went off at four, Millie reached across my chest, where she'd been sleeping, and smacked it off. Then instead of sneaking out, she snuggled into my side.

———

"WANT A REFILL?" I held up the coffee pot.

Millie nodded, holding her mug out across the island from where she was perched on a stool. "I like this look on you, Coach."

"What look?"

"You in the kitchen, cooking me breakfast."

I rounded the island, setting the pot aside to lean down and kiss the corner of her mouth. "I like this look on you too."

She was wearing a pair of my sweats, cinched at the waist and rolled up at the ankles. The matching hoodie dwarfed her and might as well have been a dress. But the look of her wearing my clothes was one I'd like to see every morning for the rest of my life.

The sound of bare feet on the wood floor made me turn from Millie.

Joey came walking our way, her hair a wild mess. "Hi, Daddy."

"Hey, princess." I dropped to a crouch, arms opening for her to fall into a hug. "Missed you yesterday."

"I missed you too." She yawned. "Did Mom leave?"

"Yeah."

"Oh." She sagged against my chest.

I didn't get a lot of cuddles these days, usually only when she was half asleep or hurting. This one was likely a combination of both.

Joey shifted, resting her chin on my shoulder. "Hi, Millie."

"Hey, Jo."

I let my daughter go, shifting so she could sit on my knee. "Millie is going to hang with us today."

"Okay." Joey leaned her head into the crook of my neck.

Millie hadn't said anything, but her nerves about being here this morning had been palpable. Now, the tension crept from her frame, noticeable to me and me alone.

"Can I paint your nails?" Joey asked.

"No," I said at the same time Millie said, "Definitely."

"Daddy, I was asking Millie." Joey rolled her eyes, standing up. Then she went to her room, coming back a minute later with her caddy of polishes.

Then my daughter painted Millie's nails.

CHAPTER THIRTY-THREE

FORD

There were times a single loss could derail an entire winning season. When players lost their confidence. When coaches started second-guessing their decisions. When a team spiraled after the chink in their armor had been found.

After last weekend's loss, I'd feared that for the Wildcats.

Except as I sat at the conference room table surrounded by my coaches, I saw nothing but iron determination to win. I suspected I'd see the same from the players at this afternoon's practice.

Everyone had returned from Idaho, well . . . mad.

And six days later, the simmering anger from last week's game had only grown hotter.

We'd played like shit last Saturday. We'd made stupid mistakes and lost focus. Maybe that loss was exactly what we'd needed.

I loved the frustration hanging heavy in the air. We'd take that rage into the final regular-season game this weekend.

The Treasure State Wildcats versus the University of Montana Grizzlies.

The biggest game of the season.

The rivalry.

Fuck, but I wanted to win.

We'd be going to the playoffs this year, and so would the Grizzlies. But this upcoming game was what mattered most. And if this was my last season in football, there'd be no better way to end it than with a victory.

"Anything else?" I asked the room. We'd just spent an hour hashing through the plan for today's last practice before tomorrow's game.

Toren leaned his forearms on the table. "I'm going to watch film on the Griz for a while if anyone wants to join me."

"I'm in," Parks said.

Everyone else at the table nodded too.

As much as I wanted to join them, I had a list a mile long of shit to take care of before the game. Besides, I'd spent plenty of time this week watching film.

Each night, Millie had come over after work. Other than the two evenings when Joey and I had been at her volleyball practice, the three of us had eaten dinner together. Then Joey had done her homework and we'd hung out before her bedtime.

Once she was asleep, Millie and I would curl up on the couch. I'd watch film for a couple hours while she read or worked on her laptop. Then I'd carry her to bed and worship her body until we both fell asleep.

Life was almost perfect.

I only wished that the world could know she was mine. That I could slide a ring on her finger and make it official.

Soon.

After the Griz game, after the playoffs, I'd quit. My heart twisted, already feeling the pain from that loss, but I shoved it aside. First things first. I'd give the rest of this season my all.

"Thanks, everyone." I rapped my knuckles on the table and stood, the meeting breaking apart.

Toren and I were the last in line to walk out of the room. I was about to head for my office when my phone vibrated in my pocket with a text from Millie.

xoxo

"You guys all good?" Toren nudged his elbow to mine.

"Yeah, man." I nodded. "We're good."

He gave me a sad smile. "You're going to quit, aren't you?"

As much as I wanted to lie, Toren saw the truth in my gaze. "I won't make her give up her career just so I can keep mine."

"Then I guess we'd better win tomorrow." He clapped me on the shoulder, then walked away to catch up to the other coaches and watch film.

Damn, but I wanted to win this game. The last time I'd felt like this had been before the Super Bowl.

The anticipation for tomorrow was a constant buzz beneath my skin. The energy was jarring, and every day that passed, it intensified. By tomorrow morning, I'd be a wreck.

The only thing that seemed to calm my nerves was Millie.

My to-do list was calling but rather than go to my office, I went to the stairwell and climbed to the second floor. I needed a dose of her calm.

So even though it was risky, I walked to her office, stopping outside her door to lean against its frame.

Millie was sitting behind her desk, her back to me as she swiveled in her chair. She was typing on her phone, and a second later, mine buzzed.

"What did you text me?"

Her eyes flew up as she spun around. The smile that lit up her face made my heart stop. "Hi."

"That's what you texted me?"

"No, I texted that I wanted pizza for dinner. And that your ass looks great in those jeans."

Fuck, but I loved this woman. Until Millie, I hadn't even known what love meant.

I wanted a lifetime with her. I wanted to see that smile every day. I wanted to watch her and Joey at the kitchen island, painting their nails. I wanted to have more kids. Another daughter with Millie's dark hair. A son with her hazel eyes.

"Why are you looking at me like that?" Her cheeks flushed.

"Do you want kids?"

She blinked, that smile faltering. "Huh?"

"Kids." I pushed away from the door, closing it behind me as I stepped into her office. Then I went to the edge of her desk, taking a seat and pulling her up from the chair, positioning her to stand between my thighs. "What if we had kids?"

Her jaw dropped. "Ford."

"I want more," I confessed.

Her eyes searched mine as the shock in her expression vanished. "Two. At least two."

"Done."

"Sooner rather than later."

"Agreed." Tonight when I got home, I'd be flushing the pills from her toiletry case. Then I'd clear half the drawers in the bathroom so she could just unpack that case. Same with the closet.

"Did we just decide to have a baby?" she whispered.

I banded my arms around her, pulling her close. "Yes."

I'd bind her to me in every way possible.

A giggle erupted from her throat before she melted against me, her face burrowing into my neck. "Do you think Joey will be okay with it?"

I loved her for thinking of my daughter. "Yeah, Mills. She'll be okay."

We'd give Joey siblings to play with and boss around. We'd build a life together with all that Joey and I had been missing on our own. *Millie.*

She leaned away, taking my face in her hands. Then she slammed her mouth on mine, her lips hard against my own.

I let her control the kiss for a moment, but when her tongue slipped past my teeth, I stood, banding my arms around her as I swept inside, swallowing a moan.

Millie's hands clung to me as I hauled her up, carrying her to the nearest wall. Her legs parted, wrapping around my hips as I pressed my arousal against her core.

As much as I wanted to fuck her in this office, I tore my lips away, dropping them to her throat. I licked her skin, tasting her sweet, then latched on to her pulse and sucked. Hard.

"Ford." Her hands threaded into my hair as her head lolled, giving me better access.

I sucked harder, this urgent need to leave my mark. To

show the world, if I couldn't tell them, that Millie was mine. For the rest of my days, she was mine.

When I finally broke away, there was a red mark on her throat where my lips had been. I smirked at that pink flesh, the same pretty color as her pussy.

"Did you give me a hickey?" she asked.

I grinned. "Yep."

She scrunched up her nose and giggled. "Good thing I wore my hair down today."

I chuckled. "I'll get out of here. Let you get back to work."

She groaned, unwinding her legs from my waist. "I'm still working on the budget. So basically banging my head against the wall."

I set her on her feet, dropping a quick kiss to her forehead. "See you at home?"

Her eyes softened. "I'll be there."

"I love you."

"Love you too, Coach."

Coach.

For a few more weeks, I was Coach. So I walked out of her office and returned to mine to get back to work.

We had a game to win tomorrow.

CHAPTER THIRTY-FOUR

MILLIE

"Holy shit, did that conversation just happen?" A laugh escaped as I collapsed in my chair, spinning it in a circle.

When I stopped, the dizzy feeling in my head had nothing to do with the twirling and everything to do with Ford. My fingers drifted to the spot on my neck where he'd kissed me. I didn't need a mirror to know he'd left a mark. A mark I'd wear with a dreamy smile.

I'd thought about having kids. Someday. With the right man.

Ford. He'd always been the right man. And this, us, felt . . . right.

"Oh my God." I swiped my phone from my desk, about to call Autumn and tell her everything, when a throat cleared.

My gaze flew to the open door.

To Adrian.

We hadn't spoken since the game when he'd kissed me.

Given the angry clench in his jaw, I doubted he was here to apologize.

"Hi," I said, my good mood fading.

He shook his head, planting his hands on his hips as his gaze dropped to the floor, like he was composing himself. Silence hung between us, and in that silence, a jolt of panic raced through my veins.

He'd watched Ford walk out of here, hadn't he?

"I loved you," he murmured, barely above a whisper. Then he looked up, his gaze so full of pain and heartbreak it made my stomach roil.

"Adrian."

"I love you, Millie." His voice cracked.

Not loved. Love.

He was still in love with me.

Oh God. "I'm sorry." There was nothing else to say.

Except it was the wrong thing. Instead of walking away, the hurt in his expression shifted to anger. No, rage. His eyes blazed with fury as he glared at me. "I knew there was something going on with you and Ford. You couldn't just tell me?"

"I . . ." I couldn't tell anyone. Even now, I couldn't admit it. "I'm sorry I hurt you."

Adrian huffed. "What happens when he leaves? What happens when he gets fired?"

Fired? The Wildcats had a winning season, and Ford was beloved by his staff and players. Plus the alumni and donors were absolutely smitten. Anyone who attended a football game could tell he'd won over the crowd.

"Why would Ford get fired?" I asked, except I didn't need Adrian to answer. "It was you, wasn't it? You're the one who complained to Kurt."

Adrian didn't answer. He just flicked a wrist, dismissing the subject.

He used to do that when we were together too. Whenever I'd bring up a topic he didn't want to discuss—the strained relationship he had with his father, the way his sister had always been rude to me—he'd flick his wrist. Discussion over.

I hadn't realized until now just how much that had bothered me.

Maybe because Ford was as open as the Montana sky.

But it had to have been Adrian who'd lodged those complaints. Or at least one of them.

All this time, I'd suspected the complaint about Joey had come from Kurt. What if it hadn't? What if it had been Adrian?

He'd been at that bar event after the first game and must have seen Ford and Toren taking a shot. He could have complained about the drinking. And he must have spotted Ford and Joey the day he'd brought her to campus.

"Ford is a good man." I sat straighter, my glare matching Adrian's. "And he's a good coach. He's good for this school. Your jealousy is showing."

"Of course you'd defend him." Without another word, Adrian stormed down the hallway, probably walking straight to Kurt's office. His footsteps thudded like nails being driven into a coffin.

A coffin that was my career.

As a cold sensation spread through my body, I wrapped my hands around my middle, staring blankly at the smooth surface of my desk.

This was it. This was the end of my time here.

For months, I'd known this day would come. This was

my choice. Ford was my choice. Except no amount of time had prepared me for this strange feeling that settled in my heart. I wasn't angry. I wasn't hurt. I wasn't sad.

I was just . . . relieved.

No more hiding. No more secrets.

A framed photo of Dad sat on my desk beside my monitors. He was dressed in his uniform, smiling at the camera. He'd be proud, wouldn't he? Dad would have loved Ford.

I picked up the picture, clutching it to my heart. Then I opened my desk drawer and slid it into my purse.

Considering how long I'd worked here, it didn't take long to pack up my office. A few special trinkets. The personal stuff like gum and concealer and lip balm was taken from my drawers. The rest was left behind for the person who'd get this chair next.

I only hoped he or she would love the Wildcats as much as I did. That they'd cheer for every athlete, no matter their gender or their sport.

With my belongings stuffed into my purse and a tote that I'd had buried in my bottom drawer, there was nothing to do but wait for Kurt. I stared at the open doorway, checking the clock.

It was like awaiting an executioner. The minutes ticked by slowly, and with every passing second, my heartbeat began to hurt. The numbness from earlier vanished.

This sucked. I wasn't waiting any longer.

So I unlocked my computer and sent one final email. Then I shoved to my feet, taking a fortifying breath before I marched from my office, chin held high, to Kurt's.

He was seated at his desk, his head buried in his hands. His gray hair caught the light streaming in through his windows, making it nearly white.

Here we go. I squared my shoulders and knocked on his open door. "Kurt."

He lifted his head. "Oh, hi, Millie."

I'd expected to see some frustration, maybe disappointment, on his face. Instead he looked . . . exhausted.

"Come in." He waved me forward to one of the chairs opposite his desk.

I eased the door closed, not wanting anyone to overhear this conversation. Then I took a seat, placing my hands on my lap. I opened my mouth, ready to speak, but he beat me to it.

"I think I'm going to have to fire another coach."

My jaw hit the floor. "What?"

"Ford." Kurt rubbed his temples. "I just had a call from the head of the foundation."

The head of the foundation? Wait. So Adrian hadn't told Kurt? He'd gone to his boss instead?

"Apparently there's a rumor that Ford is having an affair with an employee in the department."

I blinked. "W-what?"

"First, a coach who encouraged underage drinking. Now, a womanizer?" Kurt shook his head. "What a disaster."

I was too stunned to defend the womanizer accusation.

So Adrian hadn't told anyone it was me sleeping with Ford, but he'd still lodged his complaint. He could have instantly had my job, but he'd gone to his boss. To make sure it would put Ford's job in jeopardy, not mine.

That. Asshole.

My molars ground together as my hands fisted.

"I can't do this again," Kurt said. "I can't have another scandal. I won't survive it."

Kurt always spoke in *I*s.

Had he known something hadn't been right with the former coach? Had he heard the rumors and ignored them? Was that why he was so hyperfocused about them now?

Adrian had played this perfectly, hadn't he? He probably hadn't personally registered the previous complaints about Ford. He'd probably had someone else call Kurt, just like today.

The first two had been minor. Enough to raise suspicion. Enough to conjure doubts in Kurt's mind. Anyone else probably would have dismissed them.

Except Kurt.

Because this wasn't really about Ford's job.

It was about Kurt's.

Today's complaint, a third with more severe consequences, would be the end.

And it was utter bullshit.

"Ford's a good coach," I said. "He's good for this program. We both know it." And I wouldn't take this from Ford.

"He is. This season has been incredible. Beyond my wildest dreams." Kurt nodded, blowing out a deep sigh. "But—"

"Adrian Allen is the reason you've received these complaints. It has nothing to do with Ford's character or integrity. It has everything to do with my very jealous ex-boyfriend."

Kurt blinked, his attention wholly fixed on me now, his posture stiffening. "What?"

"Ford *is* in a relationship with an employee. Me." I pointed to his computer. "If you check your email, you'll find my resignation, effective immediately. Thank you for the opportunity to work here, Kurt. This job has meant the world to me."

His eyes widened, his mouth fell open. "Millie, wait."

I ignored him, standing from my chair. Then I left my boss's office—former boss's office—and returned to my own to collect my things.

The cubicles were noisy this afternoon. The eagerness for the game against the Grizzlies charged the air. I ducked into my office, my heart in my throat as I collected my things. Then, with my purse and tote slung over a shoulder, I stood in the doorway, taking one last look at my desk.

I pushed the light switch down.

Click.

The end of one chapter.

The beginning of another.

I didn't have to work at TSU to be a Wildcat. Royal blue and silver were the colors of my heart. So as I walked down the hallway, making my way to the exit one last time, I smiled and waved goodbye to the other employees, promising to see them tomorrow at the game.

No one so much as blinked at the amount of stuff I was toting home.

I slipped down the stairwell and outside to my car waiting in the parking lot.

The moment I was in the driver's seat, closed inside, my eyes flooded. I had no regrets about quitting, but the reality of it was still raw. The sting sharp.

I didn't give in to the tears, not yet. I pulled my phone from my pocket and called Ford.

"Hey, baby," he answered.

"Hi." I forced cheer into my voice.

"What's up?"

"My mom just called me," I lied. "She's making a last-minute trip to town."

"Okay. Want to have her over tonight?"

"Actually, I think it might be good for me to spend some time with her. We haven't talked much lately. And she can just stay in my guest bedroom."

"Or she can stay in mine."

My chin began to quiver but I squeezed my eyes shut, hoping he wouldn't hear the emotion clawing at my throat. "Let's work up to that. I'll spend time with her. You can focus on preparing for the game."

With any luck, Kurt wouldn't make a big announcement about my resignation. Not until Monday. And Ford needed to focus on tomorrow.

"Mills."

"Ford."

"Fine," he grumbled. "See you at the game?"

"Absolutely."

"Love you."

"Love you too." The first tear dripped down my cheek. "Good luck tomorrow, Coach."

CHAPTER THIRTY-FIVE

FORD

As I stood surrounded by my staff, I fought to keep still despite the adrenaline coursing through my veins, a buzz beneath my skin. Out of sixteen men, I was the only one not bouncing on the balls of their feet or swaying side to side. Anticipation was as ripe as the smell of the cleaner they'd used last night in the weight room.

"Everyone good?" I asked.

"Yeah, Coach," a few of the guys muttered while the rest simply nodded.

We were all standing. Normally, we held this pre-game meeting in a conference room, but I'd known this morning none of us would be able to sit trapped in a chair. So we were huddled in the empty weight room while the players geared up in the locker room next door.

"All right." I clapped my hands, the sound a clear break to the meeting. "Let's go."

The room erupted with chatter and movement. One by one, we filtered out of the weight room, most coaches heading to the locker room to check on the players. But I went to the hallway, pulling my phone from my pocket, hoping to see a text from Millie.

Nothing.

So I pulled up her name, and just like it had been this morning on the drive to the fieldhouse, my call went straight to voicemail. She was probably just spending time with her mom before the game. But the twist in my gut said there was more. That something was wrong.

Paranoia from our *pause*.

Sleep last night had been nonexistent, not without Millie to help chase away the nerves for the game. I'd spent most of the night on the couch, watching film or reviewing the play-book. It was how I'd been as a player. When I couldn't sleep, when I was on edge, I gave my attention to football.

What would I do when it was gone?

Today was not the day to worry about the future, so I called Stephanie's phone, wanting to talk to Joey.

"Hi, Daddy," she answered.

"Hey. How did the game go?"

"We won." There was a smile in her voice. It killed me to have missed her volleyball game this morning, but Stephanie had promised to take a bunch of videos and another one of the parents had recorded it on a live stream, so hopefully I could track it down on Facebook later.

"That's awesome," I said. "Did you have fun?"

"Yeah, a lot."

"What are you up to now?"

"We just got the recording for your game all set up." There was a clang in the background, like a mixing bowl hitting the counter. "And now we're making snacks and stuff to eat while we watch."

"Nice. Save some for me?"

"And Millie."

My heart squeezed. "Yeah. Millie too."

No offense to Millie's mother, but she needed to leave Mission so I could have my woman back. That, or get used to the idea of spending nights in my guest room.

Our guest room. Sooner rather than later, Millie and I were going to have the same address.

Either in Mission. Or wherever she and Joey wanted to live.

"Do you like it here?" I blurted. It was a question I should have asked Joey months ago.

This was also not the time to worry over this discussion, especially on the phone, but that twist in my gut kept wrenching tighter. We were on the cusp of a major change. Again. This time around, I didn't want to just force it upon Joey.

"In Mission?" she asked.

I nodded. "Yes, in Mission."

"Yeah. Why?"

"I want you to like it here."

"I do." Spoken so nonchalantly that it eased some of the worry.

"Better than Seattle?"

"Um . . . I guess."

That was good enough for me. "I know it's hard being this far away from your mom."

Joey went quiet on the other end of the line. When she spoke, her voice was a whisper. "Do you think she'll move here someday?"

No. "I don't know, princess."

Sienna had drifted back into her life, reverting to phone calls and video chats to stay in touch with our daughter. The reality show was filming again, the first season about to air, and her life with Jordan Powell was still broadcast on social media in a carefully curated display.

For the time being, it was just Joey and me.

Was it enough? Was *I* enough? Millie's voice rang in the back of my mind. *You're a good dad, Ford.*

"I hope I'm a good dad," I confessed.

"You're the best dad."

That. Right there. The air rushed from my lungs. If nothing else good happened today, if we lost this game to the Grizzlies, today would still be a win.

"I love you, Josalynn."

"I love you too, Daddy."

No matter how many times I heard that sentence, it would never be enough. Maybe I wasn't the best father in the world, but damn it, I was trying.

"Okay, I'd better get ready for the game. You're going to watch, right? Cheer loud?"

"Yeah. I wish I could have come to watch it for real with Millie."

"Me too." Except Millie would be working today, and I knew she'd be busy. "Next time. Bye."

"Bye."

I closed my eyes, letting that conversation sink in deep. I had put my phone away, about to head to the locker room, when I heard my name.

"Ford." Kurt walked down the hallway with one of the other assistant ADs, Drew, trailing behind. Both were dressed in winter coats.

"Kurt." I nodded.

He stopped in front of me, his frame tense and his expression apprehensive like he was, well . . . scared. Like he expected me to rip his head off. Was that how the former coach had been? A loose cannon on major game days?

Kurt should know better. I hadn't once acted like that before any of the previous games. But today was different. Every emotion was heightened to the extreme.

"Are you, um . . . okay?" he asked.

"Yes," I drawled. "Are you?"

"Oh, yes." He nodded too wildly. "Great. Excited for the game. I just wanted to check in with you, make sure you were good. Yesterday was an, er . . . eventful day."

Busy. But all Fridays before a game were busy. "Yep. Good to go."

"Let me know if you need anything," he said, then motioned to Drew beside him. "Or Drew."

Drew looked like he was about to puke. I suspected that I'd have a few players who looked green too.

"I'll be in the Stadium Club today," Kurt said.

Just like Millie had told me, when the weather was bad, Kurt was in the club. And today, it was going to be damn cold. The high was eleven. The forecast was calling for snow this afternoon.

"If you need anything, Drew will be on the field," he said.

Drew nodded from Kurt's side.

"We're covered," I said. "But thanks."

"Good luck, Ford." Kurt extended his hand for a shake. "No matter what happens, it's been a great season."

That was a lie. Yes, it had been a great season. But what happened today did matter.

With a wave, Kurt headed for the nearest exit. A blast of cold air rushed inside before the door slammed closed behind him.

Drew waited until Kurt was gone, then cleared his throat. "Could you, um . . . Kurt told me this morning about what happened yesterday. Millie left without saying good-bye. Could you tell her that we're all going to miss her? It was pretty devastating to hear the news."

Hold up. News?

What. The. Fuck.

"She was really good for the department. She balanced Kurt and made sure the other programs didn't get over-looked." Drew sighed. "Whoever takes her position is going to have a high bar to chin."

His words were muted and dull. Too quiet to combat the blood rushing in my ears as my heart hammered against my sternum.

She'd quit.

She'd fucking quit, hadn't she?

What the hell had happened yesterday after I'd left her office? How could she do this without talking to me? How could she make this sort of decision on her own? Granted, I'd planned to do the same damn thing. But still. I would have talked to her. Probably.

Except she would have refused. She would have adamantly refused.

Just like I would have if she'd run this by me first.

How long had she been planning this? Had something happened yesterday? What about sneaking around until the end of the season? *Goddamn it.*

No wonder Kurt had looked so terrified. He'd assumed I knew. Had he fired her?

My hands balled into fists, furious. At Kurt. At Millie. At the fact that she'd beat me to leaving. That she'd lied to me. Was her mother even in town?

316

Maybe the reason she'd stayed away was because she wouldn't have been able to hide this from me last night if she'd come over. I'd thought her voice had sounded different on the phone yesterday afternoon but I hadn't pressed.

I should have fucking pressed. I should have insisted she come to my place or I should have just gone to pick her up from hers.

Fuck.

Now she was avoiding me. Did she think she'd make it through the game without me finding out? Oh, we would have words about this.

Drew must have taken my silence as acceptance so he nodded. "Thanks, Coach Ellis. Good luck."

He took the same door as Kurt, leaving me alone in the hallway. Fuming.

"What the actual *fuck*?" My bark echoed off the walls.

I ripped my phone from my pocket, hitting Millie's name. Again, the call went straight to voicemail.

"Millicent," I clipped. One word. That was the extent of my message. That was all she'd need to know I was livid.

A ruckus drifted from the vicinity of the locker room, the guys pumping each other up. As much as I wanted—needed—to track Millie down and talk this out, it would have to wait.

The Wildcats had a game to play.

CHAPTER THIRTY-SIX

MILLIE

Surrounded by thousands and thousands of Wildcat fans, hidden in a sea of royal blue and silver, I yelled.

I yelled and screamed and whistled.

My noise was lost in the chaos, just a whisper compared to the collective roar whirling through the stadium. For the first time since college, I was here only as a Wildcat fan, my single responsibility to cheer for my team against the Griz.

"Thanks for coming with me." I leaned closer to Autumn, taking her gloved hand in mine.

"Anytime. How are you doing?"

"I just want to win."

Nearly everyone from the athletics department was here today. None of them had so much as blinked when Autumn and I had walked through the gates. I'd been greeted with smiles and waves, which meant Kurt must not have told anyone I'd quit.

The only person I hadn't seen today was Drew. If Kurt had told anyone, it would have been him. But Drew was probably crazy busy today if he was covering for me. Poor Drew. I felt awful for leaving him in the lurch.

But awful was the adjective for the past twenty-four hours.

I'd managed not to cave and call Ford last night. Instead, I'd called Autumn. She'd come over with a bottle of wine and pizza, both consumed while I'd told her about Adrian and Kurt and quitting my job.

Since I hadn't trusted myself last night not to call Ford and have a breakdown, I'd asked her to hold my phone hostage until this morning. He needed to concentrate on the game, not my unemployment situation.

After breakfast, we'd donned our winter gear and made our way to the stadium, my phone still tucked safely in her coat pocket. But thirty minutes before the game had started, after Ford and his team had made the trek from the field-house to the stadium and the stands had begun to fill with people, she'd given it back. So I'd slipped off my thick mittens and turned on my phone.

The first message he'd left this morning had been nice. Sweet. He missed me. Wanted me to have a good day. Told me to find him after the game. I'd breathed a sigh of relief that I'd gotten lucky. That he hadn't found out I'd quit.

But then I'd listened to his second message.

Millicent.

Oh, I was in trouble.

Ford stood on the sidelines, his undivided attention on the game. But there was an edge to his movements today. A calculation. Not once had he casually put his hands in his pockets. Not once had he smiled.

Granted, this was *the* game of the season.

Except I knew that man to the core. He was angry, and

football was his outlet. So he was giving everything he had to the game.

So far, it was paying off.

The Wildcats were leading the Grizzlies ten to seven. Both teams had scored during the first quarter, and since . . . nothing. The Griz defense had shown up to play. They weren't giving the Wildcat offense a break. Thankfully, our defense had matched theirs beat for beat to keep them from scoring too.

The clock on the scoreboard kept ticking down. With only four and a half minutes left to play in the fourth quarter, if we could just hold them off for a little while longer, we'd be the Big Sky Conference champions. A feat no one had expected this year, not with a new coach and the drama from last year's scandal.

People had underestimated Ford. Of course, he'd come here to win.

A surge of pride swelled in my chest, so strong it nearly brought me to tears for the hundredth time since yesterday.

I'd spent last night crying on Autumn's shoulder, mourning the loss of my career. But this morning, when I'd woken to a beautiful, chilly November morning, the tears of sadness were gone. Today, the only tears I'd cried had been of joy. Of pride.

Ford was magnificent. He'd been born to lead this Wildcat team.

Not once since I'd been here today, watching the game, rooting for my alma mater, had I regretted my decision. If me quitting meant Ford could stand on the sidelines, exactly where he was meant to be, I'd do it a thousand times.

The sound system buzzed with the commentator announcing a third down by the Wildcats.

"Damn," I muttered. With the time left, I'd expected the Grizzlies to get another possession, but I'd hoped that our offense would have made it farther and chewed up the clock. But they'd only managed eight rushing yards.

"The defense has got to be getting tired," I told Autumn, smacking my hands together in frustration. "We can't seem to keep them off the field."

"We're still winning," she said.

"We'll be okay." As long as the Griz didn't score on this drive. "If we can just hold them off here."

"It's scary how well you know football," she said.

"Scary awesome."

Autumn pointed to the Griz sideline. "That coach right there is smoking hot."

"No." I shook my head. "If you date a Griz coach, our friendship will never recover."

"Fine," she muttered.

The white puffs of our breaths mingled as the commentator came on again. "Maverick Houston on the field to punt for the Wildcats."

The team was decked out in special uniforms today, a vintage-inspired set of blue jerseys and gray pants with silver helmets.

Special teams took their places, the crowd on their feet as Maverick took his position. Then the long snapper sent the ball flying into Maverick's waiting hands. He kicked it, the ball sailing toward the other end of the field, where the receiver signaled for a fair catch.

The referees rushed to put the ball on the line of scrimmage as our defense once again took the field.

The next three minutes were agony.

Not a single person sat on the icy, metal benches. Thousands and thousands of people were on their feet, jumping and moving in place with the flow of the game.

The Griz managed to get a first down, advancing the chains. The fatigue on our defense was noticeable. Sluggish legs. Panting chests. But they didn't give up. And by the third down, they'd held the Grizzlies to only two yards gained. Not enough to keep the ball.

"Oh, thank God." The air rushed from my lungs as the defense jogged off the field. "This could be it. If we don't make a mistake, if we keep them from getting the ball back, we'll win."

"We're going to win." Autumn clutched my hand tight.

My heart was in my throat as the Grizzlies punted. The receiver attempted to run but was stopped at the nineteen yard line.

So the offense jogged onto the field, led by Rush Ramsey as he took his position behind the center. He shifted, stepping back as he started talking to another player. There must have been a miscommunication because when Rush should have been getting ready for the snap, he was shaking his head, glancing to the sidelines and Parks O'Haire.

The two shared hand signals, back and forth, all while the play clock ticked.

"Watch the clock!" I screamed, my arm flying toward the scoreboard. Ten seconds. Nine. Eight. "Hurry up!"

"What are they waiting for?" a man behind me asked.

My heart was in my throat, my gaze glued to the field. But then there was Ford, stepping up beside Parks to signal the play.

Twins right, special.

I'd been paying attention to Ford's playbook this week as he'd prepped for the game. This was one of the simpler plays, but nonetheless effective. Especially when you had a quarterback who could run the ball if his running back wasn't open.

Rush ran to his spot behind center, hands ready as he called it out. *Hike.*

The center snapped him the ball and Rush dropped back into the pocket, looking for his receiver. Except he was under tight coverage, that freaking Grizzly defense almost impenetrable. So Rush tucked the ball and took off.

It was one of Rush's greatest strengths as a quarterback. He was a beast, strong and fast, and wasn't afraid to get hit. Running the ball was a risk, it opened up quarterbacks to injuries, but he ran regardless, gaining the Wildcats six yards.

"Yes," I breathed, letting my shoulders sag. Then I clapped, ready for the next play like I was out there on the field myself. "Four more. Let's get four more yards."

The confusion from the first play was gone. This time, as the offense took formation and Rush waited, the delay was intentional. Let the play clock run to eat up the game clock.

The snap came and Rush handed the ball to a running back, the kid busting past the line and gaining five yards before he was brought down.

"Yes." My arms shot in the air.

"First down, Wildcats!" The commentator's voice filled the stadium along with a chorus of cheers.

While a handful of the other coaches were cheering, Ford stood stoically on the sideline, gaze locked on the field as he crossed his arms over his chest.

"You got this," I murmured, willing my words to hitch a ride on the slight breeze and float their way to Ford.

His arms uncrossed. His gaze drifted from the field to the stands.

It was ridiculous to think he could see me, but I smiled all the same.

Then, like Ford, I shifted my attention to the Wildcats.

We just had to run down the clock. "Don't fumble the ball. Do not fumble the ball."

"Should you even be putting that out in the universe, Millie?"

"Sorry." I held my breath as the ball was snapped and Rush took a few steps back, arm raised like he was going to throw it. "No," I gasped.

A pass was too risky. We couldn't risk an interception, not now.

But Rush threw the ball anyway, sending it straight into the arms of Erik Manning, our star wide receiver.

Erik took off running for the end zone. His long legs stretched, his body pushed to the extreme as he outmatched every Grizzly attempting to take him down. In that moment, he looked a lot like Ford.

And I was taken ten years into the past, to a game not all that different from this one, when I'd cheered for the man of my dreams as he'd run the ball the length of this exact field to score the winning touchdown.

Every single person in the stadium was locked on Erik.

But I only had eyes for Ford.

I watched him as he stood, unmoving, as the rest of the players and coaches were waving Erik on, screaming and cheering. I watched Ford do a fist pump, then shoot that arm straight in the air as the crowd erupted. I watched Ford as everyone around him converged, jumping and leaping on him while the cannon fired its thundering boom in the background.

I watched Ford as the football sailed through the goal posts for the extra point, the clock ticked to zero, and the Wildcats declared victory over the Grizzlies.

We won.

"We won."

My eyes flooded. My chin quivered. I sucked in a breath, willing myself not to cry. Then I started clapping with muffled thwacks of my mittens.

"Hey." Autumn nudged my elbow, then pointed toward the jumbotron.

And there I was.

Ollie, a cameraman I'd known for years, was on the field below my section. He'd zoomed in so close that my face filled the massive screen.

I smiled, then raised an arm in the air. "Go Big Blue!"

Autumn laughed as the screen changed to another group of fans. And I turned my attention again to the field.

To Ford.

Who was staring straight at me.

No hiding this time. My cheeks flushed because he did not look happy. But I simply shrugged, lifted a mitten to my face and blew him a kiss.

He pointed at me. Then he pointed to the field. A clear *get your ass down here* if I'd ever seen one.

"And that's my cue to go home and unthaw." Autumn pulled me into a hug. "Call me tomorrow."

"Thanks for coming with me."

"It was fun." Her gaze drifted to the Griz coach she'd been ogling earlier.

"Autumn," I warned.

"What?" She feigned innocence. "Maybe he needs consoling."

I rolled my eyes. "Go. Console."

She giggled, then slipped past me while I made my way to the railing that bordered the field. It was a solid eight foot drop to the turf.

But I didn't have to worry about jumping down.

Ford stalked through the crush of players and staff and fans on the field, only stopping to shake hands with the Grizzly head coach. Then he kept on walking, his long strides eating up the distance between us. People parted around him, some watching to see where he was going.

I climbed over the railing, sitting on the cold metal bar as Ford stopped beneath me, extending his arms to catch me as I dropped.

The moment I was on my feet, he planted his hands on his hips. "Millicent."

"Congratulations, Coach. Great game."

He arched an eyebrow. "You lied to me."

"Coach Ellis." A man appeared at his side but Ford dismissed him with a headshake.

"We can talk about this later," I said.

"No."

I sighed. "I'm sorry."

"No secrets, Millie. Not from each other."

"Promise."

The scowl on his face faded. "You quit your job."

"Yep."

"I was going to quit."

"You'd better not. Now that I'm not working for the school, I need you to get me VIP access passes."

Ford shook his head, fighting a grin. "Do not make me laugh when I'm mad at you."

"Don't be mad at me."

He stepped forward, his knuckles coming to brush against my cheek. Regret filled those brilliant blue eyes. "I didn't want you to quit. I don't want you giving anything up for me."

I leaned into his touch. "And I would give up anything for you."

"No. That's not how it should be."

"It's okay, Ford. Really. I'm oddly good with this."

"I'm not."

"Neither am I." President Cruz came to a stop at our sides.

Next to her stood Kurt. His chin was bowed, his shoulders hunched. This was not the look of a man whose team had just won an important game. No, this was a guy who'd just received an epic ass chewing.

I really loved President Cruz.

"Millie, you can't quit," Kurt said. "Would you please consider staying?"

My jaw dropped. He actually looked sincere. "What about the no-fraternization policy?"

"Amended," President Cruz answered for him. "Effective immediately. It's antiquated. I see no reason why two people can't be in a relationship as long as it doesn't impact the quality of their work and one party doesn't supervise the other."

Oh my God. I looked to Ford.

He grinned. "Problem solved."

"Just like that?" My gaze darted everywhere. To President Cruz. To Kurt. To Ford. This seemed too simple. Too good to be true.

"Just like that." President Cruz nodded. "Fantastic game, Ford."

"Thank you." He dipped his chin.

"So you'll come back, Millie?" Kurt asked. "Monday morning?"

"I'd lov—" *Wait*. "I want the men's basketball team under my umbrella." Kurt could keep football. He could be Ford's boss. My boss. But I wanted everything else. It was time for more equality across our sports.

Those teams that brought in more revenue would always have larger budgets, but if they were all under my supervision, I could ensure that the smaller programs weren't forced to make unnecessary cuts.

And even if football remained with Kurt, I had Ford in my corner.

Kurt opened his mouth, probably to tell me no, but President Cruz cleared her throat. "Yes," he said. "I've been thinking about delegating more your way."

That actually sounded like the truth.

"Then I'll see you Monday morning."

The relief on Kurt's face was palpable. "Thank goodness."

President Cruz winked at me. "I'll let you all celebrate. Kurt, I'll see you Tuesday at our standing meeting."

"Have a great weekend."

She disappeared into the crowd, leaving Kurt behind. He extended his hand to Ford. "Big Sky champs. It's incredible. Congratulations."

"Thanks." Ford shook Kurt's hand.

"See you both next week." Kurt turned, like he was about

to leave, but he stopped. And this time, he held his hand out to me. "We're a better department with you, Millie."

My jaw hit the turf for the second time in five minutes. More sincerity. Who was this Kurt imposter? "Um, thank you."

"Monday."

I nodded. "Monday."

With a wave, he vanished into the crowd too.

"Did that just happen?" I whispered.

Ford dropped his forehead to mine. "I love you."

"Love you too."

His arms wrapped around me, hauling me off my feet.

Movement over his shoulder had my eyes going wide. I opened my mouth, ready to warn him, but I was too late. I buried my face in his shoulder just as Rush Ramsey and Maverick Houston hefted a water cooler over their heads.

And dumped it on Ford.

He shifted, doing his best to shield me, but we both got soaked.

"Ah!" I laughed, pulling a lock of hair out of my mouth before taking off my wet beanie, stuffing it into my coat pocket. Then after Ford set me on my feet, I shoved his arm. "Go. Celebrate. I'll see you at home."

Ford just shook his head, stretched out an arm and pulled me close. Then he sealed his mouth over mine.

Catcalls from his team erupted as they circled around us.

Ford just kept kissing me.

Ollie got footage of that kiss too.

EPILOGUE

FORD

S *even years later ...*
"I'm pissed at you," I panted, shooting a glare at Millie.

"Me?" She rolled her eyes as we jogged. "This is not my fault."

There were at least a hundred blisters on my feet. My lungs were on fire, and if I didn't puke before this race was over, it would be a marvel. "Fuck. I shouldn't have had such a big breakfast."

Millie hummed.

"Just say it," I snapped.

"I told you so." No hesitation.

I really should have listened to my wife.

"This sucks." I groaned, pinching at the ache in my side.

"Do you complain this much when you're working out in the weight room?"

"This isn't a workout, Millie. This is torture."

"Are you going to complain this entire time?"

Yes. I clamped my mouth shut before I could answer but

330

then remembered the only way I could breathe was by gulping down air, so I opened my mouth again.

Millie sighed, then slowed to a walk.

"What are you doing?" I asked, running in place beside her.

"You're not ready for this. You're going to hurt yourself."

Which was exactly what she'd told me before we'd left the house this morning. I hadn't listened. Just like I hadn't listened when she'd told me that I'd need to spend weeks training for a half-marathon.

Thank fuck she hadn't signed up for a full. I wasn't going to make it thirteen miles, let alone twenty-six point two.

"Come on." I waved her on. "If I stop, you'll never get me going again."

"Ford."

"Millie, let's go." I took off, facing forward, knowing that she'd catch up.

She settled into the space beside me, but slowed down, letting me set the pace.

We were five miles in, and I was miserable. The next eight were going to be brutal, but I didn't stop.

"You can run ahead," I said. "We both know you want to."

"We're in this together, Coach." Millie reached out, her hand brushing mine. But she stayed with me, step by painful step.

This race had been my idea.

Millie hadn't done the Mission Mountain Marathon for years, not since before our boys were born. She'd wanted to register for it but hadn't wanted to run alone. So I'd volunteered to run too, thinking this would be something fun the two of us could do together.

I worked out five days a week. I wasn't in the same, peak shape as I had been playing in the NFL, but I was still in damn good shape. Or so I'd thought.

My toes were going numb. Was that normal?

As much as I wanted to ask Millie, I kept my mouth shut and kept on running. Mile six. Mile seven. It was by sheer, stubborn will that I made it to mile eight.

And Millie looked barely winded.

Maybe I should have followed the running program she'd set out for me after all. I'd figured two or three miles a day would be fine.

A ding chimed from Millie's pocket and she dug out her phone, smiling at the screen. Then she lifted it up so I could see the photo Joey had texted.

It was of Joey standing with Jack and Jameson.

Stephanie had brought them here to wait for us at the finish line.

Joey didn't need a nanny these days, not when she'd just gotten her driver's license, but Stephanie had been with us for years, looking after the boys while Millie and I worked.

Jack, named after Millie's dad, had just turned five. And Jameson was three. Millie teased that they were my carbon copies and that the only thing they'd inherited from her was dark hair.

Except whenever I looked at them, whenever those precious boys smiled, all I saw was my Millie.

Jack was wearing a Wildcat jersey in the photo. He had seven of them, one for every day of the week because he refused to wear anything else. So Millie had bought enough jerseys to save us from constantly doing laundry.

Jameson was wearing his earmuffs. I doubted the finish line was loud, but he'd gotten a new pair to wear to the stadium for yesterday's game, and they'd been on his ears ever since.

Only Millie and the boys had come to the stadium to watch yesterday's game. Sienna had been in town and she'd spent the day with Joey.

Sienna's visits were as rare now as they had been after we'd moved to Mission. She and Jordan had gotten married about six years ago, not all that long after Millie and I had exchanged vows in a simple ceremony surrounded by our family and closest friends. Except while Millie and I'd had a baby a year later, Sienna had gotten divorced.

Afterward, we'd all wondered if Sienna would move to be closer to Joey, but she'd chosen to stay in Seattle. And in doing so, she'd broken our daughter's heart.

Joey's relationship had been different with her mother ever since. There was a distance between them. A strain. Joey was disappointed in her mother.

Sienna had called me seething late one night about five years ago, blaming the rift on Millie.

The truth was, Joey and Sienna's rift *was* because of Millie. Because Millie would sacrifice anything for my daughter or my sons. Anything in the world. And Joey saw that unconditional love every single day.

Sienna didn't stand a damn chance.

"Look how old she looks, Ford." Millie stared longingly at the photo, glancing up every few steps. Then she let out a sigh and tucked her phone away.

Joey, my little girl, was growing up too fast.

"President Cruz asked me if Joey was starting to think about colleges," she said.

"Millie." I scowled. "This run is painful enough. Pick another topic. *Any* other topic."

If Joey wanted to leave Mission and head to college somewhere else, I'd understand. Probably. I just wasn't ready to talk about it yet.

"Sorry." She laughed.

How she could laugh, how she could talk, was beyond me. I was close to projectile vomiting.

"We're going to need to get a wheelchair so you can make it to practice tomorrow, aren't we?"

I nodded.

Not a chance I'd be able to walk after this race. But I kept on going, refusing to make Millie stop simply because I'd been too cocky to follow her training plan.

God, I was a fool. My only salvation was that she hadn't told anyone else about this half-marathon. If anyone from the team saw me like this, I'd never live it down.

We kept on running, past mile nine, then ten. Three to go and I did what I always did when I was miserable. I tuned out the pain and focused on football.

Mile eleven was spent mentally reviewing plays. Mile twelve was spent dreaming up drills to pitch to the assistant coaches and the director of strength and conditioning.

Running. Maybe we should incorporate more distance running. This was the biggest ass-kicking I'd had in ages. Maybe the players could benefit from some endurance training. Though I was hesitant to change a program that was clearly getting us results.

The Wildcats had won the Division I FCS national championship last year. It would be a hard season to follow, but I was up for the challenge, especially with the support from the university's administration.

Kurt was, well . . . Kurt. This would be his last year before retirement, and though he still irritated me, I'd learned to tolerate him as my boss. Mostly, he stayed out of my way, having learned to give me space to do my job.

I doubted I'd ever like the man, not after the way he'd acted during my first season at TSU, so paranoid he would have fired me because of some trivial complaints. But since, he'd backed off. Maybe because he'd realized that I wasn't going to cause a scandal. Or maybe because he'd realized just how beloved Millie was around campus.

She had her job as an assistant AD, managing every program but football. That allowed us to both work for the same department without violating the updated no-fraternization policy. And although it meant that as long as I was the head coach, she couldn't take over as director when Kurt retired, he'd given her much more freedom with her position.

She loved her job and when I'd asked her a few months ago if she wanted to go for the director, that I'd step down as a coach, she'd refused. Being the director would mean even more responsibility. More nights and weekends away from home. So she was content to do exactly what she was doing.

A win-win. For us both.

We rode to work together. We ate lunch in one of our offices. The TSU campus was our second home. And it was even better now that that prick Adrian Allen had quit his job at the foundation, finally leaving Mission this past winter.

"Last mile." Millie pointed to the marker as we passed the final water station. "You got this."

I gulped, too drained to speak. Every ounce of energy went into pushing my legs to keep on running.

The applause from the finish line echoed from behind a bend in the road. It reached us before the archway came into view.

"Keep pushing," Millie said, like she could tell I wanted to quit and walk. "Almost there."

Almost there. I summoned the feeble remains of my strength, willing my body to keep pushing. And then, with my wife at my side, I crossed the finish line and immediately came to a stop.

"The kids are up there." Millie pointed down the line of clapping spectators to where Joey had both hands in the air, flagging us down. The boys, like always, copied her every move and shouted for us.

Autumn had come too. She stood beside Joey, holding a sign that said *Run, Millie! Run!*

And behind our crew was what looked to be the entire Treasure State University football team.

"Go, Coach Ellis!" one of the guys yelled, his hands cupped to his mouth.

Rush Ramsey stood in the mix, a recent addition to our coaching staff, with his son perched on his shoulders. The boy's hair was the same strawberry-blond as Faye's.

The team cheered louder, a few of the upperclassmen starting a chant.

"Coach. Coach. Coach. Coach."

"You've got to be fucking kidding me." I shook my head. My feet fell in step with the chant, and I dragged a hand through my sweat-drenched hair as we headed toward the kids. No doubt I looked like I'd just been put through the wringer. The teasing at practice tomorrow would be unforgiving. "Did you tell them?"

Before Millie could answer, I spotted Toren in the group wearing a shit-eating grin. "Never mind."

Millie just giggled, brushing a lock of damp hair off her temple.

Thirteen miles beside my slow ass, she looked as beautiful as ever. Not a day went by when I didn't feel like the luckiest man on earth to be hired as the Wildcat coach. Not for the job. Not even for the home I'd built with Joey.

But for Millie. My Millie.

I tossed a sweaty arm around her shoulders, pulling her close to kiss the top of her head. "There isn't a woman in the world besides you I'd run thirteen point one miles with."

"Oh, that's not true." Millie looked up, her hazel eyes sparkling. Then she cast them to Joey.

Yeah, I'd hate it. But if Joey ever asked me to run a half-marathon with her, I'd do it. Begrudgingly.

"Thank you for running this with me," she said.

"I love you." I leaned into her.

She leaned into me. "I love you too, Coach."

Then she gave me that beautiful smile that still made my heart skip. Or maybe that was my heart finally crapping out after all those miles.

If it did, I'd die a happy man.

ACKNOWLEDGMENTS

Thank you for reading *Coach*! For those who follow me on social media, you know that I am a loyal Montana State University fan. As much as I wanted to write a book about my beloved Bobcats, I also wanted the creative freedom that comes with a fictional setting. Now I've got two teams of Cats, one real, one pretend, but both cherished by me all the same.

A massive thanks to my amazing team. My editor, Elizabeth Nover. My proofreaders, Julie Deaton, Judy Zweifel and Kaitlyn Moodie. My cover designer, Sarah Hansen. My publicist and agent, Nina. And to Logan and Vicki for all you do.

Thanks to all the influencers who read and promote my books. To my family, every book reminds me of your unending love and support. And lastly, another thanks to you for reading. I am so grateful that with all the books in the world, you'd choose to get lost within the pages of mine.

ABOUT THE AUTHOR

Devney Perry is a *Wall Street Journal* and *USA Today* bestselling author of over forty romance novels. After working in the technology industry for a decade, she abandoned conference calls and project schedules to pursue her passion for writing. She was born and raised in Montana and now lives in Washington with her husband and two sons.

Don't miss out on Devney's latest book news.
Subscribe to her newsletter!
www.devneyperry.com

PREVIEW TO INDIGO RIDGE

Enjoy this preview from Indigo Ridge, book one in The Edens series.

WINSLOW

"Could I get another . . ."

The bartender didn't slow as he passed by.

"Drink," I muttered, slumping forward.

Pops had told me that this bar was where the locals hung out. Not only was it within walking distance of my new house in case I decided not to drive, but I was a local now. As of today, I lived in Quincy, Montana.

I'd told the bartender as much when I'd asked for his wine list. He'd raised one bushy white eyebrow above his narrowed gaze, and I'd abandoned my thirst for a glass of cabernet, ordering a vodka tonic instead. It had zapped every ounce of my willpower not to request a lemon twist.

The ice cubes in my glass clinked together as I swirled

around my pink plastic straw. The bartender ignored that sound too.

Main Street had two bars—tourist traps this time of year, according to Pops. But I regretted not choosing one of those to celebrate my first night in Quincy. Given his attitude, the bartender, who must have thought I was a lost tourist, regretted my decision too.

Willie's was a dive bar and not exactly my scene.

The bartenders downtown probably acknowledged their customers, and the prices were listed on a menu, not delivered using three fingers on one wrinkled hand.

He looked about as old as this dark, dingy building. Like most small-town Montana bars, the walls were teeming with beer signs and neon lights. Shelves stacked with liquor bottles lined the mirrored wall across from my seat. The room was cluttered with tables, every chair empty.

Willie's was all but deserted this Sunday night at nine o'clock.

The locals must know of a better place to unwind.

The only other patron was a man sitting at the farthest end of the bar, in the last stool down the line. He'd come in ten minutes after I'd arrived and chosen the seat as far from me as possible. He and the bartender were nearly carbon copies of one another, with the same white hair and scraggly beards.

Twins? They looked old enough to have established this bar. Maybe one of them was Willie himself.

The bartender caught me staring.

I smiled and rattled the ice in my glass.

His mouth pursed in a thin line but he made me another drink. And like with the first, he delivered it without a word, holding up the same three fingers.

I twisted to reach into my purse, fishing out another five because clearly starting a tab was out of the question. But before I could pull the bill from my wallet, a deep, rugged voice caressed the room.

"Hey, Willie."

"Griffin." The bartender nodded.

So he was Willie. And he could speak.

"Usual?" Willie asked.

"Yep." The man with the incredible voice, Griffin, pulled out the stool two down from mine.

As his tall, broad body eased into the seat, a whiff of his scent carried my way. Leather and wind and spice filled my nose, chasing away the musty air from the bar. It was heady and alluring.

He was the type of man who turned a woman's head.

One glimpse at his profile and the cocktail in front of me was unnecessary. Instead, I drank this man in head to toe.

The sleeves of his black T-shirt stretched around his honed biceps and molded to the planes of his shoulders as he leaned his elbows on the bar. His brown hair was finger-combed and curled at the nape of his neck. His tan forearms were dusted with the same dark hair and a vein ran over the corded muscle beneath.

Even seated, I could tell his legs were long, his thighs thick like the evergreen tree trunks from the forests outside of town. Frayed hems of his faded jeans brushed against his black cowboy boots. And as he shifted in his seat, I caught the glimmer of a silver and gold belt buckle at his waist.

If his voice, his scent and that chiseled jaw hadn't been enough to make my mouth go dry, that buckle would have done it.

One of my mom's favorite movies had been *Legends of*

the Fall. She'd let me watch it at sixteen and we'd cried together. Whenever I missed her, I'd put it on. The DVD was scratched and the clasp on the case was broken because I'd watched that movie countless times simply because it had been hers.

She'd always swooned over Brad Pitt as a sexy cowboy.

If she could see Griffin, she'd be drooling too. Though he was missing the hat and the horse, this guy was every cowboy fantasy come to life.

Lifting my glass to my mouth, I sipped the cold drink and tore my gaze from the handsome stranger. The vodka burned my throat and the alcohol rushed to my head. Ol' Willie mixed his cocktails strong.

I was unabashedly staring. It was rude and obvious. Yet when I set the glass down, my gaze immediately returned to Griffin.

His piercing blue eyes were waiting.

My breath hitched.

Willie set down a tumbler full of ice and caramel liquid in front of Griffin, then, without giving him the fingers to pay, walked away.

Griffin took a single swallow of his drink, his Adam's apple bobbing. Then his attention was on me once more.

The intensity of his gaze was as intoxicating as my cocktail.

He stared without hesitation. He stared with bold desire. His gaze raked down my black tank top to the ripped jeans I'd put on this morning before checking out of my hotel in Bozeman.

I'd spent four and a half hours driving to Quincy with a U-Haul trailer hitched to my Dodge Durango. When I'd arrived, I'd immediately jumped into unloading, only breaking to meet Pops for dinner.

I was a mess after a day of hauling boxes. My hair was in a ponytail and whatever makeup I'd put on this morning had likely worn off. Yet the appreciation in Griffin's gaze sent a wave of desire rushing to my core.

"Hi," I blurted. *Smooth, Winn.*

His eyes twinkled like two perfect sapphires set behind long, sooty lashes. "Hi."

"I'm Winn." I held out a hand over the space between us.

"Griffin." The moment his warm, calloused palm grazed mine, tingles cascaded across my skin like fireworks. A shiver rolled down my spine.

Holy hell. There was enough electricity between us to power the jukebox in the corner.

I focused on my drink, gulping more than sipping. The ice did nothing to cool me down. When was the last time I'd been this attracted to a man? Years. It had been years. Even then, it paled in comparison to five minutes beside Griffin.

"Where are you from?" he asked. Like Willie, he must have assumed I was a tourist too.

"Bozeman."

He nodded. "I went to college at Montana State."

"Go Bobcats." I lifted my drink in a salute.

Griffin returned the gesture, then put the rim of his glass to his full lower lip.

I was staring again, unashamed. Maybe it was the angular cheekbones that set his face apart. Maybe it was the straight nose with a slight bump at the bridge. Or his dark, bold browbone. He was no ordinary, handsome man. Griffin was drop-dead gorgeous.

And if he was at Willie's . . . a local.

Local meant off-limits. *Damn.*

I swallowed my disappointment with another gulp of vodka.

The scrape of stool legs rang through the room as he moved to take the seat beside mine. His arms returned to the bar, his drink between them as he leaned forward. He sat so close, his body so large, that the heat from his skin seeped into mine.

"Winn. I like that name."

"Thanks." My full name was Winslow but very few people ever called me anything other than Winn or Winnie.

Willie walked by and narrowed his eyes at the sliver of space between Griffin and me. Then he joined his doppelganger.

"Are they related?" I asked, dropping my voice.

"Willie Senior is on our side of the bar. His son is mixing drinks."

"Father and son. Huh. I thought twins. Does Willie Senior have the same glowing personality as Willie Junior?"

"It's worse." Griffin chuckled. "Every time I come through town, he gets crankier."

Wait. Did that mean . . . "You don't live in town?"

"No." He shook his head, picking up his drink.

I did the same, hiding my smile in the glass. So he wasn't a local. Which meant flirting was harmless. *Bless you, Quincy.*

A hundred personal questions raced through my mind, but I dismissed them all. Skyler used to criticize me for going into interrogation mode within ten minutes of meeting someone new. One of many critiques. He'd used his profession as a life coach as an excuse to tell me anything and everything I'd been doing wrong in our relationship. In life.

Meanwhile, he'd betrayed me, so I wasn't listening to Skyler's voice anymore.

But I still wasn't going to bombard this man with questions. He didn't live here, and I'd save my questions for the people who did: my constituents.

Griffin looked to the far end of the room and the empty shuffleboard table. "Want to play a game?"

"Um . . . sure? I've never played before."

"It's easy." He slid off his stool, moving with a grace that men his size didn't normally possess.

I followed, eyes glued to the best ass I had ever seen. And he didn't live here. An imaginary choir perched in the bar's dusty rafters gave a collective *yeehaw*.

Griffin went to one end of the table while I walked to the other. "Okay, Winn. Loser buys the next round of drinks."

Good thing I had cash. "Okay."

Griffin spent the next ten minutes explaining the rules and demonstrating how to slide the pucks down the sand-dusted surface toward the point lines. Then we played, game after game. After one more round, we both stopped drinking, but neither of us made a move to leave.

I won some games. I lost most. And when Willie finally announced that he was closing at one, the two of us walked outside to the darkened parking lot.

A dusty black truck was parked beside my Durango.

"That was fun."

"It was." I smiled up at Griffin, my cheeks pinching. I hadn't had this much fun openly flirting with a man in, well . . . ever. I slowed my steps because the last place I wanted to go was home alone.

He must have had the same idea because his boots stopped on the pavement. He inched closer.

Winslow Covington didn't have one-night stands. I'd been too busy wasting years on the wrong man. Griffin wasn't the right man either, but I'd learned in my time as a cop that sometimes it wasn't about choosing right from wrong. It was choosing the *right* wrongs.

Griffin. Tonight, I chose Griffin.

So I closed the distance between us and stood on my toes, letting my hands snake up his hard, flat stomach.

He was tall, standing two or three inches over six feet. At five nine, it was refreshing to be around a man who towered over me. I lifted a hand to his neck, pulling him down until his mouth hovered over mine.

"Is that your truck?"

———

"Shit." I cursed at the clock, then flew into action, flinging the covers off my naked body and racing for the bathroom.

Late was not how I wanted to start the first day of my new job.

I flipped on the shower, my head pounding as I stepped under the cold spray and let out a yelp. There was no time to wait for hot water, so I shampooed my hair and put in some conditioner while I scrubbed Griffin's scent off my skin. I'd mourn the loss of it later.

There was an ache between my legs that I'd think about later too. Last night had been . . .

Mind blowing. Toe curling. The best night I'd ever had with a man. Griffin knew exactly how to use that powerful body of his and I'd been the lucky recipient of three—or had it been four?—orgasms.

I shuddered and realized the water was hot. "Damn it."

Shoving thoughts of Griffin out of my head, I hurried out of the shower, frantically swiping on makeup and willing the blow dryer to work faster. Without time to curl or straighten my hair, I twisted it into a tight bun at the nape of my neck, then dashed to the bedroom to get dressed.

The mattress rested on the floor, the sheets and blankets rumpled and strewn everywhere. Thankfully, before I'd headed to the bar last night, I'd searched for bedding in the boxes and laid it out. When I'd finally gotten home after hours spent in the back of Griffin's truck, I'd practically face-planted into my pillows and forgotten to set my alarm.

I refused to regret Griffin. Kicking off my new life in Quincy with a hot and wild night seemed a little bit like fate.

Serendipity.

Maybe on his next trip through town, we'd bump into each other. But if not, well . . . I didn't have time for the distraction of a man.

Especially not today.

"Oh, God. Please don't let me be late." I rifled through a suitcase, finding a pair of dark-wash jeans.

Pops had told me specifically not to show up at the station looking fancy.

The jeans were slightly wrinkled but there was no time to find whatever box had stolen my iron. Besides, an iron meant fancy. The simple white tee I found next was also wrinkled, so I dug for my favorite black blazer to hide the worst offenders. Then I hopped into my favorite black boots with the chunky heels before jogging for the door, swiping up my purse from where I'd dumped it on the living room floor.

The sun was shining. The air was clean. The sky was blue. And I had no time to appreciate a minute of my first

Quincy, Montana, morning as I ran to the Durango parked in my driveway.

I slid behind the wheel, started the engine and cursed again at the clock on the dash. *Eight-oh-two.* "I'm late."

Thankfully, Quincy wasn't Bozeman and the drive from one side of town to the police station on the other took exactly six minutes. I pulled into the lot and parked next to a familiar blue Bronco and let myself take a single deep breath.

I can do this job.

Then I got out of my car and walked to the station's front door, hoping with every step I looked okay.

One disdaining look from the officer stationed behind a glass partition at the front desk and I knew I'd gotten it wrong. *Shit.*

His gray hair was cut short, high and tight in a military style. He looked me up and down, the wrinkles on his face deepening with a scowl. That glare likely had nothing to do with my outfit.

And everything to do with my last name.

"Good morning." I plastered on a bright smile, crossing the small lobby to his workspace. "I'm Winslow Covington."

"The new chief. I know," he muttered.

My smile didn't falter.

I'd win them over. Eventually. That's what I'd told Pops last night when he'd had me over for dinner after I'd returned the U-Haul. I'd win them all over, one by one.

Most people were bound to think that the only reason I'd gotten the job as the Quincy chief of police was because my grandfather was the mayor. Yes, he would be my boss. But there wasn't a nepotism clause for city employees. Probably because in a town this size, everyone was likely related in some manner. If you added too many restrictions, no one would be able to get a job.

Besides, Pops hadn't hired me. He could have, but instead, he'd put together a search committee so that there'd be more than one voice in the decision. Walter Covington was the fairest, most honorable man I'd ever known.

And granddaughter or not, what mattered was my performance. He'd take the cues from the community, and though my grandfather loved me completely, he wouldn't hesitate to fire me if I screwed this up.

He'd told me as much the day he'd hired me. He'd reminded me again last night.

"The mayor is waiting in your office," the officer said, pushing the button to buzz me into the door beside his cubicle.

"It was nice to meet you"—I glanced at the silver name-plate on his black uniform—"Officer Smith."

His response was to ignore me completely, turning his attention to his computer screen. I'd have to win him over another day. Or maybe he'd be open to an early retirement.

I pushed through the door that led into the heart of the station. I'd been here twice, both times during the interview process. But it was different now as I walked through the bullpen no longer a guest. This was my bullpen. The officers looking up from their desks were under my charge.

My stomach clenched.

Staying up all night having sex with a stranger probably hadn't been the smartest way to prepare for my first day.

"Winnie." Pops came out of what would be my office, his hand extended. He seemed taller today, probably because he was dressed in nice jeans and a starched shirt instead of the ratty T-shirt, baggy jeans and suspenders I'd seen him in yesterday.

Pops was fit for his seventy-one years and though his hair was a thick silver, his six-three frame was as strong as an ox. He was in better shape than most men my age, let alone his.

I shook his hand, glad that he hadn't tried to hug me. "Morning. Sorry I'm late."

"I just got here myself." He leaned in closer and dropped his voice. "You doing okay?"

"Nervous," I whispered.

He gave me a small smile. "You'll do great."

I could do this job.

I was thirty years old. Two decades below the median age of a person in this position. Four decades younger than my predecessor had been when he'd retired.

The former chief of police had worked in Quincy for his entire career, moving up the ranks and acting as chief for as long as I'd been alive. But that was why Pops had wanted me in this position. He said Quincy needed fresh eyes and younger blood. The town was growing, and with it, their problems. The old ways weren't cutting it.

The department needed to embrace technology and new processes. When the former chief had announced his retirement, Pops had encouraged me to toss my name into the hat. By some miracle, the hiring committee had chosen me.

Yes, I was young, but I met the minimum qualifications. I'd worked for ten years with the Bozeman Police Department. During that time, I'd earned my bachelor's degree and a position as detective within their department. My record was impeccable, and I'd never left a case unclosed.

Maybe my welcome would have been warmer if I were a

man, but that had never scared me and it certainly wasn't going to today.

I can do this job.

I would do this job.

"Let me introduce you to Janice." He nodded for me to follow him into my office, where we spent the morning with Janice, my new assistant.

She'd worked for the former chief for fifteen years, and the longer she spoke, the more I fell in love with her. Janice had spiky gray hair and the cutest pair of red-framed glasses I'd ever seen. She knew the ins and outs of the station, the schedules and the shortcomings.

As we ended our initial meeting, I made a mental note to bring her flowers because without Janice, I'd likely fall flat on my face. We toured the station, meeting the officers not out on patrol.

Officer Smith, who was rarely sent into the field because he preferred the desk, had been one of the candidates for chief, and Janice told me that he'd been a grumpy asshole since the day he'd been rejected.

Every officer besides him had been polite and professional, though reserved. No doubt they weren't sure what to make of me, but today I'd won Janice over—or maybe she'd won me. I was calling it a victory.

"You'll meet most of the department this afternoon at shift change," she told me when we retreated back to the safety of my office.

"I was planning on staying late one evening this week to meet the night shift too."

This wasn't a large station, because Quincy wasn't a large town, but in total, I had fifteen officers, four dispatchers, two administrators and a Janice.

norrow, the county sheriff is coming in to meet you," said, reading from the notebook she'd had with her all ing. "Ten o'clock. His staff is twice the size of ours but he has more ground to cover. For the most part, their team stays out of our way, but he's always willing to step in if you need help."

"Good to know." I wouldn't mind having a resource to bounce ideas off of either.

"How's your head?" Pops asked.

I put my hands by my ears and made the sound of an exploding bomb.

He laughed. "You'll catch on."

"Yes, you will," Janice said.

"Thank you for everything," I told her. "I'm really looking forward to working with you."

She sat a little straighter. "Likewise."

"Okay, Winnie." Pops slapped his hands on his knees. "Let's go grab some lunch. Then I've got to get to my own office, and I'll let you come back here and settle in."

"I'll be here when you get back." Janice squeezed my arm as we shuffled out of my office.

Pops simply nodded, maintaining his distance. Tonight, when I wasn't Chief Covington and he wasn't Mayor Covington, I'd head to his house and get one of his bear hugs.

"How about we eat at The Eloise?" he suggested as we made our way outside.

"The hotel?"

He nodded. "It would be good for you to spend some time there. Get to know the Edens."

The Edens. Quincy's founding family.

Pops had promised that the fastest way to earn favor with the community was to win over the Edens. One of their relatives from generations past had founded the town and the family had been the community's cornerstone ever since.

"They own the hotel, remember?" he asked.

"I remember. I just didn't realize there was a restaurant in the hotel these days." Probably because I hadn't spent much time in Quincy lately.

The six trips I'd taken here to participate in the interview process had been my first trips to Quincy in years. Five, to be exact.

But when Skyler and I had fallen to pieces and Pops had pitched the job as chief, I'd decided it was time for a change. And Quincy, well . . . Quincy had always held a special place in my heart.

"The Edens started the hotel's restaurant about four years ago," Pops said. "It's the best place in town, in my opinion."

"Then let's eat." I unlocked my car. "Meet you there."

I followed his Bronco from the station to Main Street, taking in the plethora of out-of-state cars parked downtown. Tourist season was in full swing and nearly every space was full.

Pops parked two blocks away from Main on a side street, and side by side, we strolled to The Eloise Inn.

The town's iconic hotel was the tallest building in Quincy, standing proudly against the mountain backdrop in the distance. I'd always wanted to spend a night at The Eloise. Maybe one day I'd book myself a room, just for fun.

The lobby smelled of lemons and rosemary. The front desk was an island in the grand, open space, and a young woman with a sweet face stood behind the counter, checking in a guest. When she spotted Pops, she tossed him a wink.

"Who's that?" I asked.

"Eloise Eden. She took over as manager this past winter."

Pops waved at her, then walked past the front desk toward an open doorway. The clatter of forks on plates and the dull murmur of conversation greeted me as we entered the hotel's restaurant.

The dining room was spacious and the ceilings as tall as those in the lobby. It was the perfect place for entertaining. Almost a ballroom but filled with tables of varying sizes, it also worked well as a restaurant.

"They just put in those windows." Pops pointed at the far wall where black-paned windows cut into a red-brick wall. "Last time I talked to Harrison, he said this fall they'll be remodeling this whole space."

Harrison Eden. The family's patriarch. He'd been on the hiring committee, and I liked to believe I'd made a good impression. According to Pops, if I hadn't, there was no way I'd have gotten my job.

A hostess greeted us with a wide smile and led us to a square table in the center of the room.

"Which of the Edens runs the restaurant?" I asked as we browsed the menu card.

"Knox. He's Harrison and Anne's second oldest son. Eloise is their youngest daughter."

Harrison and Anne, the parents. Knox, a son. Eloise, a daughter. There were likely many more Edens to meet.

Down Main, the Eden name was splashed on numerous storefronts, including the coffee shop I wished I'd had time to stop by this morning. Last night's antics were catching up to me, and I hid a yawn with my menu.

"They're good people," Pops said. "You've met Harrison. Anne's a sweetheart. Their opinion carries a lot of weight around here. So does Griffin's."

Griffin. *Did he say Griffin?*

My stomach dropped.

No. This couldn't be happening. It had to be a mistake. There had to be another Griffin, one who didn't live in Quincy. I'd specifically asked him last night if he lived in town and he'd said no. Hadn't he?

"Hey, Covie."

So busy having my mental freak-out that I'd slept with not only a local man, but one I needed to see me as a professional and not a backseat hookup, I didn't notice the two men standing beside our table until it was too late.

Harrison Eden smiled.

Griffin, who was just as handsome as he had been last night, did not.

Had he known who I was last night? Had that been some sort of test or trick? Doubtful. He looked as surprised to see me as I was to see him.

"Hey, Harrison." Pops stood to shake his hand, then waved at me. "You remember my granddaughter, Winslow."

"Of course." Harrison took my hand as I stood, shaking it with a firm grip. "Welcome. We're glad to have you as our new chief of police."

"Thank you." My voice was surprisingly steady considering my heart was attempting to dive out of my chest and hide under the table. "I'm glad to be here."

"Would you like to join us?" Pops offered, nodding to the empty chairs at our table.

"No," Griffin said at the same time his father said, "We'd love to."

Neither Pops nor Harrison seemed to notice the tension rolling off Griffin's body as they took their chairs, leaving Griffin and me to introduce ourselves.

I swallowed hard, then extended a hand. "Hello."

That sharp jaw I'd traced with my tongue last night clenched so tight that I heard the crack of his molars. He glared at my hand before capturing it in his large palm. "Griffin."

Griffin Eden.

My one-night stand.

So much for serendipity.